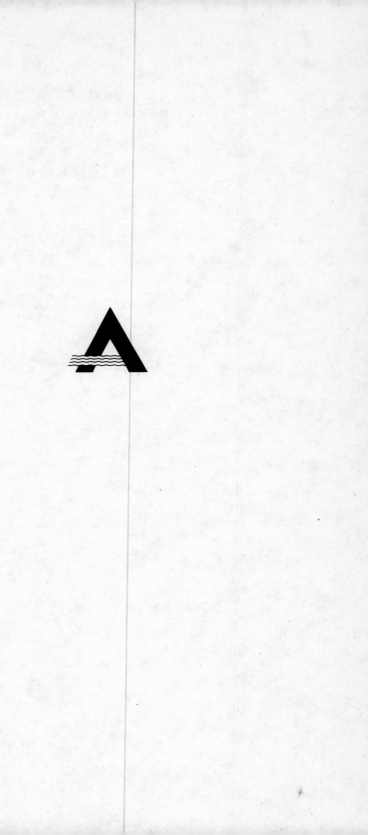

SPILL

SPILL

Les Standiford

THE ATLANTIC MONTHLY PRESS
NEW YORK

I would like to extend a special thanks to Dale Walker, Director of the Texas Western Press, for his invaluable assistance and unflagging encouragement. To Art Wills, Robert Canzoneri, and David Kranes, fine writers and generous teachers all. To the National Endowment for the Arts, which helped me make the time. And finally, to Nat Sobel and to Watson's Pop, without whose help this surely could not have come to pass.

Published simultaneously in Canada
Printed in the United States of America
FIRST EDITION

Library of Congress Cataloging-in-Publication Data

Standiford, Les.
    Spill / Les Standiford. — 1st ed.
    ISBN 0-87113-438-1
    I. Title.
    PS3569.T331528S65   1990   813'.54—dc20   90-19750

The Atlantic Monthly Press
19 Union Square West
New York, NY 10003

FIRST PRINTING

This is for Pat and Stany,
Rhoda and Lew,
and for my mainstays,
Kimberly, Hannah, and J.R.

"No pestilence had ever been so fatal, or so hideous. Blood was its Avatar and its seal—the redness and the horror of blood. There were sharp pains, and sudden dizziness, and then profuse bleeding at the pores, with dissolution."

—*Edgar Allan Poe, "The Masque of the Red Death"*

"Whatever sun and moon may be,
the hearts of men are merciless."

—*James Wright, "Two Poems About President Harding"*

Part
1

RESEARCH
AND
DEVELOPMENT

Monday, July 18

FENWAY PARK. Announced attendance 19,407. An uncharacteristically cool day for mid-July, perfect baseball weather, if you cared about baseball. Some fans were packing up, heading happily toward the exits. Skanz couldn't leave. He had someone to kill.

"Top of the ninth," the man next to him said, grinning, loony. Skanz nodded, his mood neutral. He glanced at the scoreboard. Unless the Visitors—the "Indians," according to the sign—were to score seven times, he'd soon be out of the park, able to complete his business.

Skanz's neighbor bent to a thick briefcase, unsnapped it, lifted a panel, and revealed a cooler in disguise. He took a beer out of a can-shaped Styrofoam nest and offered it, a Schaefer, to Skanz. Skanz declined. The man shrugged, closed his briefcase, popped his beer, and turned to exhort the Red Sox.

Skanz stared at the false briefcase. A vendor passed by, offering the same beer from paper cups. The first Indian went down, swinging. How much effort expended on a device for smuggling beer into the baseball park?

The second batter tapped the ball back to the pitcher, who threw him out. Skanz's neighbor finished his beer and cheered, jostling him as he stood, then again as he dropped

5

back. Skanz considered killing *this* man. It could be managed.

There was a policeman standing at the top of the aisle above them. He could be managed too, and no one in the park would notice. Somewhere in his mind a plaintive voice begged for control. Skanz shook his head and turned his concentration on the game.

The third Indian swung at the first pitch and sent a line drive back at the pitcher, who threw up his glove to protect his face. The ball caromed high in the air and was snared by the second baseman before it hit the ground. The crowd was ecstatic. Skanz's neighbor turned and clapped his arm.

"You see that?" he asked.

Skanz looked at him. One quick movement. It would seem he'd stumbled. The man would die before he reached the ground.

"See what?" Skanz said, fighting to contain himself.

The man turned and jabbed his finger toward the pitcher's mound. "Ah Jesus, it was terrific . . . ," he began, but when he turned back Skanz was gone.

Skanz wore thick-soled cordovans, khaki trousers, and a short-sleeved blue shirt with a button collar. He had picked up a hot dog on the way out and chewed it mechanically as he shuffled along in the departing crowd, his eyes flickering here and there, but always coming back to the narrow-shouldered man in the baggy white shirt up ahead.

Skanz, who didn't drink beer, looked as if he'd had a lot of it in his time. He had thick hands, not much of a neck, and soft brown hair that wasn't thick but fell softly over his broad forehead. He looked like a good-natured cabdriver. The pale, balding man he followed was central casting's image of a scientist. His desert boots were run down. His shirt pocket was full of pens. He carried a soft-sided briefcase. There was a snag in his pantleg and a long thread fluttered from it as he walked.

Skanz followed him out of the stadium and onto a crowded downtown train. The thread irked him. He ought to be killed for the thread alone. As the train rocked and dived underground, the scientist took a small computer from his briefcase and began tapping its keyboard.

Skanz watched the man work, thinking that it was a foolish way to spend one's final minutes. On the other hand, how could he know what was going to happen? He was just a man. Skanz had read an article that argued the ability of animals to sense their status as prey, that they knew when some predator's death ray had locked in on them. Skanz believed it. Too bad for this one that humans had evolved away from it.

He noticed that a man wearing a Celtics ball cap and cowboy boots had edged his way through the crowd to stand near the scientist. His stomach bulged over the belt of his jeans, straining the fabric of a plaid, pearl-button shirt. Skanz dismissed him as a prototypical tourist, but then, as the train slowed for a stop, he saw the man carefully hook his finger into the scientist's briefcase and slip it off the seat. The scientist tapped on, apparently unaware of what had happened. The man in the Celtics cap merged with a group of departing passengers, the briefcase firmly in hand. Skanz started up from his seat, then fell back.

As the train pulled away from the station, the scientist looked up from his tapping, glanced about the train compartment, then went back to his work. *It had been arranged,* Skanz thought. He hurriedly craned his neck toward the platform that was receding behind them, but the man in the Celtics cap was gone.

The scientist was still tapping as the train slowed for their downtown stop, and they very nearly missed getting off. The scientist stopped for the paper at a kiosk before they went up into the world.

Halfway across the vast plaza that fronted one of the insurance company buildings, Skanz caught the scientist by the arm. The man started, then pulled away, annoyance replacing his surprise.

"Schreiber sent you?" he said.

Skanz gave a nearly imperceptible nod. They were standing by a large fountain and the noise would wash out their conversation. Still, one needed to be cautious.

"I said I'd call when I was ready."

"Some things cannot wait," Skanz said.

The scientist thought a moment, then seemed to relent. "Do you have what I asked for?" he asked.

A woman pushing a baby carriage cut between them, heading for the fountain that shot water high into the air and sent a mist over a group of cavorting children. Skanz waited until she was out of earshot, then drew close and took the scientist firmly by the arm.

"Inside," he said, and the scientist went along.

Skanz took them to a service elevator in an alcove off the main lobby. As he pushed the button, he inserted a key in the panel lock. If the scientist noticed, he didn't say so. The elevator doors jittered open and they went inside.

Skanz stopped the car between the sixth and seventh floors. Six was vacant. Seven was undergoing renovation. The roar of automatic hammers echoed in the car, which was cluttered with paint cans, tools, chunks of wallboard.

The scientist looked at him, seemingly at ease. "So where is the money?"

Skanz affected apology, lifting his hands. "All in good time."

The scientist bunched his hands in his pockets and looked at the floor. "I'm protected. There's nothing Schreiber can do but pay. If I don't see the rest of the money today, the price is going up."

"I see. You're only a businessman." Skanz pulled one of his sausagelike fingers and the pop sounded in a momentary silence. "You do some work for your employer, then you threaten to tell the world about this work, and you want your employer to pay you to keep silent." Skanz nodded, and it almost sounded as if he approved. "That's business."

The scientist heard something else in Skanz's voice. He looked up and withdrew his hands from his pockets. One of them held a small pistol, which he pointed at Skanz. "You start the elevator. Schreiber knows I've taken precautions. Anything happens to me . . ."

"Yes, there was a safe-deposit box in Miami. We have found that, destroyed the contents." Skanz nodded. "You can't put your trust in anything, not these days." He smiled at the pistol. "Everybody wants to make a killing."

The scientist shook his head. "You don't know what I've arranged," he said. He rubbed his left arm as if something were stinging him there.

Skanz leaned back against the wall of the elevator, waiting. The scientist waved the pistol in his face. "Let's go," he commanded. Skanz shrugged, and reached up to push the button. He hesitated, his thick finger poised above the control panel. He studied the seconds flickering across the face of his watch, counting to himself.

He turned. The scientist was pale. Sweat beaded his forehead. His left arm had begun to buck and jerk with a life

9

of its own. The scientist turned from Skanz to stare in disbelief at his own unruly limb. Skanz reached out to take the pistol.

The man fired. The explosion was drowned by the roar of the hammers. Skanz felt a sharp pain in his hand, but he could still grip. He wrested the gun from the man and fought the urge to shoot him in the face with it.

He pushed the scientist away and held the tiny pistol on him. The scientist seemed more interested in his left arm than in Skanz. The skin of his hand had turned a deep violet. Blood seeped from his fingertips and oozed from beneath his nails. The scientist held his hand aloft, examining it with an infant's fascination. It had swollen to an impossible size and seemed ready to explode from the pressure of his blood.

He turned to Skanz, terror in his eyes at last. Skanz unfolded his hand and showed him the device with which he'd been injected: it was made of stainless steel and slipped over one's fingers like a double ring. Take someone by the arm, apply gentle pressure, and a needle the size of an asp's tooth did the work. It was the failed patent design of a German doctor who'd concocted it for children afraid of their vaccinations.

Skanz slipped the device into his pocket and pursed his lips in an understanding way. "They told me what I've given you is something you worked on yourself," he said. "Something you wanted to sell them, when it was already theirs."

The scientist was wobbling. A dark stain had worked its way up from his collar toward his chin. He tried to speak, his eyes imploring, but the words only gurgled in his throat.

"Who was the man on the train?" Skanz asked. "What did you give him?"

The scientist spat blood upon Skanz as he began to slide down the wall of the car. Skanz jerked back, and fired.

Quickly, he drew his sleeve across his cheek. He had not meant to fire.

The scientist was on the floor now. Skanz stared down at him. The man's eyes blinked wildly, saw nothing. His mind would race, would remember Skanz taking his left arm and squeezing, the sharp pinprick, and the fountain pulsing bright jets of water into the air where the gulls wheeled and squawked.

"It will take you too," the scientist gasped. Skanz shook his head. It seemed a terrible way to die.

When the scientist was quiet, Skanz turned to examine his hand. A bullet had split the skin between his thumb and palm. The scientist heaved once more and a sigh bubbled through the froth at his lips.

Skanz bent and opened a can of paint, poured it over the body. He stood, pushed buttons on the elevator panel. He shouldn't have shot. He wiped his face again. He looked down on the thing that had been human. He picked up a can of thinner, poured that atop the yellow paint. He looked away and focused on the whir of the elevator as it caught and drew him down. All he wanted was out.

And then he felt the hand on his ankle. He jerked back and began to kick at the pitiful creature there. *"Out of control, out of control,"* a voice inside Skanz intoned, and his heavy sole rose and fell to its rhythm.

By the time they reached bottom, all was still. Skanz wiped his shoe on a rag, then touched a match to the cloth. He let the flaming rag flutter to the bright collage of paint and blood at his feet and stepped out. He was well across the plaza before the fire alarms began to ring.

Thursday, July 21
West Yellowstone,
Montana

FAIRCHILD TOOK HIS eyes off the narrow road to steal a glance at the woman beside him. She looked good. Still.

Anybody who saw her on the street or at a party would think she was a prize. For a moment, he was dreadfully sorry she was leaving him.

The wheel bucked in his hands and he turned back to the road. There was a curve up ahead, a three-hundred-foot drop to his left and a sheer wall of granite on his right. He thought briefly about flooring the pickup and never mind the turn, just launch them out into space, a cannonball soaring into the forest below.

"Don't fool around," his wife said.

Fairchild floored the truck anyway and took the curve hard, the soft macadam tearing underneath them. He heard the sharp hiss of her breath and smiled, then noticed what was coming and took a quick little breath himself.

An RV the size of a house was boring into the turn from the other direction, taking up most of the road. Fairchild wrenched the truck to the right, catching a brief glimpse of the RV driver's panicked face. Berm gravel thundered on the floor pan of the pickup. Lena jerked her arm inside as the rock wall neared the passenger door.

Fairchild caught the bucking wheel, eased the tires back

onto the pavement, and checked the rearview mirror. The RV was gone, though not over the cliff, he hoped. He hadn't heard a crash, but then it was a long, straight drop.

He imagined the RV plummeting nose first into the tinder-dry sweep of pines where Little Murky Creek normally meandered. With butane tanks and fifty gallons of gasoline, it could start a fire that could burn for weeks.

"I'd like to get where I'm going, if you don't mind." Her voice was surprisingly even. She had already opened a pocket mirror and was inspecting her makeup, dabbing at the sweat freckling her forehead. She'd added some frosting to her normally dark brown hair. She probably thought it made her seem older and more sophisticated. He thought that it didn't suit her, which was probably the point.

"And where is that, anyway?" he said.

She gave him a neutral look. "To the bus station."

He wanted to punch her. Instead, he turned his attention back to the road. His mood swings amazed him. Since she'd told him she was leaving, he might be furious one moment, consumed by depression the next. He had taken up the habit of country music, which he had always detested. Now, even Tanya Tucker could move him to tears. And last night he had watched *All-Star Wrestling,* reveling in every body slam and burst blood capsule.

A station wagon approached, and when the kids inside saw the Park Service truck and his Smokey the Bear hat, they leaned out the windows, waving madly until they passed. He ignored the station wagon and looked at Lena.

"I know you're going to the bus station," he said, forcing himself to sound reasonable. "What if somebody calls. What about your mail?"

"Nobody will call."

The rest of the trip was silent, a steady downhill shot

into the town of West Yellowstone. Even at eight-thirty the streets were busy, tourists looking for breakfast, more tourists heading out toward the high country, merchants hurrying toward their shops, Ranger Fairchild taking his runaway wife to the bus station.

He made the first light, passed Alpha Beta and the Texaco station, then turned right and into the graveled parking lot that served the Buckaroo Lounge and the Western Stage Lines. The lounge was closed and the lot was empty save for an Olympia beer truck with a sleeping driver inside. Fairchild shut down the pickup and turned to his wife, who stared out at the concrete wall of the bus station.

"You sure this is what you want to do?" He was trying to sound like the one in charge. The heat was palpable now that they had stopped. Another day pushing one hundred.

She smiled to herself and finally turned to him, a trace of the old familiarity in her eyes. She took his hand and squeezed it. "We're not going to have any more conversations, Jack. Now get my suitcase, okay?" She gestured toward the door, her familiarity gone. The bus was pulling into the lot.

As he brought Lena's lone suitcase around from the bed of the truck, two Indians in Forest Service greens, and Jessie, the Buckaroo's daytime barmaid, emerged from the bus. This was the milk run that ran north and south from the park's gateway back into Idaho.

Jessie took one look at him, then at the set of Lena's jaw. She raised her eyes at Fairchild and moved on toward the bar. Lena tried to take her suitcase, but Fairchild held it stubbornly and walked toward the bus. The driver was cranking the sign over from West Yellowstone back to Pocatello.

The driver came down, took the suitcase from Fairchild, opened up the bay, and slid it inside. He smiled professionally

17

at Lena. "I'm gonna get a cup," he said, moving off toward the tiny station where a coffee machine sat just inside the double doors.

Lena took the first step up. Fairchild touched her arm. She turned around. He opened his mouth to say something, though he had no idea what. She cut him off. "You shouldn't stay here the rest of your life. That's what you're thinking you'll do, but take it from me, it'd be a big mistake."

It took the edge off his sentiment. "What the hell do you know about it," he said. He meant to sound assured but he doubted she was impressed. She'd never liked it here—trying to talk her into an appreciation of the wilderness was like reasoning with a Klansman about miscegenation.

"More than you think," she said, solemnly. And then she was gone. Fairchild stood toeing the gravel for a moment.

"How's things in the park?" the driver asked, on his way back.

"Absolutely fucked," Fairchild said, and went for his truck.

THE SAME HEAT that had scorched the entire West for nearly two weeks pressed down upon Denver, fraying tempers and igniting brush fires in the canyons and arroyos.

Skanz approached the PetroDyne headquarters without his customary care. Normally, he'd have spent half an hour circling through the lobbies and shopping plazas of the downtown office sprawl, making sure that no one could be following him. But it was hot, the thin air filthy, and he was tired. If someone wanted to trace him to PetroDyne, let PetroDyne worry about it. He hadn't called this meeting.

He entered the lobby of the building through a revolving door. An old man with a cane was going out, tottering along in the wedge of door space opposite him. The old man glanced his way as the glass revolved, and Skanz stopped abruptly. It was a moment's trick of light and mirrored reflection. His own image overlay the features of the old man, and it was as if he were staring at himself grown old and thin, wearing a tattered suit, his scabrous hand dragging at the glass for purchase.

Then the trailing edge of the door hit him from behind, gouging his heel sharply, propelling him into the lobby. Skanz realized his heart was pumping wildly. He glanced outside, but the old man had disappeared, swept up in the

19

swirl of pedestrian traffic. The guard at the reception desk was staring at him oddly. He turned and forced a smile, a salesman on his way up.

"That old man was lost," the guard offered, pushing the register across the smooth marble surface of the counter.

Skanz nodded, signing an unreadable scrawl. He produced a PetroDyne ID with a name he had forgotten.

The guard nodded and pressed a button. A gate in the low teakwood barrier snapped open.

"He thought he was in Florida," the guard added, shaking his head.

Skanz glanced at the guard. The man wore an affable smile, was doing his best to ease the passage of the day, to get along. Skanz felt an unaccountable impulse to hammer him to jelly.

The guard looked away, and Skanz moved on. He passed the bank of public elevators and went down a narrow hallway that led past a series of maintenance closets. He stopped before one that was labeled HYDRO and withdrew a key. He was inside in a moment, the door whisked shut behind him. A soft glow emanated from a control panel on the wall before him: it was not a closet, but a small waiting room. In moments, a pair of doors slid open and he entered the private elevator.

It rose swiftly and quietly, all sound muffled by the thick carpeting, the heavy wood panels of its interior. Somewhere along the rise, a mild tremor shook the compartment, and for a moment the lighting wavered and cast a glow that seemed almost red. Skanz glanced down at the scar that marked the flesh between his thumb and forefinger. It might have been an old burn. He shook his head. He had been careless. Unaccountably careless.

When the doors opened, Skanz found himself staring

across the vast expanse of Schreiber's office and out a bank of floor-to-ceiling windows. The view of the distant Rockies would have been breathtaking if not for the smog, which was even thicker at this height. Schreiber stood at a massive antique sideboard near the doors. He was a tall, thin man wearing a dark suit that draped him with the ease of a doge's cloak. His hair gleamed silver in the soft light. He'd poured one snifter with what looked like brandy and held the decanter aloft as Skanz stepped out of the elevator.

Skanz shook his head at the unasked question and went toward one of the leather chairs that had been arranged about a huge slab of gnarled, polished wood meant to serve as a coffee table. A second man, much younger than Schreiber, was seated there. He too wore an expensive suit, his hair trimmed stylishly. A corporate clone, Skanz thought.

"This is Mr. Reisman," Schreiber said over his shoulder. "Our security director."

Reisman nodded and rose to extend his hand. Skanz ignored him. He turned back to Schreiber, a question in his eyes.

"Dr. Skanz is from the East, one of our consultants," Schreiber continued, his gaze on Reisman. "We don't see much of him, but his work is invaluable to us."

Skanz felt himself relax. He turned back to Reisman with a curt nod. Reisman had pulled his hand back, his demeanor changed. Skanz knew he had become a nonentity in the man's eyes, just another hatcher of polymers and esters.

"I've got a plane to catch," Reisman told Schreiber. "But we're agreed on the switchover to rail?"

"Go to Utah," Schreiber said, showing him out. "We'll talk again soon."

When the man was gone, Skanz sat stiffly on the edge

of the thickly cushioned seat, annoyed at the sensation of comfort. It was as false as the liquid in Schreiber's glass, all part of a design meant to lull him into carelessness.

"You wanted to see me," he said.

Schreiber nodded, apparently distracted. "Mr. Reisman has many ideas for efficiency," he said. "He feels we are in a position to resume rail shipments to our storage points."

Skanz shrugged. It was no concern of his whether they smuggled their deadly cargo by truck or rail.

"Certain environmentalist pressures have eased. The sponsor is amenable. It's really a matter of approaching the appropriate officials in the state governments." Schreiber gazed out his lofty windows toward Wyoming.

"You're dreaming," Skanz said. "You're getting old."

Schreiber turned back, smiling faintly. "We're all getting old," he said. "That is why we must talk."

He gestured toward the door where Reisman had gone out, then put his glass down and came to sit in one of the chairs across from Skanz. "You were successful?"

Skanz paused before he spoke. It wasn't really a question. He felt a faint pounding of his pulse where the bullet had grazed his palm. "This man, this scientist," he said slowly. "He mentioned before he died that he had arranged something."

Schreiber shrugged. "Of what nature?" His tone was of studied disinterest. Another sham.

"He didn't say."

Schreiber nodded. "He was bluffing. An idiot. An amateur."

Skanz shrugged. He thought of the man on the subway with the ball cap and boots slipping away with the briefcase. What had been inside? A payoff? Company secrets? Some arcane recipe for death? He considered telling Schreiber of

22

the incident but knew he would not. It could only make him look worse. What would be gained by it now?

His thoughts moved on to the suddenness with which the scientist's face had blackened with his own blood. The man had been good at chemical research, bad at extortion. It didn't matter. He knew that this line of questioning was not where Schreiber's interest lay. Far beyond the smoked windows he could see the glint of airliners circling the distant airport, each waiting for its chance to land. In his mind, he saw them erupting, one by one, into bright blossoms of flame.

He turned back as Schreiber leaned forward in his seat. Schreiber glanced toward the distant airliners, looked at Skanz thoughtfully, then gestured toward the gleaming wood between them.

"This is *eruguayo*," he said, rapping the surface of the table with his knuckles. "It comes from an area of Brazil . . ." Schreiber shrugged, barely disturbing the soft folds of his suit. He meant that it would mean nothing to name the place. Skanz stared at the wood. It was variegated red and orange, with pockmarks of black. It must have weighed a thousand pounds.

"Those black spots you see," Schreiber continued, "are holes. Which were not there when I had the piece installed."

Skanz looked up at him, realizing that now the conversation was on track. He enjoyed these moments, knowing something important was under way yet wondering what was to come. They were very rare in his life now.

"One night I had stayed late. So late I fell asleep in that chair." He pointed at Skanz and took a sharp breath through his thin nostrils. "When I woke up, I heard a strange noise. I was still groggy, and as I looked around the room in confusion I heard a glass shatter." He indicated the table again.

"I looked to find my drink on its side, pieces of glass

23

dancing on the surface of that table." His pale blue eyes met Skanz's gaze and held. "I looked closer, disbelieving, and found that the entire surface of the table had come alive. Worms, strange horned worms the size of your finger, were erupting through the finish, chewing through a quarter inch of marine varnish as if it were tissue paper."

Skanz glanced at the table once more, hoping to see it happening again. Finally he looked back at Schreiber. "And what did you do?"

Schreiber smiled his thin smile again. "At first I did nothing. I simply watched. I was sure I was dreaming. Then, when I realized that the creatures were real, I thought of going for something with which to smash them. And then I thought, as I was about to rise, I will do nothing. I will not have to."

Skanz nodded. "They did not live long."

Schreiber smiled. "Not even an hour. Horrible-looking creatures. Such violent power. And yet once they had expended that energy, burst those incredible bounds, they found themselves in a place they could not survive. They expected to find themselves at home in their jungle and instead they died, hundreds of feet above an arid plateau."

Skanz held Schreiber's gaze. "He tried to kill me, you know."

"Yes. And is that the first time?" Skanz heard the patient tone of an aggrieved schoolmaster.

"It was—," he began another protest, then gave it up. "A mistake," he concluded.

Schreiber nodded thoughtfully. "He was to appear a mere robbery victim. You turned it into a Viking funeral."

Skanz turned away. "Who cares what they think now?"

"I do not like loose threads," Schreiber said firmly, and it was as near anger as Skanz had ever seen him.

Skanz thought about how easy it would be to kill him. Slip back down the elevator, disappear. But to what?

"You're not afraid of me, are you?" he asked Schreiber.

"I'm not afraid of men," Schreiber said calmly.

"I don't believe that," Skanz said. "But I know you're not afraid of me."

Schreiber laughed and reached across the table to grasp his shoulder. His grip was surprisingly strong. "I count on you." He withdrew his grip and stood, saluting Skanz with his drink. "Take care. Who knows when I will need you."

"Not soon," Skanz said, already moving for the elevator. "I will be taking some sun now."

"Good," Schreiber said. "You should rest. Enjoy yourself."

Enjoy himself, Skanz thought, as the elevator sank down its shaft. Yes, he should do that. It was a long drive back to the airport and he had rented a heavy car. With any luck, something would step into his path along the way.

FAIRCHILD STOOD IN front of his idling pickup, looking down over the edge where he'd had his earlier adventure in driving. Evidently the RV had not plunged to its fiery demise. The dry course of the Little Murky was unmarred by flame or twisted wreckage and he felt a little wistful about it. The driver was more than likely filing a complaint about Fairchild's driving at this very moment.

Once during a trip to visit Lena's folks, he'd seen an even higher cliff in Wheeling, where legend had it that a man had jumped off, on horseback. There'd been other men chasing after him with guns. As his purpose was noble, the man lived, and so did his horse, according to the story. Anything was possible.

It was nearing lunchtime, but he didn't feel very hungry. He turned back to the truck, took off his Smokey hat, and tossed it in on the seat, working at the crease it left in his hair. He didn't like the hat on general principles—maybe it was all right if you were a bear, but it was heavy, hot in the summer, and probably promoted baldness. He took it off more often than proper rangers were supposed to.

Lena hadn't much cared for it either, but then she hadn't much cared for anything that reminded her of the

National Park Service. For her, the mission of that agency was to deny her access to civilized America.

They'd been happy enough, the first few years, when it was all an adventure, a natural rebellion against her Main Line upbringing. Her father had been a Philadelphia attorney, her mother an interior designer. They'd decided Lena should be a physician. Fairchild met her in an Ecology of the West class at the University of Utah. He was on leave for the summer, working on his master's. She had just dropped out of medical school at Boulder and had hitchhiked to Salt Lake City on a whim.

The professor was describing a recently published novel full of the exploits of a group of eco-raiders. This merry band of anarchists sabotaged machinery involved in various road, dam, and forestry projects, generally creating havoc around the West. Though the professor pretended neutrality, Fairchild had finally lost it.

He broke into the prof's recitation, standing to tell the story of a friend who'd lost his hand. His chain saw had struck a spike hidden in a pine by someone distressed by a logging operation in the Absaroka Range. The saw bucked and clipped his friend's hand off at the wrist. The friend drove forty miles into town with a belt tourniquet in his teeth, his hand in his lunch box, but he'd been too late.

The friend had never gotten used to his prosthesis and had stopped going to the free government physical therapy two hundred miles away in Casper. The state employment office hadn't been able to find him a job, either, but were still telling him not to worry, it had only been a year and a half since the accident.

When Fairchild sat down, the professor gave the class a break and never mentioned the book again. Lena stopped

27

Fairchild after the class that night. She wanted to know what he did for a living. He told her; she suggested they go for coffee. By the end of the summer they were married and on their way to Park Service housing, West Yellowstone, Montana. She'd loved it, for six months.

The echoes of a shot rolled down the canyon and Fairchild broke off his reverie. He glanced about him. Though he was outside the park boundary, it was still Forest Service land, and posted against firearms. He got in the truck and swung back on the road. Not five hundred yards uproad, he topped a mild rise and saw an old GMC pickup drawn off in a pullout. He knew who it was.

He cut his engine and quietly coasted in behind the battered truck. He looked about, but the turnout was otherwise unoccupied. He got down and approached the Jimmy.

It was hot outside, but the wind cutting through the shallow canyon began to dry the sweaty patch at the small of his back at once. It was quiet and he could taste the dust in his mouth. The bed of the truck was empty. He stared at it for a while, then reached to fiddle with something that looked like a tie-down near the tailgate release. The cleat twisted in his hands with a tiny squeak of metal and the entire floor of the truck bed gave way.

He shook his head and was about to curl his fingers under the trapdoor that had opened when there was a sound in the gravel beside him and a hand slammed the false bottom shut.

Fairchild turned. A big man whose features were mostly hidden behind a bushy, unkempt beard stood glaring down at him. He wore bib overalls, a T-shirt, and a gimme cap that was embroidered PROUST.

"How you doing, Joss?" Fairchild said.

28

The big man grunted and leaned his bulk forward, but Fairchild didn't step back. Fairchild had played ball, a one-step-too-slow linebacker in high school. Joss Humphries had never played tackle, but he looked as if he could. This close, Joss smelled like damp grass.

"I like your hat," Fairchild said, looking up.

Joss seemed to relax. He stepped back, and pulled off the cap as if he'd just discovered it. He smiled, revealing some good teeth, some bad. "What the fuck kind of company is Proust, anyway?" Joss said.

Fairchild shook his head. "Hydroelectric, I think." Joss nodded as if he'd accept that, then stared out into the dry canyon nearby. Fairchild watched him. He would not be surprised to learn that Joss could quote from Proust's work.

"Super's on my ass, Joss. Somebody's been poaching deer in the park again."

Joss thought about it, then pointed toward the forest below. "Superintendent's a Mormon asshole," he said mildly. "Lookee down there."

Fairchild scanned the yellowing line of trees above the dry creek bed. Two months ago there'd been a fine trout stream filling the banks.

"It's dry all right," Fairchild said. He turned back to Joss, trying to come up with a formidable expression. "There's rangers that would like to bag a poacher," he added.

Joss didn't register it. He took Fairchild's arm and pointed. "Right there. See 'um?"

Fairchild caught a glance of something big, a dusty brown creature wobbling uncertainly behind the skein of trees. Joss moved quickly to the cab and came out with a scoped deer rifle. He gave Fairchild a look, then leaned across the hood of his pickup, taking aim at the animal.

29

"Joss!" Fairchild felt tired now, as if he were coming down with a summer cold. He heard a car approaching behind them.

"It's rabid, dammit." Joss turned to fire.

Fairchild lunged for his arm and the shot crashed through the bushes wide of its mark. The creature, whatever it was, vanished.

"Damn, Jack," Humphries said, complaining.

A station wagon sped by on the roadway. An elderly woman had her face pressed to the passenger window, staring openmouthed at Joss and his smoking rifle. The wagon sped on out of sight.

Fairchild felt an ache starting up behind his right eye. Every time he tried to be decent to people, it ended up costing him. Joss shook his head and spat into a dry clump of rye grass. He flipped open the false bottom. There, in a compartment where two deer could have fit, was a tangle of cables, empty beer cans, and tools. Across the top of the mess lay the stiff carcass of a coyote.

"There's rabid animals all over these parts," Joss growled. Fairchild grimaced as the lid slammed back down.

"I got a real bad feeling, Jack," Joss continued. He gazed out over the forest, searching the skyline as if for something approaching, flying in low over the horizon. "This drought, the heat, the rabies—things just ain't right." He trailed off, turning back to Fairchild. "We're lookin' at hard times, old buddy."

Fairchild felt a chill tracing his neck, despite the heat. It was typical backwoods superstition, but when it came from someone like Humphries, it could catch you.

Joss hadn't waited for a reply. He was in his truck, grinding the starter, jamming the gears. He stuck his head out the passenger window and grinned back at Fairchild. "Hope you boys find your poacher," he called.

Fairchild watched him roar away up the canyon. The shadow of a rainless cloud cut the sun and he turned away with a shudder. He had the unreasonable feeling that evil was gathering in the trees that crowded down upon the road, and he didn't want to be around when it came hurtling out. It was the sort of thinking you might expect from an eight-year-old, he realized, but he didn't care, and he didn't look back before he pulled away.

CARL RIPLEY GUNNED the eighteen-wheel tanker heavily as he downshifted his way to the guarded exit gate. He smiled at the racket that bounced off the walls of the tin warehouses on either side of them.

"Shit, man, cut that out." Norton bounced nervously in the seat beside him. "What's wrong with you?"

Ripley laughed. "You're a nervous turd, Norton." He turned back to the wheel. A man in stiff khakis, with a sidearm in a shiny, intricately tooled holster, was already storming out of the guard shack. Ripley pulled the rig to a stop.

"That's going in your file," the uniformed man snapped.

"You can stick it anywhere you want to, Harris," Ripley called over the roaring idle. He checked his reflection in the outside mirror. He smoothed his hair and winked at the image of a grinning tiger that was emblazoned on the side of the tanker. So they were a major oil company this trip. He turned back to Harris, who gritted his teeth and jabbed a clipboard up at him.

Ripley took it and scrawled "Burt Reynolds" in the place reserved for his checkout signature. He handed the clipboard down to Harris, who snatched it back without looking. Harris gestured to someone inside the guardhouse.

A second man in starched company greens came out to hand Harris a manila envelope. Harris checked the label, then handed it up to Ripley. Ripley tipped an imaginary hat at Harris then revved up his engine. He started toward the still-closed gates. A guard near the barrier hesitated.

"Ripley!" Harris shouted. He'd noticed the signature at last.

The truck picked up steam.

"Goddammit, Ripley!" Harris was purple. The truck caught a gear. Frantic, Harris gestured at the gate attendant, who threw a switch. The gates swung open just ahead of the huge silver tanker. Harris glared after the departing truck, then stomped inside and picked up a telephone.

They rolled down Colfax, over the speed limit. Norton was beside himself. "You're crazy, you know that?" Ripley wasn't paying any attention. Norton turned and stared out the passenger window, fuming. Ripley cuffed him good-naturedly on the shoulder.

"Look over here."

Norton wouldn't turn his head. Ripley pinched his ear. Norton slapped it away. Ripley grabbed his skinny knee and squeezed. Norton sat up, banging his head a good one on the window frame. Ripley laughed as Norton rubbed his knobby head.

"Now look over here," he said, braking for a light.

Grudgingly, Norton looked. The tanker pulled up beside a white Caddy, a convertible, carrying two women with hairdos you could hide things in.

Ripley leaned out of the cab. "How you girls doin'?" He grinned. The driver, a blonde in a leopard-skin jumpsuit, gave him a bored look. The passenger, a redhead with a T-shirt that read PINK PUSSYCAT, looked at him and smiled.

"We're in that new Burt Reynolds movie," Ripley called down to them. "I'm his double."

The driver rolled her eyes and picked up a pair of rhinestone-studded sunglasses from the dash. She turned and stared at Ripley before she pushed them up on her nose. "Must be the ass end you double."

Ripley whooped as the Caddy shot away from the light. He turned to Norton, delighted.

"Isn't she something?"

Norton rubbed his head ruefully. "You're gonna get us fired."

"Shoot, Norton. Open the envelope. Which way they want us to go this week?" Ripley caught third gear, watching sadly as the Caddy made a snappy turn off Colfax into the crowded lot of a cocktail lounge. He blasted the air horn as they went by. The blonde didn't look up. The redhead waved as she got out.

Ripley laid on the horn again. Norton winced, looking up from the papers in his lap. "I got a headache, okay?"

Ripley made a mournful face. Norton stuffed the papers over his visor and looked away, in a huff. Ripley punched his shoulder, rocking him. "They got us on 80, all the way to Rock Springs," Norton said.

Ripley nodded, maneuvering across two lanes of traffic toward a freeway ramp. A chorus of horns sounded behind them. Ripley waved a reassurance to the angry drivers and ran the caution light above the turn lane. He dug in his shirt pocket and laid a small black capsule on his tongue, then flipped it back in his throat and swallowed. He looked somberly at Norton.

"La cucaracha, la cucaracha," Ripley sang.

Norton looked ready to cry.

"I'm tired of driving that I-80," Ripley said.

"Aw, Jesus . . . ," Norton whined.

"I mean it. It's a safety matter. I could go to sleep out of sheer boredom."

"Carl, we haveta go the way they say. Let me drive, then." Norton's voice was pleading. He leaned out his window as if he were thinking to jump, but they were clipping it off now, piling into the slow lane ahead of a wave of outbound commuters.

"Norton," Ripley said, shaking his head. "I don't have to do nothing except die." He nodded, his hands wringing the wheel, his eyes glittering straight ahead. "Besides"—he turned to smile at Norton—"we got us a new boss this trip."

Norton's expression fell from despair into suspicion.

Ripley turned back to the road, shrugging. "Wait'll we get down the road a piece. I'll tell you all about it." A Jaguar swooshed by them, offering a glimpse of blond hair and bare shoulder at the passenger window.

Ripley shook his head, indicating the Jag. "There goes a man getting a handjob at a hundred miles an hour."

Norton rubbed the stubble on his chin, pondering it. "What do you mean, a new boss?"

"It's okay, Bo. We're making a little extra this haul." Ripley smiled. "Kinda money a man ought to, carry the kind of things we carry."

Curiosity seemed to have wormed its way into Norton's brain. He rubbed at the knot on his head and glanced over at Ripley, waiting for the rest of it.

"We're going to drive her right off the map," Ripley went on happily, patting the dash. "That's the only thing there is to it. And then we're gonna hide."

Norton looked painfully confused. Ripley caught high

gear and yahooed. He reached back into the daybed compartment, found a green gimme cap embroidered with the logo of the Boston Celtics, and mashed it down around Norton's ears. They were flying now.

FAIRCHILD WAS DOING his best to concentrate on the list of holiday-weekend procedures he'd found on his desk when he came in, but it wasn't easy. He was not unaffected by Joss Humphries and his prophecy of gloom and besides that, he kept on seeing Lena disappearing into the maw of the bus, kept hearing her know-it-all voice telling him he was a failure.

She was right, of course, from her point of view. He had a college degree and a number of hours toward a master's. He could have done something practical a long time ago. One of his classmates was now the director of a famous zoo and had appeared on *Good Morning America* with unusual animals. His partner on his senior research project worked for Weyerhauser, managing their "ecological planning"; he probably knocked down twice what Fairchild made.

Fairchild sighed. He'd seen an ad in the Salt Lake paper the other day; even rookie cops were getting close to his present salary. He tried to imagine being a Salt Lake cop, idling away the hours in an air-conditioned cruiser, moving from doughnut shop to doughnut shop, always on the lookout for polygamists, rousting loiterers out of Temple Square. Maybe he could play on the department softball team, find a girl who liked the badge.

37

A door opened behind him and footsteps approached his desk. Fairchild feigned interest in his mimeographed list of procedures. "We got a complaint somebody in a Park Service truck was driving erratically on the West Yellowstone road." The voice belonged to Perry Christensen, the district supervisor. It was after six, and the portable office was otherwise deserted. Only the occasional crackle of the dispatch radio cut the background silence. "Early this morning. You know anything about it?"

Fairchild stared at the last item on the list. "REMEMBER THAT COURTESY PAYS DIVIDENDS." All caps and underlined. Something Christensen had added, to be sure. Fairchild shook his head without looking up.

Christensen continued. "Also, a couple of concerned citizens stopped in here to tell me somebody was discharging a firearm alongside the same road, in the presence of one of our rangers. They wanted to be sure this man had been arrested."

Fairchild finally took his glance from the paper. Christensen had whitish blond hair, red-rimmed eyes, and an almost transparent mustache. There was a habitual twitch at his upper lip that made him look like a rabbit.

"Joss Humphries spotted a rabid coyote in Little Murky draw. When he brought it to my attention, I suggested he go ahead and shoot it. The report's on your secretary's desk."

Christensen thought it over for a moment. "Why didn't you call Animal Control?"

"For one thing, we weren't in the park. For another, the animal would have been gone by the time they got there."

Christensen bit his lip, annoyed. "We oughtn't to be encouraging civilians to go tracking down rabid animals. We ought to be doing our jobs ourselves."

"I agree," Fairchild said. "I just felt I did what had to be done."

Christensen ignored him. "That Humphries is going to get his ass in a sling sooner or later," he said. "I know damn well who's been shooting deer up by Wilson Lodge."

"I'm not so sure about that."

"I just wish somebody else would put a little effort into stopping him," Christensen said, glaring.

"I asked Joss to keep an eye out for us. He said he'd report any suspicious parties to me personally."

Christensen snorted, then turned for his office. He stopped abruptly and turned back. "You're on tonight, right?"

Fairchild nodded.

"Well, the superintendent called me this afternoon. He wants somebody to stake out the hot pots over by the lodge. The kids are skinny-dipping again and we've had a dozen complaints."

Fairchild groaned. "Come on, Perry."

"He wants some citations. This is a serious public relations matter. I promised him we'd see to it."

Christensen turned and moved into his office, slamming his door on any further discussion. Fairchild leaned back in his chair and stared up at the huge action map on his wall. The map was flagged with pushpins, different colors designating various trouble spots. A yellow pin near Antler Peak indicated the place where two hikers from New Jersey had disappeared—it had been ten days now, and though the search continued, it was likely that they had long since become scavenger food.

There was a dark blue pin near the Falls on South Canyon Loop. The road had slipped away there, creating a

considerable chasm, and they'd already lost a party of bicy-
clers who ignored the barricades and shot off into the ride of
their lives.

There were several red pins scattered about where a
series of brush fires had been keeping the fire teams busy over
the last week. Only luck had kept any one of them from
jumping the line into disaster.

Then there was the green pin by the West Thumb hot
pots, where tourists were complaining about nude bathers. It
was common knowledge that the offenders were the college-
aged employees of the concessionaires who ran the lodge
and gift shop and that they were simply reenacting a long-
standing local tradition. After the shops closed, there wasn't
too much for inventive young people to do, and most of the
workers came from parts of the country where nude bathing
was not high on the list of public menaces. However, they'd
been getting too bold to bother trekking to the more remote
pools, and worse yet, were also reported to be smoking marijuana. Now Fairchild had been ordered to do something
about it.

He slumped down in his seat. His wife had left him,
forest fires were threatening, tenderfoot campers were lost in
the wilderness, Farily Junction was the focus of a massive bear
invasion, the drought was driving rattlesnakes into all the
campgrounds, the elk herds were regularly stampeding the
Meadows walking tours, and he had been ordered to arrest
skinny-dippers and confiscate their thirty-dollar stash of
dope.

Obviously, when Lena demeaned the entirety of his life,
she was only being reasonable. Maybe he was cut out for
better things. He would give it some thought while he staked
out the nudists. He picked up his Smokey hat and walked
wearily out the door.

SPILL

* * *

Fairchild sat alone at the bar of the Buckaroo, toying with the last of his beer, trying to get up the spirit to go back to his gloomy married quarters for a shower and a fresh shirt. It being Happy Hour on the eve of the Frontier Days weekend, he was not exactly alone, though he felt like it. He was thinking that he had absolutely nothing in common with a single one of the two hundred or so ranch hands, roughnecks, cowgirls, and assorted locals who jammed the bar.

He was about to ask Jessie for another beer when she threw down her bar rag and focused her glance on something evidently evil coming their way.

"I'm tired of your shit, Isaac," she cried. "Don't even look cross-eyed at me, or you're gone." Her voice cut the din of the place easily.

Jessie could joke roughhouse with the best of them, but there wasn't a trace of humor in her expression. Though Fairchild didn't have to turn around to see who it was, he did anyway.

Isaac Brigham Smith was still several steps from the bar, but he was easy to spot. His mother was a Nez Perce, the tallest Indian in the Bureau of Indian Affairs school; his father, a jack-Mormon logger big enough to flip jeeps out of parking spaces he wanted. Isaac was a head taller than the crowd fighting for the ten feet of free submarine sandwich on a table just behind the bar. He had stopped, apparently considering the seriousness of Jessie's warning.

Jessie stared up at him, her jaw thrust, one hand out of sight beneath the bar. Isaac pursed his lips, finally nodding his agreement to be a good boy. As she started away, Isaac saw Fairchild and winked, then crossed his eyes. Jessie went off, shaking her head.

41

"A beer?" Isaac called after her. She appeared not to notice. He reached over the shoulder of an outfitter and took up a foot or so of the submarine in one of his big hands, then came to join Fairchild.

"We'll never get a beer now," Fairchild told him.

Isaac shrugged and checked his watch. "Hell, she's off in ten minutes. Somebody'll take pity on us."

Fairchild nodded. "I could use some pity."

Isaac looked him over. "Nothing worse than a man feeling sorry for himself."

"Thanks, Isaac."

"You ought to be like me, give up women," Isaac said.

"Who said it was about women?"

"I didn't figure it was about money, all you make with the Park Service."

Fairchild smiled, feeling himself falling into the rhythm of buddy talk. He and Isaac went back a ways, to the time when Fairchild had hired on with the Park Service. He'd started as the lowest of grunts, collecting tolls at the east entrance to the park, up the road from Cody.

On a Fourth of July weekend, Fairchild had a trio of bikers at the gate. Two of their buddies had run past him without paying a few minutes before, and Fairchild had, in a rush of misplaced bravado, swung the snow gate closed when he saw the next bunch approaching. The three had stood down from their bikes and were moving in on Fairchild, who was alone at the isolated station, when Isaac arrived in his Bureau of Public Roads dump truck.

Isaac dropped the plow blade in front of the truck and scraped the three choppers off the road and down into the ravine that flanked the entrance. The bikers made the mistake of rushing the cab. By the time they saw whom they were dealing with, it was too late. All three had been taken away by ambulance.

Fairchild and Isaac had ended up at the Buckaroo that evening, a college boy buying a taciturn Indian a drink in thanks. They'd been thrown out at 2:00 A.M., fast friends, and had been coming back ever since.

Isaac knew about him and Lena, of course. Fairchild knew Isaac had never been convinced their marriage would work, and he also knew that Isaac would have had his fingernails pulled out before he'd have said so.

Fairchild turned to feed Isaac the line he was waiting on. "You gave up women, huh?"

Isaac nodded. "Nearly every night."

Fairchild laughed and turned to signal Jessie. She gave him a grudging look, then finally slid them a pair of Rainiers.

Isaac took most of his down with his first swallow. He banged the bottle down on the bar and sighed. "It don't taste like anything at all," he said. "But as long as they don't sell it east of the Rockies, I'll keep drinking it."

Fairchild nodded. It was a kind of isolationism he could understand. He'd grown up in Ohio, discovered the West through 3-D View-Master slides and old copies of *Arizona Highways* in the family doctor's office. Fairchild had fallen immediately, desperately, in love with the look of that dramatic landscape, so distinct from the fenced-in, glacier-flattened land where he'd grown up, impatient with the predictable life around him.

His parents, decent if unimaginative factory workers, dismissed it as one of those fleeting passions of adolescence. It was the sixties, after all, and young people were passionate about many things. His folks were happy he wasn't into drugs, and that he was keeping his hair cut reasonably far off his shoulders.

They'd underestimated him, of course. The afternoon he graduated from Findlay High, Fairchild was standing beside U.S. 24 with his thumb out. He didn't stop until a trucker dropped him in Aspen. He spent the summer busing dishes and by fall had managed a modest scholarship at the state university in Fort Collins. He found a room that overlooked the Cache la Poudre River, with a tough landlady who chain-smoked Lucky Strikes and raised Labrador retrievers. He had never looked back.

He shook his head at the memories and smiled at Isaac. He saw no reason to set foot east of the Rockies again himself. Isaac finished his beer and placed the empty out where Jessie couldn't miss it.

"You on this weekend?"

Fairchild nodded.

"Me too," Isaac said. "Maybe it'll keep me out of trouble."

Fairchild looked at him. Isaac made a big target for trouble, but then again, he had always been able to handle it.

"I been seeing this woman down by Crowheart," Isaac said. "A Gros Ventre."

Fairchild nodded. Isaac's leathered face showed no expression, but his eyes had narrowed. There had to be a story coming.

Isaac tried to get Jessie's attention, but she was ignoring them again. He turned back to Fairchild. "One of her brothers got him a new pickup with his annual allotment check from the BIA, and her and me took it for a ride while he was passed out the other night." Isaac shrugged. "Anyhow, we went over the side about halfway down to Jackson. Ended up in a geyser pool. By the time we got out, the damn geyser had gone off. There was steam and mud and water flying out from all around that truck, it looked like some kind of a monster." Isaac allowed himself a smile. "Hell, I couldn't even get back in to turn off the lights."

Fairchild laughed. "How'd you get it out?"

Isaac shook his head. "I didn't. We hitched on down to Jackson and Sophia called her brother from this bar to tell him what happened. I guess he must have pulled it out."

Fairchild stared. "You haven't seen him?"

"I never even met the guy. He was passed out, remember."

"Jesus Christ, Isaac."

"I know. I been one or two steps the other side of the line for a while now."

Fairchild thought about it a minute. "It's okay," he said finally. "We all get there at one time or another."

They were sitting in silence when Jessie stopped to pick up Isaac's empty. She checked it, then stared at him. Isaac shrugged. "They ought to make a bigger bottle."

"Or smaller Indians," she said.

Fairchild put a bill on the bar and Jessie took it with a glower. She was no rookie. With her meanness and Isaac's size they could solve the Broncos' problem at defensive end, he thought, watching her bend into the cooler for the beer.

She was not unattractive, nor had she spread too much across the beam. But as far as he knew, she lived a celibate life. She'd been married to a lineman for Utah Power and Light who'd been killed by lightning while he worked on a transformer during a storm. You had to forgive her for her moods.

45

"A testy woman is more interesting," Isaac said, following Fairchild's gaze. "Sophia's pretty testy," he added.

"I suppose you could call it interesting," Fairchild said. He was thinking of Lena again. Rolling the fact of her departure around in his mind was like probing a broken tooth with his tongue: he wondered when the serious pain would start.

Jessie turned and placed two dripping bottles of beer in front of them. "Why don't we run off for the weekend?" Isaac said to her.

She gave him a withering glance. "There's about a million reasons why, but I don't have time to run through them right now." She turned to a barmaid who was frantically tossing lime slices into a tray full of gin and tonics and added several beers to the load.

"I need a reason to live," Isaac said good-naturedly.

Jessie turned to scorch him, then froze, her mouth open. The outfitter on the other side of Isaac was backpedaling furiously. Curious, Fairchild turned on his stool just in time to see a small Indian in a pearl-buttoned shirt roundhousing a pool cue toward Isaac's head.

A table of cowgirls sitting between the pool table and the shuffleboard bowling machine ducked in unison as the cue whooshed over them. The pool game and bowling continued in the background. Isaac had finally turned and had thrown up his hand instinctively, but he was too late.

Abruptly, the plug in the butt of the pool cue gave way and the lead weight in the handle flew across the room, crashing into a Hamm's sign on the far wall. The sign, which created the illusion of a river running along snowy peaks, sprayed plastic fragments onto the empty dance floor but did not go out. The river continued to pour around a jagged hole in the wilderness.

46

The cue stick, considerably lightened, soared up and missed Isaac entirely. The little Gros Ventre came off his feet and fell across the table of cowgirls, who grabbed their purses and fled. Fairchild, who'd made a futile lunge for the cue stick, crashed into the undiminished knot of cowhands gathered around the free buffet.

Isaac was still staring at the broken sign, disbelieving his good fortune, when the Gros Ventre got to his feet, growling and charging, this time tugging at a skinning knife sheathed at his belt. The knife, however, had got hung up during the fall. When the Gros Ventre finally ripped it free, he brought a large, flapping chunk of his shirttail with it. He was trying to pull the cloth away when Isaac hit him.

The small Indian flew back across the cowgirls' table, past Fairchild, glanced off the rail of the pool table, and slid backward down the shuffleboard bowling outfit. He skidded, sitting up, into the plastic pins and lodged between the hardwood surface and the pin tray. The machine began a terrible buzzing, and the Gros Ventre's mouth opened in a soundless howl, his eyes sightless, his limbs rigid and jittering. The jukebox had lapsed and there was an uncharacteristic silence in the place.

"He's being electrocuted," somebody yelled.

One of the cowgirls dove under the machine and yanked the power cord out of the wall. The Gros Ventre relaxed. His head sank to his knees.

A man in a gimme cap stood at the head of the bowling machine, staring at the unconscious Gros Ventre in disgust. "I had a perfect game going," the man said.

Fairchild stepped gingerly through mounds of spilled sandwich and pulled the small Indian out of the pins.

Isaac turned to the bar where Jessie stood with a riot stick braced. "Damn, Jessie, it wasn't my fault."

47

"Get out of here, Isaac." She moved forward menacingly.

"I'll pay you—"

"You don't ever come back," she added, her face reddened.

"Ah, damn," Isaac said, as Fairchild came to pull him away. The jukebox picked up again, and the two of them moved on toward the door.

Outside, they found a Ford pickup parked askew on the walkway, an error of judgment sure to warrant a tow job from Jessie or one of her cohorts. The truck had a terrible scrape along one side where it had apparently cozied up to a tree. Its front bumper sagged low to the ground and the grille was caked with gray and black mud. It looked like a truck that had been driven down a forest embankment and into a geyser pool.

"You recognize that?" Fairchild asked.

Isaac gave a soundless laugh. "Somebody asleep in there," he said, pointing. "Let's see who he brought for backup."

They walked to the driver's window and looked in. There was a terrible stink of liquor in the cab, with a litter of beer cans and a couple empty pints of J. W. Dant strewn about the mats. There was a sizable rip in the seat and a spot where somebody had puked and apparently tried to clean it up with a rake.

Snuggled in the far corner, fast asleep, was a dark-haired Indian woman, a beatific smile on her face.

"Sophia?" Fairchild asked.

Isaac nodded. He leaned through the window and nudged her, but she hardly stirred. She looked innocent in

48

her sleep, and decidedly not testy. The testiness was probably something Isaac had invented.

Her shirt had hiked up and a little roll of her tummy hung over the edge of her stiff new jeans. She rolled her head to the side then, and Fairchild noted a heavy bruise on the side of her face. She might have got it in the wreck but it looked fresher than that, a souvenir from her brother more likely. He glanced back at the Buckaroo and shook his head.

"It was her driving that night," Isaac said, his voice soft. "I didn't want her to, but hell, it was *her* brother's truck. She was looking at me and laughing when the turn came up. I went for the wheel but we were off the road before I could do anything. We go about twenty feet down and then there's this tree coming up at us like God's last judgment. My head went into the windshield then and the next thing I know, I'm smelling sulfur and there's this awful hissing sound like the truck's gonna blow up."

He turned to Fairchild, a rueful smile on his face. "It was a dumb thing, Jack. But hell, this last month I been losing ground, you know. I quit going to night school, I slept through that state trooper exam, I even answered a chain letter." He shook his head in disgust and looked off toward the mountains that rose up to the east, behind the town.

Fairchild felt an aching sadness growing inside him. Take this girl and run away with her, he wanted to say. Find a new place, make a nest. Have babies. Make a new life. Wouldn't that be nice?

He put his hand on Isaac's shoulder. "Lena took off," he said. Isaac nodded, as if he'd known all along. There was the sound of an ambulance approaching the Buckaroo, and soon its flashers broke past the screen of pines between them

49

and the highway. Sophia gave a little snore and shifted in her seat.

Fairchild studied the ruined truck. There was a considerable star in the safety glass where Isaac's head had apparently tried to go through it. Several jagged cracks radiated out from this point, dividing the windshield into a map of some insane country. He checked the odometer. Twelve hundred miles. There'd been plenty pulled out of the reservation canyons with less. There were many new pickups sold when the yearly allotment checks went out, and a fair number of them never made it home. As far as he was concerned, the runty little Gros Ventre was lucky. His truck still ran and nobody was dead yet.

The ambulance, actually a van with GALLATIN COUNTY RESCUE emblazoned on its side, uttered one last whoop and slid to a stop in front of the Buckaroo. After a moment, two young attendants stepped down, looking decidedly unconcerned.

As they started toward the building, the doors opened and the little Gros Ventre appeared, awake but groggy, supported by one of the cowgirls and the bowler in the gimme cap. The attendants took their patient away toward the back of their rig and the two patrons went back inside.

As the ambulance pulled off, Isaac turned to Fairchild. "You lend me twenty?" he asked.

"Sure," Fairchild said. He found a bill in his wallet and offered it to Isaac, who took it, opened the pickup door, and leaned across the seat to tuck it into Sophia's pocket. She smiled in her sleep and Isaac worked his fingers loose with a little smile of his own.

"She's a sweet kid, really," he said.

Fairchild nodded. Asleep, she appeared something like the twenty-five she was. Awake, she'd look forty.

Isaac put his arm around Fairchild's shoulders and they walked away together, after the departing ambulance.

"Happy Frontier Days," Isaac said. "See you in the park."

"Good luck to you too," Fairchild said. It could be a worse life, he told himself. Surely.

NORTON WAS TRYING to make sense of what Ripley was telling him, but it was a tough job. For one thing, Ripley tended to make the simplest things sound difficult and complex. For another thing, Norton would have much preferred to concentrate on eating his chicken-fried steak, his favorite meal. It was a sorry trial, trying to concentrate on a speed freak's fantasies when all you wanted to do was enjoy your dinner. He was going to end up with indigestion and the heck of it was, he was paying good money to do it.

"You just got to make yourself available when opportunity comes knocking, Norton."

Norton swallowed a bite of his steak, then scooped up some of the cream gravy with his bread. The gravy was the color of old white socks and tasted like chalk. It was perfect and he was only sorry to be using brown bread to sop it up with. He'd asked for Wonder, but they didn't have it.

"Why you think I come to work for an outfit like this? You hear they run all these checks and tests on you, you know there's gonna be some kind of chance to cash in." Ripley beamed with satisfaction.

"Why don't you just come right out and say what it is you done?" Norton said. He glanced toward the counter, hoping to catch the waitress's attention, but she was checking

52

her lipstick in the mirror. It was only three-thirty and he and Ripley were the only customers in the place, a roadside diner a few miles northeast of Laramie.

"Could I have some more bread please," he called. The waitress looked up, raised an eyebrow, then went back to her makeup. After a moment, she sighed heavily, rolled her eyes, and moved off into the kitchen.

When she reappeared she had a loaf of whole-wheat bread in her hands, which she brought to the table and plunked down by Norton. She gave Ripley a lingering glance, however, then switched her hips at him all the way back to the counter.

"We shouldn't be on this road," Norton said, opening the new loaf of bread.

Ripley's eyes were on the waitress. "We use this route all the time," he said.

"But they told us to use I-80 this week—"

"Opportunity, Norton. Opportunity." Ripley stared unabashedly at the waitress, who smiled and ran her tongue around her lips for him.

"You could get a blowjob on your own time, it seems to me. Instead, you have to go and jeopardize my career just because you're horny."

Ripley turned patiently. "Lucy is just a side dish, Norton, a teensy little diversion." He looked over his shoulder as if there might be someone in the deserted place trying to listen in on their conversation, then leaned close to Norton. "The fact is, we had a man pay us good money to take this truck up into Montana and lose it for a little while."

Norton stared blankly at him. "What do you mean, lose it?"

"Christ, Norton. I mean *hide* it."

"Why would someone pay you to hide our truck?"

"It's complicated."

Norton raised one hand to hold Ripley off. With his other, he swiped up the last of the gravy and chewed the bread as slowly as he could. He was hoping there was some decent pie for dessert. If this was going to be his last run for PetroDyne, he might as well get what pleasure he could from it.

Ripley continued. "But it ain't exactly bug spray we're hauling. In fact, we're not supposed to be moving this stuff at all." He bent close, nudging Norton's empty plate aside. "Truth be told, Norton, some of the shit PetroDyne's making, it's illegal, germ warfare stuff. It's in violation of an international treaty."

Norton stared. "How the hell would you know?"

Ripley seemed happy with the question. He sat back in his chair with a shit-eating grin. "A little bird told me."

Norton shrugged. It was not his concern. His concern was a steady paycheck and now that seemed lost.

Ripley studied him a moment, then, still grinning, pulled his wallet from his back pocket and tossed it on the table between them. It was one of the heavy tooled leather jobs with a brass zipper that ran along one seam. He kept it hooked to a belt loop with a chain thick enough to choke a Doberman. He pulled the zipper down and parted the flaps so Norton could look inside. Norton gaped. He was staring at a wad of hundred-dollar bills.

"That's just the deposit," Ripley said. He looked over at the waitress, gauging the effect of his theatrics. She was watching, all right, and cocked an eyebrow at Ripley's stare.

"Where'd you get that?" Norton was dazed.

"I picked it up in Boston," Ripley said, proud. Ripley leaned close enough for Norton to smell his awful breath.

"A man who works for the company back east came to me with a proposition, Norton, and I took him up on it."

"You're crazy."

"Like a fox, Norton. Like a fox." Ripley tapped the wallet with one grimy finger. "We get the rest after we're finished." Ripley zipped up his wallet and stuck it back in his pocket.

"Finished what?"

"There's nothin' to it. We take the truck to this out-of-the-way spot up by Rexburg, you tie me up, give me a little knock on the head, and when they find us, we tell them we were hijacked, that's all we know."

"How about me? Who ties me up?"

"We'll do it before you hit me."

"Then how'm I supposed to hit you, all tied up?"

Ripley sighed. "The trouble with you is, you lack imagination. We'll work something out. Maybe we'll both just take a run and butt head-on against a tree."

The thought did not appeal to Norton, but he was still focused on the wad of hundreds in Ripley's wallet. "Maybe I just lack criminal tendencies," he said cautiously.

"You're going to make five thousand dollars for this," Ripley replied.

Norton swallowed, not sure he had heard correctly, but Ripley was nodding in assurance. Norton felt a sudden burning in his bowels and thought for a moment that he'd have to run to the bathroom. He stole a glance at the counter and saw that the waitress had wormed her way closer in an effort to hear. She was leaning over far enough to reveal the considerable cleavage that had attracted Ripley's attention some months ago.

"Five thousand ought to set your thinking straight,"

Ripley said. He leaned back in his chair. Evidently, the issue was settled. He winked at the waitress, who smiled back.

There was the sound of a car pulling into the gravel lot then, and the three of them turned to watch a faded bronze Pacer nose up against the front of the place. An obese woman in a white uniform emerged and came through the door, jingling a little bell in the process. The woman walked around the counter and nodded at the waitress, who looked critically at the clock.

"You're late," the waitress said to her colleague.

"File a grievance."

The waitress shrugged, untied her apron, and came around the counter toward the truckers' table. "Ain't it a shame how a jealous woman will act?" She took Ripley's hand and squeezed it. "Come on, honey. Let me show you what I bought."

Ripley rose and clapped Norton on the shoulder. "Be right back," he said, following the waitress out the door. Norton watched the two of them walking hand in hand toward a battered Airstream trailer that sat on blocks at the far side of the parking lot.

The waitress plunged her hand down the front of Ripley's pants. Ripley's whoop echoed through the diner's window. He pressed her up against the side of the trailer, her skirt hiked to her waist. They were clutched together, heaving, Ripley struggling to keep his feet under him. The waitress flailed out, caught hold of the trailer door, and maneuvered them sideways until they fell through the opening without missing a stroke.

"That's a crying shame," Norton heard the big woman behind him saying. "She ain't nothing but a common whore."

Norton turned around and stared at the woman, apparently thinking hard. She looked back at him, awaiting his thoughts on the matter.

"What kind of pie you got?" Norton said finally. He thought his voice sounded just like a rich man's would.

FAIRCHILD HAD BEEN too absorbed in the fly-fishing tackle to notice Larraine's approach. It was her store—her's and her daddy's, that is—one of the largest outfitters outside the Intermountain cities, and there was plenty to be absorbed in.

"I didn't think you'd be fishing this weekend," she said.

He smiled wistfully. "Just killing time. I'm on tonight, then Saturday and Sunday."

She nodded sympathetically. They stood together in silence for a moment. Abruptly, she stepped to pull a slender rod from the rack in front of them. "As long as you're dreaming, look at this."

He inspected the sleek graphite shaft, the intricately wrapped ferrules and guides. He tested the tip, which had a lovely blend of give and firmness, then handed it back to her. "Nice," he said. His eyes met hers briefly, then flicked away.

"It ought to be. It's three hundred dollars. I picked up four of them from Bill Simms over in Livingston." She shook her head. "Not much good in the wind, but it's a beauty for a sure hand. I'll be lucky to sell them before the snow flies." She waited for him to look at her. "How come you're so talkative?"

He shrugged. "Maybe it's the holidays. I read about this syndrome some people get. I could be one of them."

"That's just at Christmastime."

He shook his head. "They've never researched Frontier Days. There's a terrible Frontier Days syndrome just waiting to be written up."

She laughed, and then the silence fell upon them again. She reached to fiddle with the rods. "So, how's things at home?" She adjusted a price tag.

"Okay," he said. "Sort of empty."

She turned to him.

He looked away. "Lena took off."

She considered it for a moment. "You surprised?"

"Not really."

She glanced about the shop. It was suppertime and there were more sales clerks on the floor than customers. "Why don't we go get some coffee?" she said.

"Let's make it a beer," he said, and led her toward the door.

He took her to Tom Clancy's, the one bar in town that made some pretensions to serious saloon decor. Clancy referred to it as "Early Lowenbrau Commercial." Clancy was a retired adman from Hartford who bought the place cheap, just after the earthquake, from a paranoid former bronc rider who lit out for Hawaii. Clancy took down the elk and antelope trophy heads, fired the cowboy band, and set about making his nest.

There were oversized red leather booths and a mahogany bar, rescued from a condemned hotel in Denver; backlit glass panels along the walls, with etchings of nudes and flamingos, from a dive in Butte; and, from a whorehouse in Casper, cut-glass sconces with bulbs that looked like gaslights.

Clancy endured a year of shunning from the local clientele philosophically. "I don't give a shit if nobody comes in. *I* like to drink here," he said. Over time the place had become popular with the tourists and certain of the townspeople, "the ones who clean the shit off their boots," as Clancy referred to them.

He was behind the bar when Fairchild and Larraine entered, polishing glasses and watching the *MacNeil-Lehrer NewsHour* on TV. Fairchild led Larraine to a seat at the opposite end of the bar. They noticed the program and looked at each other.

"How'd you manage to get PBS?" Fairchild asked when he came for their order.

"Satellite dish." Clancy juked his head toward the ceiling, an ornate patchwork of pressed tin panels scavenged from a local restaurant. "I bought it from that screenwriter lives over by Chico Hot Springs. He got a bigger one."

"Do you ever feel isolated out here, Tom?" Larraine looked at the TV as she spoke.

"Naw. I like it. I wouldn't go back east for anything." He swept his hand about the bar. "When I come to work, it's like I'm on this ship, like one of those old clippers, you know. I just sail along past all this exotic country and whenever I feel adventurous, I get off and mingle with the locals."

"I'd like a martini, straight up. With a twist," Fairchild said.

Clancy and Larraine turned to stare at him.

"And a chilled glass," he added.

"I didn't think they allowed that in the Park Service. I thought you guys were into Miller Lite," Clancy said.

"Make it two," Larraine said.

"It's a holiday," Fairchild said.

Clancy shrugged and went off to bury two glasses in the

ice bin. Larraine turned to face Fairchild, an expectant look on her face.

"So?" she said.

"So what?"

"So, how do you feel?"

"Like I had this enormous blister and it finally popped."

She drummed her nails on the marble bar top. "I thought maybe we'd have a real conversation, Jack."

He turned and stared out the window at a family of four who were crossing the broad main street. They stood at the median, waiting for an RV to pass, arranged like a photograph: Papa, Mama, Sister, and Little Brother, in descending order, all in matching plaid shirts, blue jeans, and straw Stetsons.

"Do you suppose they're singing somewhere tonight?" he said. Clancy had arrived with their drinks. He followed Fairchild's gesture.

"You know, when I bought this place, the guy had a whole family of antelope hung up on the wall, four of 'em, just like that crew outside." Clancy shook his head and went to draw beers for an older couple at the other end of the bar.

Fairchild watched the tourist family disappear, then forced himself to meet Larraine's steady gaze. "I don't know, I'm just glad it's over with. There hasn't been much there, not for a long time."

"You sure about that?"

He took a sip of his drink, which went down like liquid ice. "I wonder if it happens to everybody."

She raised an eyebrow inquisitively.

"You get married the first time, you don't have the slightest idea what you're doing."

She nodded. "I didn't."

"From there on, it's just dumb animal luck."

61

"That's a pretty good description of my husband," she said.

He glanced at her, smiling. "I thought we were going to have a real conversation."

She raised her glass and smiled. "Here's to smart animal luck." She took a drink, and then told him of the boy she'd met at college, a classmate in drama school. They married the day after graduation, despite her parents' wishes. They moved to Hollywood and they tried out for parts. When their cash ran out she waitressed and stocked panty hose racks in supermarkets from North Hollywood to Los Felis. He took a nonpaying job with a local theater, "for exposure," and kept going to calls. After two years of exposure she got pregnant, and he walked out. It wasn't until she had the miscarriage that she broke down and called home. Her father drove his van straight through from West Yellowstone to Los Angeles and brought her home.

"I wasn't happy to come back here, then," she finished.

"And now?" he asked.

"Where would you rather be?" It wasn't a question.

They raised their glasses together.

"But, I do need to change my life," Fairchild said. "I've got a buddy that runs this zoo back in the Midwest."

She put her glass down and turned to him, incredulous. He raised his hands. "It's just a thought," he said.

"Some thought," she said.

"Yeah, you're right." He looked at the TV, which was now into the daily financial report. Clancy stood beneath the glow of the set, rapt.

"I just wonder where it says you can't make out doing what you like to do," Fairchild said.

"It doesn't. It doesn't say that anywhere."

"Billy Bob Parks wants me to go to work guiding."

She nodded. "Billy Bob does all right."

"*He* does. I don't know how I'd do, working for him." He lifted his drink and stared deeply into it. "Actually, he's an asshole and I'd probably end up shooting him."

"You don't seem like the violent type."

"I try to keep away from situations." He finished his drink.

She was thoughtful for a moment, then turned abruptly to him. "How about going in with me, then?"

He stared at her as she continued. "With the store, I mean. We've got the capital. I just need somebody with the time. We could set up raft trips, fishing, hiking, the works."

He pursed his lips. "Billy Bob would be sad to hear you talking like this."

"Fuck Billy Bob," she said. "This is the free-enterprise system."

He nodded. It was a pleasant fantasy. He could burn his hat on Perry Christensen's desk by way of resignation.

"Well," she said. "Why not? I think we could do a lot of business."

"In the summer," he agreed. "Winter'd be tough."

"There's always snowmobile tours."

He glanced at her. "I hate snowmobiles."

She nodded. "Me too."

"Everything needs a rest, even a park."

"I agree. Snowmobiles are out."

"Have to do a whale of a summer business, then."

"We will," she said. "It's settled, then?" She raised her glass.

He smiled. "It'd be nice."

"Jack, I'm serious."

He noticed that her eyes were green, and that they crossed ever so slightly when she looked at something close.

63

It was endearing. It had been a while since he'd been endeared.

"I don't know," he said. "Working for a friend might be worse than working for somebody like Billy Bob. I wouldn't feel bad about shooting him."

She laughed. "You wouldn't be working for anybody. We'd be partners."

He smiled. "I'll come and see you about it, then."

"When?"

"The first of the week. Soon as I run these naked teenagers to the ground."

She laughed. "I wish you'd believe me. I've wanted to do this for a while."

"I do believe you," he said. "I'll just have to get over my civil servant mentality. You know, pension plans and steady paychecks."

She nodded, backing off. "Whatever. I told you I mean it."

"I appreciate it," he said. He reached automatically for his hat, then remembered he'd left it in the truck. "I'll come in next week."

She nodded, but he doubted she believed him. He didn't blame her. He had his doubts himself.

RIPLEY STOOD BY the pay phone in the parking lot of a shut-
tered auction pen, listening to the infuriating sound his quarter made as it slid once again through the works of the phone
and into the coin return. He turned to the cab of the idling
truck.

"You got a quarter?" he called to Norton, who looked
down at him sorrowfully. "For Christ's sake, Norton, I just
want to trade you. This one won't catch." He held the coin
up, but Norton shook his head.

"I left my change for the waitress," he said. "It was good
pie."

Ripley turned away. He stared at the phone, which was
mounted on a post and surrounded by a little metal housing
with a dim fluorescent light glowing inside. Suddenly, he
stepped forward and, thinking of the phone box as the side
of Norton's head, slammed his forearm heavily against it. The
box vibrated wildly on its base, shaking the receiver from the
hook. There was a chunking sound from inside the box and
a clattering of coins loosed into the change box. Ripley
rubbed his forearm, then picked up the receiver and checked
the coin return. Three quarters and a brand-new dime. He
dropped one of the quarters back in the phone and nodded
with satisfaction as he got his dial tone. He punched in the

series of numbers, glancing up at Norton, who looked more forlorn than ever.

There was the usual lengthy series of electronic grunts and peeps as his call was relayed along some endless route and then the sound of the quarter coming back as the machine finally answered.

"Unit number and coordinates," the synthesized voice droned.

"Four-twelve," Ripley said. He felt a prickling on his neck as he got ready to lie. He knew it was just a machine, but he was still uneasy. "I-80, westbound, marker 283." They were in fact sitting off U.S. 26, a good two hundred miles northwest of what he was claiming.

There was another series of whoops and beeps and Ripley felt the receiver grow slippery in his hand. He licked his lips and swallowed, waiting for the confirmation to sound. He fished in his shirt pockets, found another Black Beauty, and popped it into his mouth, nearly choking as he forced it down his dry throat.

There was a terrible electronic shriek then, causing him to hold the phone from his ear. When he brought the receiver close again, he thought his heart would stop.

"Where are you, four-twelve?" The voice was quite clearly human and just as clearly accusatory. Never had he spoken to anyone human during his check-in. Then again, he'd never told anything but the truth. He felt the capsule still in his throat, swelling, threatening to strangle him. How in purple Jesus would they know he wasn't where he said he was? He stared at the phone a moment, his mind racing.

"Uh, just off the interstate by, uh, just a minute." He tried to think clearly. He had driven I-80 a hundred times in the past year. He knew every place to take a leak, where to get coffee that wouldn't kill you, where to get a blowjob without having to shut down your rig.

"Creston," he nearly shouted, then forced himself to be calm. "Right around Creston. There was a slide, I think, or a wreck. They detoured us." He heard the desperation in his voice and gritted his teeth, fighting for control.

"Just a minute, four-twelve." The voice did not sound convinced. Another series of beeps sounded over the line. Ripley sagged against the phone box, staring at the receiver. Could the fucking machine read his mind? Maybe it could. And if it could do that, it might just as easily send an electronic signal over the line that would kill him on the spot. He jerked the receiver from his ear and stared at it.

"Hey, the cops are waving me on. I gotta go, you hear?" he shouted into the receiver. "I'll call later," he added, then hung up. He started toward the truck, then came back, lifted the receiver, and tore its wires out of the phone box. Norton stared down from the truck in disbelief.

Ripley flung the receiver off into the darkness, then leaped into the cab and ground into reverse. He'd backed off about twenty feet and was about to swing onto the highway when he paused. The phone box sat at the edge of his vision, glowing like a mechanical troll. Possibly it was feeding its own little distress signals back to the computer as he watched. Tearing the receiver out might not affect a thing. He took a deep breath, hit first gear, and wrenched the wheel away from the highway.

"Holy shit," Norton said, grabbing the doorframe.

By the time they plowed into the phone standard, Ripley had caught two gears. It went over with a terrific snap of its wooden post and lodged beneath the rigging of the tanker, making a terrible racket as they surged on, making for the highway now.

"God almighty," Norton wailed.

The rig jolted against the raised bed of the highway, and the phone box dug into the asphalt curb. As the truck moved onto the highway, the box tore away down the long under- belly of the trailer tank with the sound of a huge metal fingernail raking a steel blackboard, showering sparks into the night.

When the sound finally died away, Norton looked back down the black highway. There was a vague lump of twisted rubble visible in the glow of their taillights for a moment, but it quickly disappeared. Norton pulled his head back in the cab and stared at Ripley apprehensively.

"That thing's laying right in the road. Somebody could get killed."

Ripley turned to him, his eyes glittering. "They were trying to trace us, Norton. Sneaking sonsabitches."

Norton looked out the window as if to calculate his chances of jumping. "Maybe we ought to get back where we belong," he said lamely.

Ripley laughed. "That's where we are, old buddy." He laid his hand on Norton's shoulder and squeezed until Nor- ton caught his breath. He let go then, and pointed at a grocery sack on the floor at Norton's feet. "Hand me another beer. I got a little edge on."

Norton quickly dug out a beer and cracked it for him. He handed it over, hesitated, then got one for himself. Ripley looked over and banged his beer against Norton's. Foam flew against the windshield.

"That's the spirit, Norton." Ripley turned on the wip- ers, which flung themselves madly about outside while the foam dripped undisturbed down the inner glass. He rubbed his aching forearm absently.

"We're in it now," he whooped as their speed increased. "We're sure as hell in it now."

FAIRCHILD STAYED IN his pickup as Larraine got out, gave him a last wave, then disappeared into Outback Outfitters. He felt oddly disconnected, as if he were watching a film through the hazy glass of the windshield, and by the time he thought to lift his hand in return she was gone. When he reached for the ignition there was an awful grinding noise, and he jerked his hand away. The truck was already idling.

It had nothing to do with the drinks, he decided as he pulled away from the curb. There were simply too many thoughts clamoring for his attention all at once. He pulled to a stop at the first signal and a horn sounded. He glanced back in annoyance at a massive Winnebago that loomed behind him, then checked the light, which was green. He popped the clutch, nearly stalled out, and finally bucked on through the intersection. The traffic light, meanwhile, turned red on the Winnebago.

For the next five minutes he concentrated resolutely on his driving, and by the time he reached the incline that led into the canyon he was feeling a little more like himself. As the lights of the city fell away, wrapped behind increasing layers of ridgeline and forest, his breathing evened out and the muscles in his back and stomach relaxed. It was a gift, what the rugged country gave him, and all it required in turn was that he enjoy it. What would he replace the feeling with if he left?

He wondered where Lena was. Pocatello? Salt Lake City? On a plane headed east? She'd been carrying on a correspondence with a college friend in Maryland who'd come through the park the previous summer. The woman had listened politely during Fairchild's rhapsodic tour of the Yellowstone country, and then, before they were out of sight of the Falls, had begun her own litany about the beauties of the Eastern Shore. She and Lena sat up night after night, reminiscing, and Lena had moped about for days after her friend left.

It was true what he'd told Larraine. For a long time he and Lena had been more like grudging roommates than anything else. In a way, he was glad she'd made her break. Though there'd been nothing he could do to make her happy, he'd have hung on, hoping time would somehow make a difference. Now, it was out of his hands. He was weak and shaken, but in the way of a patient who'd had a serious operation in the nick of time.

A canyon owl cut his headlights, swooping toward something moving in the grass at the shoulder, and he eased back on the gas, savoring his ride and the air that was cooling noticeably as he climbed. Maybe she'd go to Maryland and love it. Or hate it. She might call him, contrite, surprised by her own heart. He tried to imagine that phone conversation, how he'd feel. He wouldn't ask her back, but would he savor her distress?

He shook his head and swung hard into a switchback, downshifting the old truck for the series of climbing turns that were coming. Of course he'd savor it. He was about as grown up as a high school kid, and wasn't that a pity. He wouldn't ask her back and yet he'd be happy she was unhappy. So much for the myth of adulthood.

Atop the ridge, he could make out the glow of the lodge and the surrounding shops a few miles ahead. He slowed, searching the screen of trees on his right, then abruptly swung off onto a dirt track protected by a drooping chain slung between two posts.

It took him a moment, fishing in the glove compartment, to find the key for the padlock, and then there was another delay when he found a wasps' nest built over the recess where the lock rested. He rousted the insects with a long stick, waited for them to fly groggily away, then wrestled with the tightly fitted mechanism. By the time he got back into the truck he was sweating.

He followed the narrow forest track for a few minutes, then spotted an opening in the trees. He wrestled the pickup off the road and up onto a mound that offered an unobstructed view of a meadow below, where a series of small pools glistened and steamed in the moonlight. The distant lights of the main lodge and store still flickered brightly through a screen of pines beyond. It was a good half hour until closing time.

He reached to switch the parking lights on and an amber glow settled on the high grass around the truck. He turned up the squelch on the CB and heard the racket echo off the nearby pines. After a moment he switched off the CB and fished around in the glove compartment until he found a little pocket radio he kept there. It took some patience, but he finally caught the all-night station out of Del Rio. The announcer was just coming down off a speed riff about Preparation H. "Rock Around the Clock" cut in before he had quite finished "hours of relief."

Fairchild propped the radio on the dash and settled back, reasonably happy. Listening to the Del Rio station was like tuning in to the planet Mars. They transmitted from the Mexican side of the Rio Grande at about six million watts, alternating turkey-necked preachers and rock and roll on through the night. All the disc jockeys were wired and it sounded as if they'd been taped years before and spliced randomly into the proceedings. They never referred to the music that surrounded them, nor the weather, nor events of the day. He'd tuned in on purpose the night after Reagan had been shot. It was business as usual, Granu-Tex Chick Meal and plenty of Eagles music, not a problem in the world.

Bill Haley faded into the Pointer Sisters and Fairchild reached for one of the beers he'd picked up at Clancy's. With proper pacing he could nurse the eight-pack through until morning and keep his mind off what he was supposed to be doing. He took a sip of beer and leaned on the horn for a moment. It sounded suitably annoying and surely carried to the clearing below. He'd try that every ten minutes or so. Anything to keep the kids out of those pools.

The Pointers wanted someone with a slow hand. It sounded all right to him. He checked his watch and wondered what Larraine was doing now that the store was closed. He hadn't felt a pang of curiosity like that in years. He should have invited her along. She might have taken him up on it, and he'd have had someone to talk to. Maybe she really wanted to set up a guide service; and maybe she could talk him into it. There were worse prospects. He felt ready to be talked into something. He drained the beer and glanced doubtfully at the remaining cans, then at his watch. So much for pacing.

He leaned for another beer and brushed the radio with his elbow. The thing fell to the floorboard with a sharp crack and instantly went dead. He fumbled around for it, and held

73

it up to the light to find that the battery had bounced out of its slot. He had bent back down to grope about the dusty floorboard when he heard the voice at his window.

"Are you okay?"

Fairchild started up, banging his head on the underside of the dash. He had to blink tears out of his eyes to see who was there.

"I think it's the fuzz, Teresa." It was a girl, talking to someone still in the shadows, who giggled in response. Fairchild found his pocket flashlight and flicked it on. The girl squinted and put up her hand.

"Geez, you're blinding me," she protested.

Fairchild lowered the beam and stared momentarily. She wore a skimpy bikini, her breasts pushing heavily at the sheer fabric. He flicked off the light altogether.

She stared at him until her eyes adjusted, then turned again to her unseen friend. "It's that ranger from the Visitors' Center, Teresa."

"Ask him if he wants a hit." Teresa's voice collapsed into giggles again.

"She's really wasted," the girl said. "What are you doing?"

Fairchild rubbed his hands heavily over his face. "I'm arresting people who smoke dope and skinny-dip in the pools," he said wearily. "Why don't you and Teresa beat a hasty retreat."

She leaned against the cab, her breasts brushing his arm. "We were just taking a hike. Is that against the law?" Her gaze settled on the beers by Fairchild's side.

He drew a breath, edging his arm away. "Look, just go someplace else, okay?"

She smiled. "Couldn't we hang around? They have citizen ridealong in Montauk. I used to go out with a cop."

"I'm not a cop."

They stared at each other. Finally, she glanced down at his crotch, back at him, and shrugged. She turned to the shadows. "Okay, Teresa, we're gonna get busted. Let's go." She hesitated, turning back to him. "How about a beer?"

Fairchild shook his head, but pulled a can from the pack. She smiled and quickly bent to kiss his cheek. Her lips were full and dry. He smelled perfume and fried onions.

"You'll be sorry tomorrow," she said huskily, disappearing into the shadows.

"I already am," he said, staring after their noisy, invisible departure. Even after the sounds had died away, a wisp of a breeze carried the heavy scent of marijuana back to him.

After a moment he bent and retrieved the radio battery and found, with relief, that things had not changed in Del Rio. He fell asleep, soothed by a preacher's insistence that he was doomed.

ALEC REISMAN, director of internal security for the PetroDyne Corporation, glanced at the computer printout in his hand, then up at the young operator who stood waiting at his desk. Though there were fifty feet of solid granite between him and the clear Utah night above, he felt unusually vulnerable.

"What do you think, Allred?"

The young man shrugged. "There's no confirmation of any closings on I-80. We're still checking."

Reisman sucked hard on the third cigarette he'd had since he'd been called in. He knew just exactly which cigarette it was, because he was trying very hard to quit. He had been trying hard for a week now, ever since the morning of his forty-second birthday, when he had awakened to a coughing fit that brought up blood. He exhaled a thick, blue ribbon of smoke.

"I can read, Allred. I asked you what you thought. You spoke to this"—he broke off to check the printout—"this Ripley."

Allred looked pained. "It wasn't much of a conversation. He sounded—" Allred looked over his shoulder at the glittering array of tracking maps, monitors, and blinking communications consoles that covered the vast office outside

Reisman's cubicle. There were few operators on at this hour. "I don't know. Nervous, in a hurry."

Reisman nodded. "Wired to the gills." Allred didn't respond. Reisman sighed. "You didn't get a trace?"

Allred shook his head. "It was just a random voice check. By the time I put on the trace, he was gone."

Reisman checked the printout again, then glanced at the clock. "He's due to call again at one. We'll give him that before we get too worked up. Meantime, let's see his manifest."

Allred gave him an uncertain look. "I already brought it up. It says he's carrying diesel fuel."

Reisman sagged. Diesel fuel was the company euphemism for a varied group of particularly toxic products. It only figured. Now it was a choice between calling Schreiber, thereby starting a real shitstorm, or waiting an hour in the hope that this speed freak had gotten his rocks off and was back on the road where he belonged.

Reisman took a huge drag, burning the ash right into the filter. He grimaced and ground the cigarette out. This was just the sort of situation he'd worried about. He'd spent two days in Denver, trying everything to get Schreiber to turn back to rail shipments of these products, to no avail.

It shouldn't have surprised him. He'd gone to work for the robber baron of the chemical products world, and he knew going in how it would be. Take orders, pick up a paycheck. At least it was a fat paycheck.

He scanned the printout once more. "Any prior problems with Ripley?"

"Nothing."

"And Norton?"

Allred shook his head. "He's new."

Reisman considered what the pair might be hauling about the red-light district of Rock Springs. Anthrax? Synthetic LSD? Plague? There was a varied menu. He reached for his cigarettes, then willed his hand back.

"Let's give it the hour, Allred."

The young man nodded and started out.

"Anything to eat around here?"

Allred stopped at the door. "Just the machines, sir."

Reisman looked glum. "Can we call Domino's?"

Allred laughed and went out.

Reisman leaned back in his chair and looked up at the ceiling, where the haze of his smoke still clung. Fifty feet up through a shelf of rock that could withstand a direct nuclear hit was the fresh air of Red Rock Canyon, a black night with stars sharp enough to hurt your eyes. Down here, smoke clouds, and fake, freezing air.

Originally, the Mormon Church had burrowed into this shoulder of the Wasatch Range, creating a warren of impregnable storage dens for the genealogical records compiled by their researchers. As Reisman understood it, the idea was to trace the existence of just about anyone who had ever lived so that they could be baptized posthumously into the church and thus become eligible for passage into heaven. They'd need these chambers back someday, but in the meantime, a sympathetic elder had arranged a lease to PetroDyne at terms quite favorable to the church.

As far as Reisman's neighbors in the Salt Lake City suburb of Olympus Cove knew, he and his twenty or so counterparts who manned this communications center were simply a group of environmental scientists and technicians assigned by the company to maintain Red Rock Canyon in a pristine state and to perform various ecological studies therein.

They kept a few pickup trucks moving back and forth, pulling up ribboned stakes in one area, pounding them back down in others. They kept the stream and its three lakes stocked with plenty of trout for the occasional outing of VA inmates or state politicos. And the dodge worked just fine. From time to time they'd have to haul in an overeager fisherman trying to scale down the thousand-foot sidewalls in quest of a fabled Red Rocks lunker, and occasionally a real scientist from the nearby university would apply to study something or other in the preserve, and huff and puff at the company's polite refusal.

But by and large the operation was a model of government-business cooperation. Reisman and his co-workers could pogo up and down the deep elevator shafts, keeping careful track of enough death-dealing agentry to wipe the earth clean of organic life a hundred thousand times over. It was a clean, efficient operation that operated much as it had for the forty years PetroDyne, under one guise or another, had been in the business, brewing up versions of everything from amebic dysentery to viral meningitis to the really bad ones with numbers instead of names.

Reisman reached to the computer keyboard on his desk and tapped out a series of commands. A detailed map of western Wyoming flashed onto the screen in crisp gold. He tapped more keys and the known route of the vehicle began to pulse in red, breaking off at Rawlins. The various alternative routes toward the Idaho storage compound glowed in colors of their own.

Goddamned Wyoming legislature, thought Reisman. If they'd approved rail transport, there wouldn't be all this hassle. The company had been freely shipping its products to various depots about the West for years until the international treaty of 1972, which had called for an end to produc-

79

tion of offensive chemical and biological weapons and for the destruction of certain stockpiled agentry. Officially, the company had been ordered to cease production of offensive weapons and transport its designated matériel from the Denver facilities for "neutralization" at certain desert sites. Of course, the company—under top-secret orders from Washington—planned no cessation of production, nor any destruction of costly stockpiles, just as their Arab and Russian counterparts had not.

If anyone needed proof, just look at what had happened in Iran and Afghanistan. Or Svedlosk in '79, when there was an explosion in a supposed military parts depot 850 miles east of Moscow. Within days, a thousand Soviet citizens had died of anthrax, a disease that hadn't claimed a dozen human lives on the planet in the last century.

Not that the U.S. ever *intended* to use the stuff on the battlefield, of course. For one thing, you never know when the wind might shift and suddenly send the bad shit drifting down on the wrong side of the lines. The air force had learned that lesson at Dugway, only a few years before Svedlosk: thousands of sheep, horses, cattle, even a few ranching families were wiped out, the result of a lurch in the desert winds.

But despite all the denials and the contraversions of common sense, production went on. There was no doubt that the others were stirring and cooking their own little vats of horror. And if they were doing it, we had to do it. That was the way things worked.

In any case, the formalization of transport would have provided a convenient guise for PetroDyne, because their ongoing, covert agreement with the Department of Defense required dispersal of inventory for strategic purposes. You couldn't keep all your Asian flu canisters in one basket, just begging for an enemy warhead to wipe you out, after all.

It seemed like a great plan: keep production up and ship it for storage as neutralized chemicals, as required by the treaty. Until the legislators of the surrounding states got into the act. No way would they allow trainloads of potentially lung-rending, brain-busting chemicals rattling across their pristine territories. The resultant storm of media coverage and public indignation had ultimately forced an announcement of on-site detoxification and the supposed conversion of the Denver facility to research and development in "petroleum refraction and agricultural products." In reality, it was business as usual, with the imposition of an incredibly complex system of production and transport. Reisman understood: the shit had to go somewhere, permits or no. But now that the controversy had died down, it was time for Schreiber to spread some grease around and get them back to rail.

The phone on Reisman's desk rang and he reached for it, hoping for good news. Maybe he could still get a few hours' sleep and bring his boys back up the canyon for a little Saturday fishing.

It was Allred. "We've had units all over Rock Springs. They're not there, and they haven't passed any of the I-80 checkpoints in the last hour."

Reisman scanned the map. There were only so many ways you could go out of Rawlins, especially in an eighteen-wheeler. He checked his watch.

"Could they have cleared Evanston already?"

"Not unless they traded in for a 'Vette."

Reisman grimaced. He hesitated, staring at the possible northwest route. "Do we have anyone in Lander?"

"There's a unit on the way, but they're driving, all the way from Rock Springs."

Reisman punched in a rapid series of commands. A pulsing blue line sprang northwest from I-80 at Rawlins and shot on past Lander an inch or more. It slowed to a throbbing crawl halfway across the Wind River Indian Reservation. If the truck had gone that way, then it was well past the town already, nearly into the national forest beyond. "I hope your guys are driving fast," he said.

"We can put something in the air as soon as it's light."

"Terrific. We'll just have a nap meantime."

"Sir?"

Reisman hung up. Through the glass he saw Allred turn from his console and look toward him with concern. He held up his hand wearily and sank back in his chair, staring at the tracking screen. The blue line was still inching along. According to that scenario, the truckers would catch U.S. 191 in an hour or so, then drop down to Jackson and work west across the desert toward the compound—if they had simply screwed up or gotten bored and taken the wrong route, that is.

He prayed for a simple explanation, staring wistfully at the huge cross-hatching that was Yellowstone National Park. Up there, people were camping, fishing, drinking beer around their fires, getting laid in sleeping bags. A big happy weekend in the wilderness, for Chrissakes. That was what life was for, and here he was, looking for rednecks in a haystack.

He checked his watch. Twenty minutes past twelve. He would wait forty minutes. Then he'd call the boss and try to find out just what sort of death was on the loose, anyway.

RIPLEY WAS FEELING much better now. The beers had kicked in and he was on a pleasant slide, about halfway down the slope from teeth-grinding, dick-throbbing hysteria, heading toward the pool of near-catatonic depression at the bottom. He wouldn't get that far, of course. He had a shirt pocket full of sleek black torpedoes that would shoot him right back up the mountain, whenever he chose. It was a great ride, and you never had to stand in line for a ticket.

It was nearly 2:00 A.M. They'd be all over I-80 by now, and probably had people on the northern alternate too. A damn shame. Soon enough they'd figure out he hadn't turned south toward Jackson and was off the map for real, but they would never get a chopper up until morning, and by then they'd be safely stashed away.

He stared dreamily out along the path his brights cut on the narrow two-lane road. They were heading north toward Yellowstone Park, and there was no traffic at this hour. His eyes were beginning to hood. There appeared to be a huge black octopus up ahead, its mouth open to swallow the rig. He blinked, forcing himself to wrench the wheel into a turn he'd almost missed. Cans slid along the floor and under his feet. The octopus was a gap in the trees just where the road bent away.

He swallowed, feeling his heart race. He nudged Norton, who grunted in his sleep but did not stir. He reached down, scattering the trash on the beer-soaked mats, groping through the mess until he found a full can. He cracked it with one finger, trying to calm himself. The road was climbing now, and he clutched the can in his crotch, reaching to drop a gear.

He scanned the roadside, looking for the turn he'd scouted on his last run. It wasn't much of a road, but they could handle it. It would get them west, skirting the south boundary of the park, toward Rexburg. There was an abandoned ranch not far from there, with a barn big enough to hide the truck and a car for his departure. He had the key right there on his ring. He glanced at Norton, feeling some remorse. He didn't want to kill him, but he didn't see how he could take him along.

Out of the corner of his eye he saw that a line of small Indians had stepped out of the roadside brush to wave the rig on. He turned, forcing his eyes to focus. The Indians became a row of stunted poplars, their silver leaves glittering in the reflected side lights of the truck.

He shook his head. They'd stopped to take a piss at some roadside markers a few hours back. The graves of Sacajawea and Washakie. Chiefs of some kind. Now he had Indians on the brain.

He turned back to the road, fighting the thought that he'd already passed his turn. Of course it was easier to see in the daylight, but he had night vision enhancers with him. He flipped another capsule onto his tongue and washed it down with the beer. It wasn't until the liquid had cleared his throat that he sensed something wrong. He held up the can in the light and instantly wanted to puke. Yoo-Hoo? That fucking Norton had snuck Yoo-fucking-Hoo into his beer stash?

He fired the can out the open window and turned to shake Norton awake. Then froze. He jerked his hand back and slid into the corner of his truck, his balls shrinking, climbing toward his belt buckle. Where Norton had been there was now an Indian, a dead Indian, with his face rotting away, a huge knife raised.

Ripley felt his heart swelling as if to burst. His breath was ragged. He clutched the door handle, ready to bail out.

"What the fuck? Where are we?" It was Norton's voice, muffled. As he fought out from under the jacket that he'd covered himself with, the dead Indian vanished.

Ripley stared at his partner for a moment, then grabbed the wheel as the rig jounced onto the shoulder. He eased them back up onto the narrow roadbed, fighting a chill, clutching the wheel as if it were a lifeline. Norton glanced out at the unfamiliar road, still groggy.

"Never mind, I don't even want to know. When they catch us, I'm saying I was asleep the whole time."

"You do that, Norton." Ripley bit his tongue, drawing blood, clearing his vision.

"I don't want the money. The hell with it."

"You'll feel better once we're in the clear."

"That's a fool's wish," Norton said.

"Well, you're a goddamned fool," Ripley said. Maybe he would pull over and kill him right now.

He was about to turn and backhand him when he saw a break in the trees up ahead. He hit his brakes, downshifting frantically, and just managed the turn. It was more like a tunnel into the forest than a road, the tank scraping the overhanging branches as he dropped another gear for the sharp climb immediately before them.

"The fool's the one driving," Norton said.

Without warning, Ripley shot his fist out, catching his

partner flush in the face. Norton's nose split open, and blood splashed onto the windshield. His head fell back against the doorframe with a crack.

Ripley stared as Norton slumped down in the corner. "Ah shit, Norton. I'm sorry. I didn't mean it."

Norton didn't budge. Ripley wanted to stop but they were halfway up the grade, and for some reason the road was suddenly gravel. But it wasn't supposed to be a gravel road. He knew it wasn't. He'd driven it, all forty-five shitty asphalt miles of it.

Then his stomach lurched as he realized. He'd taken the wrong turn. He was halfway up some goddamned gravel road on a twelve-degree slope. *The wrong goddamned road.*

Norton's breath had turned to a gurgling. It sounded as if he were drowning in snot, but Ripley suspected it was blood. He reached to shake his partner's shoulder, but there was no response. The truck was laboring. Gravel shot from beneath the tires and crashed against the stainless tanker as it fought for purchase.

Ripley turned his attention back to his driving, flooring the accelerator. The reports of the gravel on the steel under-belly were deafening. The tanker shuddered, sliding toward a deep trench cut alongside the road by spring runoff. He forced himself to ease off the gas and turned the wheels in the direction of the slide, holding the course until it seemed he would drive directly into the trench. At the last instant the rig steadied, and he guided them away from the trench and up over the crest of the hill.

For a moment he felt elation. He would pull over, get Norton straightened out. He'd get them turned around. This was no problem, nothing that couldn't be handled. Maybe he wouldn't have to kill him. He fought to control his breathing.

But suddenly, the road dove downward, plunging into a sharp turn to his left. Norton pitched forward, sliding from the seat onto the floorboard.

Ripley fought the slick wheel wildly and instinctively hit his brakes. Nothing happened. He slammed his foot down harder on the brake pedal, but it wouldn't budge. The curve loomed closer and the truck seemed to pick up speed.

Frantic, Ripley flipped on the cab lights and looked beneath the dash. Norton's head, his face covered in blood, was jammed up against the accelerator. His shoulder was lodged against a wad of crushed beer cans that were keeping the brake pedal up.

Ripley jerked him away by the blood-soaked front of his shirt and felt the surge of the truck begin to slow. He tore madly at the cans, got them cleared away, and swung back into his seat, slamming the brakes to the floor in the same motion.

He actually had made it upright in time to see the shoulder of the road rush up and away under his wheels. There was a terrific series of snapping noises as the tanker jackknifed and swung its enormous weight over the side, shearing off a line of pines clinging to the cliff side.

He felt something like hope, that maybe they would somehow hang up on the side, and then his head snapped back violently as the tanker's weight whipped them around backward and they soared off into an endless sickening blind plummeting. Then a terrific series of back-wrenching jolts, his head firing up into the roof of the cab, his teeth splintering through his gums, a bright blossom of pain behind his eyes that was surely the prelude to his death, and finally, stillness.

He lay there for an indeterminate time, not fully aware he was still alive until the pain returned in force. His back, his neck, his legs seemed on fire. His skull throbbed. His first movement was to run his tongue along his jaw, feeling the places where teeth had been.

He became aware of the sound of liquid running somewhere nearby, and thought he'd come to rest in a streambed. He realized that he could move his right arm and groped upward toward his face. He encountered his other hand then, strangely numb and lifeless, as if it had gone to sleep. His fingers raced along the sleeve, pinching, massaging, trying desperately to bring it back to life. Then, he touched the shard of bone and the ragged stump of flesh and realized the arm had been torn away.

He uttered one brief agonized sob, clutching at his dismembered limb, knowing he was going to die, then felt the watch at the limp wrist he held and felt the watch on his own good arm and felt his stomach turn over and empty itself, his vomit spewing across the wreckage of the cab, as he realized what it was he was holding, what he was now wildly trying to fling away. Dear God, it was Norton's shredded arm, he thought, and then blacked out.

Part
2

DEPLOYMENT

Friday, July 22

FAIRCHILD STOOD AT the fender of his idling pickup, guiding a ribbon of piss into a clump of Johnsongrass. An ache rose in the small of his back as his bladder emptied, matching the throbbing pain at his temples. Finally, he zipped up and moved gingerly back to the truck.

He started to climb in, then stopped to stare at the one last Budweiser on the seat, still collared by the plastic holder. How had he missed it? He hesitated, then stepped back down, grabbed the warm beer, and cracked it. He drank it quickly, trying not to taste anything, then tossed the empty into the bed.

When he got behind the wheel he was a little lightheaded, but the pain had dimmed. He hesitated, trying to form a plan. He could backtrack to the highway, stop by the office to make his report and sign out, but that would mean a possible encounter with Christensen.

Instead, he dropped into gear and moved back onto the service road, heading deeper into the forest. He would hook up with a series of jeep trails and firebreaks that would eventually bring him out of the park south of West Fork and closer to his house. He'd check out the Little Murky campground on the way, and call that in as an excuse. Perfect. If his head didn't split open before he made it into bed.

By the time he reached the ridgeline that paralleled the south boundary of the park, he was sure he'd made a mistake. There would have been stores that sold aspirin if he'd taken the normal route. He could have ignored Christensen. He'd already be at home in a cool tub of water, instead of in the cab of a pickup that was heating steadily in the sun. The jouncing over the rock-strewn, deeply rutted roads had aggravated the pain in his kidneys and he stopped the truck again, sure that this time he would piss blood.

Instead he dribbled a few pale drops onto his dusty shoes and the ache at the small of his back only intensified. He stared down at his offending prick and shook his head. "You're not worth a shit," he said, and stuffed it away.

He looked down into the fold of the canyon below him. In a cartoon world, there would have been a dotted line a half mile or so ahead, marking the edge of the park, but instead there was simply an uninterrupted sweep of pines that rose back out of the canyon, a nearly imperceptible dent where the state road cut east and west, and another gathering of mountains to the south.

It was an impressive sight, punctuated by the echoing call of a crow somewhere in the trees. If he weren't so hung over, if he weren't thinking of how quick the tinder-dry pines could burst into flames, of how many rabid coyotes, foxes, raccoons might be lurking beneath the shadows of their limbs, he might have been moved. Instead he found himself imagining he had invited the skinny-dipper twins into his truck last night. He looked down at himself and decided he'd been too harsh on his prick. He gave his hard-on a comforting pat. Not Teresa and her buddy, though. But maybe Larraine.

The crow called again, now cruising an updraft at the

ridge. The bird's shadow cut across his face and he shook off his groggy dreaming. He oughtn't to be thinking about fooling around with his new partner, ought he? He got back into his truck, the pounding in his head relieved a bit. Just the thought of telling Christensen to shove his Smokey hat up his ass was a tonic.

He started to turn the engine over, then pulled back from the key. He preferred the quiet. He eased off the parking brake and let the truck coast, making its own way down the steep series of switchbacks toward the Little Murky below.

Opposite, somewhere beneath the thick canopy of pines, was the campground, which had been closed for the season. Because it was so far from the regular patrol routes, it had gotten pretty well beaten up from overuse and neglect, so the biologists had gone to work on it and shut it down so it could revive. A pair of logging chains wouldn't keep out the intrepid holiday traveler, however, and he suspected he'd find somebody to roust off the tender grass.

The truck creaked and groaned as it moved, occasionally bottoming out on the rough talus of the roadbed. It didn't look as if anyone had been down this way since the spring runoff. He came off a switchback and stopped, confronted by a boulder about the size of a doghouse in the middle of the road.

He set the parking brake and got down from the truck again. It was hotter here, beneath the ridge, and his head was ready to come apart. He prayed there'd be a pool left in the stream where he might soak himself. He leaned into the boulder and found that it would move. A scattering of smaller rocks clattered down by his feet and he glanced up at the cliffside that loomed above him. There was an over-hang that looked large enough to squash him and his pickup several times over. On the other hand, it had been overhanging long before Teddy Roosevelt.

He turned back to the boulder and shoved. It rocked up, then back, and on the second heave he got it rolling. It took two or three turns, flipped off the precipice at the side of the narrow trail, and soared out into space. There was a crack as it took off the limb of a jack pine clinging to the cliffside about twenty feet down, then a satisfying series of thuds as it hurtled down the slope out of sight.

He stared down through the dust the boulder had raised, vaguely sorry there wasn't another to launch. He smiled. It was probably the dignity of his job that most appealed to him.

He got back in the truck and sat for a moment, willing his head to stop throbbing. Over the crackle of the CB he heard the faint voice of Betty Monell, the operator who'd worked weekend days for as long as he could remember. Though she and her husband Clyde had moved to West Yellowstone from south Georgia twenty years ago, she'd maintained her accent carefully. She had repeated her call three times before Fairchild realized she was calling him.

He groaned, wondering if he should acknowledge. It might be Christensen wanting him for something and he could always say he hadn't copied. In this rugged country, it was a solid excuse. You could have crystalline radio contact one moment, and the next second sound as if you were coming in from Mars.

Then again, there might be something important. The litany of potential calamities and emergencies was already ticking itself off automatically in his mind. He sighed and reached for the mike. He pictured Lena watching him, sadly shaking her head. Maybe he was a chump, dedicated to a job that didn't pay and had all the opportunity of the British civil service. Still, what the hell were you supposed to do, just go through the motions and pray for retirement to hurry up and eat you?

No, until he figured out something better to do with his life, *if* he ever did, he'd have to keep on keeping on. Besides, if watching out for the park and the people in it were left up to the Perry Christensens of the world, it'd take about forty-five minutes for the whole mess to go under. He shook *his* head and snapped on the mike.

He identified himself, then had to wait to catch Betty's acknowledgment. Her transmission had begun to break up badly. Not surprising, since he was already deep into the canyon. "I'm on the fire road just above Little Murky," he said, his voice echoing inside the cab. "I'll check things at the campground, then clock out. Over." With Betty, this would be fine. Some of the newer girls would refuse to sign out for you, afraid of Christensen.

As he gained speed on the last long grade toward the bottom of the canyon, he switched the ignition on and popped the truck into gear. The rear tires slid in the dry gravel, then bit, and the engine came to life with a roar. If there were any trespassers, he'd given them fair warning. He caught sight of the nearly dry streambed up ahead.

So far, no sign of anyone. The far bank of the stream rose up sharply, and he hurried the truck out of creeper gear into third. He hit the gas and braced himself for the jolting ride across the shallow ford of the stream.

The truck slammed into a series of potholes left from the scouring of spring runoff and he had to grip the wheel tightly to keep his head from ramming the roof. He felt the rear wheels break loose, headed downstream, and saw the opposite bank coming up broadside on his right.

He whooped, jerked the wheel into the slide, and floored the accelerator. The rear end slammed down, chewing into a dry hummock between thin ribbons of water. The truck shot forward toward the road break in the bank, pounded up over a shoal of gravel, and racketed onto the deeply rutted trail. His headache was lost in exhilaration. He'd bit his tongue somehow, and tears had come involuntarily to his eyes. "The *hell* with it," he called. He began to laugh and dropped the truck into second, hauling ass up the incline into the campground proper.

When he saw the little girl in front of him, he cried out more from surprise than alarm. He hit the brakes and slid to a stop well short of her, though a cloud of dust rolled out from under the wheels and swept over her. She did not move. She stood in the middle of the road with a heavy stick raised over her shoulder in a threatening gesture. This would surely get him another complaint.

He sat for a moment, waiting for his heartbeat to subside, then got down to approach her. There was no sound but the pinging of the truck's cooling manifold. "I didn't mean to scare you," he said.

She took a wary backward step and lifted her club. He swept his gaze over the terrain behind her. There was a flash of yellow nylon beyond a screen of pines, probably a tent.

He turned his attention back to the girl and felt a prickling sensation at the back of his neck. She might have been eight or nine, her blondish hair awry, face mottled with a strange blue and pink splotching. At first he thought it was birthmarking. Then he saw her eyes and a chill swept over him. There were no whites surrounding the irises. Instead there were deep red pools in which dark pupils floated. Heavy streams of mucus flowed from her nose. The front of her T-shirt was soaked with the same foul discharge. He stopped a yard away from her, his stomach heaving.

She screamed something that was drowned in a gargle at her throat. She stepped forward, swinging her club at him. He sidestepped and she went over, face-first into the gravel. Before she could struggle up he was beside her, pinning her arms. She fought him wildly for a moment, then gave a little sob and went limp. He rolled her over and found her eyes closed. Quickly, he checked at her throat for a pulse.

He forced himself to stay calm and pressed more lightly against the tender skin until he thought he could detect a faint fluttering. He looked about the silent campground. "Is anybody there?" His words died away in the underbrush.

Finally, a jay screeched in response. He turned back to the girl. She was not breathing. He put his hand under her neck and raised it to clear her air passage. He forced his fingers inside her mouth and probed, but found nothing. He checked the empty campground again. There was a fluttering sound from the direction where he'd seen the tent, a flapping of nylon fabric in the wind. "Anybody there?" He waited, but there was nothing but the grinding of two pines leaning together in the light breeze.

He glanced down at the girl's rapidly bluing face, hesitated, then swiped away the dirt and slime that covered her cheeks. Finally, he bent and gave her his breath.

On the third cycle, as he pressed down lightly upon her diaphragm, he felt her respond. By the fifth, she was breathing steadily. He waited for a moment, then when he was sure she'd caught hold, he slid his hands beneath her and lifted her to the truck, surprised at the lightness of her frame. He managed to get the passenger door open, and slid her onto the seat with her head propped in the corner. She was still unconscious, but her breathing was steady now.

He turned and ran quickly toward the screen of trees where he'd seen the flash of yellow nylon. As he came through the pines he saw that it *was* a tent, though it had the look of something long deserted. He looked for a vehicle but there was none around. Maybe the chains had forced them to park on the road.

He slowed as he stepped into the clearing. There was an aluminum table set up with the remains of a meal scattered about. A campfire lay cold in a nearby ring. He turned and approached the tent carefully. It was a good one—AAA TENT AND AWNING, SALT LAKE CITY stenciled on its side—a yellow dome supported by fiberglass stays. Its entrance flap had slid down, closing off the view inside. He willed himself forward and jerked the flap up.

Three empty sleeping bags lay inside, accompanied by the familiar musky odor of tent living. He saw scattered clothing, a woman's makeup bag, a pair of small tennis shoes with pictures of Scooby Doo stenciled on the fabric. He turned and surveyed the deserted place, then, as he started for the truck, he caught sight of a trail someone had made, crashing out of the clearing directly into the underbrush toward the stream. He followed the trail, swiping at the alders and tangling vines that brushed his face. As he bent under a low-hanging willow branch, he saw a man, facedown in a muddy seep a few yards ahead. He approached on his hands and knees. When he touched the man's leg he knew he was dead. The flesh was cool and rigid, even through his jeans.

He edged along the muddy ground, caught the man's shoulder, and turned him over. Beneath the mud and slime was the same horribly mottled face he'd seen on the little girl. The man's eyes were deep red pools, staring sightlessly at his own. He eased the man back into the muck and stood up, fighting to control his breathing, fighting to think.

The broken trail led onward, down the streambank just ahead. The woman. The woman was out there somewhere.

He stepped over the body and hurried on, mindless of the serrated vines that tore across his face and clung to his sleeves and legs. He slid down the bank of the stream and came out of the tangle of underbrush atop a massive deadfall.

It was a spot he knew, a place where in better times the water piled up, always harboring a trout or two. Upstream was the flat outcropping of rock that jutted out from the bank and served as the perfect launching place for his casts. Normally a foot or so beneath the stream's flow, the rock now jutted three feet into the air. The deadfall he usually beheld as a few limbs shuddering in the stream's current had become fully exposed: it lay there, a tangled mass of dry limbs and junk the size of a shattered cabin cruiser.

And there, ten feet above him, crouched at the tip of the deadfall, he found her. Naked, her face blackened, her mouth slack, she had evidently made her way to the far end of the pile, and then turned, exhausted, stymied by the sheer drop to the shallow stream below.

At first he thought she was alive, simply mute as she watched his approach, but as he struggled over the tangle of limbs and detritus toward her, he became less sure. Her eyes were open, but it was impossible to tell where they were fixed. Still, she seemed to tremble slightly as he closed the gap between them.

"It's okay," he said. "I'm going to help you." She did not speak, but her head seemed to nod in acknowledgment.

He grasped a thick branch for support and took another step onto a slender limb, almost close enough to reach her. There was an odor now, something foul and rotted. He eased his other foot forward and was about to reach out for her, when he felt the limb beneath him give way.

He plunged down, into the mass of the deadfall, branches snapping like gunshots in his wake. He landed on his back, sunk three feet or more into the pile. As he struggled upward, clawing at the unsteady tangle, a shadow fell over him and he looked up to see the woman lurching toward him, her arms flung outward to embrace him.

She fell heavily into him, her odor vile, her flesh as cold and taut as the dead man's in the forest. He slammed back into the grasp of the brush, willing himself to faint, then wake up and find it was only some terrible dream. But he knew it would not happen.

He struggled out from under the body, snapping wildly at the tendrils of dried vines and branches that clutched at him. His arms felt oddly heavy, his breath ragged, as if, on top of everything else, he were coming down with the flu.

He staggered back from the deadfall and steadied himself against a tree. A few feet away, by the last water that still cut the streambed, he saw a clutch of pots and pans, thick with unwashed food. The very concept of food choked him. His tongue seemed huge and heavy.

His head felt strange. He knew he had to get back to the little girl, but a terrible lethargy had swept over him. He heard the hum of a truck motor on the main road above the canyon, sometimes strong, then again faint. As he rested against the trunk of the tree, something caught his eye, just upstream, fluttering on a branch that poked up out of the water.

He moved out across the gravel of the streambed, his head wobbling, his feet shifting unsteadily beneath him. When he bent down, he saw that it was a piece of paper, and as he got closer he realized that it was, in fact, what he

102

thought it might be. He reached out to pluck it from the branch, his fingers trembling.

A money tree, he thought, smoothing the damp bill in his hands. He'd seen that movie once. He was holding a hundred-dollar bill. His throat was thick, and he had to swallow to catch his breath.

He caught movement further out in the stream and looked up. He'd taken it for the underbelly of a trout, but instead it was another bill slithering along in the current. Sweat covered his forehead, and he felt dizzy.

He'd have thought he was dreaming, but knew it was real. He lunged for the bill, and fell onto his hands and knees, finally trapping it against the slick, mossy surface of a stone beneath the water. The engraved face of Benjamin Franklin stared up at him through the rippling of the water.

He pinched the bill between his fingers and staggered up. He felt as if he were moving in slow motion. He'd lost the sound of the truck in the hissing in his ears. He wobbled, sliding about on the slick stones. He clutched the wet money in his fist and stared upstream, his breath stuck in his throat. The surface of the water was covered with hundred-dollar bills, all coming his way. He blinked. A river of money. There was a pink film at his eyes.

He knew now it was a dream. Wads of wet money piling up at his feet. And what good would it do him? All a dream. He staggered backward toward the campground, toward the girl. And fell.

IN HER DREAM, Larraine found herself living in a strange house made of wood and smoked glass that backed onto a swift-running canal. Beyond the canal lay endless flat fields of green alfalfa, with no familiar mountain skyline and no other homes in sight.

She stood on a redwood deck that was cantilevered over the water. She had a fishing rod in her hand. It seemed hot and it seemed as if she didn't really want to be fishing off the deck of her house. The water looked deep and treacherous. The current buffeted the supports of the porch; she could feel the power of the water in tremors that coursed her thighs.

Then something struck her line with such force that it nearly pulled her over the railing. Her shins and forearms cracked into the wood crossbeams of the railing, but she did not let go. Slowly, she backed away from the railing, her back taut with the effort of holding the line, though she wanted more than anything to let it go. There was something very heavy at the other end.

When the tension left the line and something burst from the water onto the deck, she dropped the pole and tried to scream.

The thing was black, the size of a seal, but it lacked a head, or fins, or any recognizable features. It was slick, slug-

104

like, covered with some clear, oozing slime. It rippled beneath its revolting skin, as if gathering strength. Somewhere in its mass there was a mouth, a terrible leechlike mouth. She backed away, whimpering silently, toward the house, unable to take her eyes from the horrible thing.

She reached behind her for the door, groping blindly, afraid to breathe. She clutched what she thought was the handle of the door. When she tried to pull it open, the handle became hands—hard, bony hands that gripped hers and pulled back. The beast from the canal shuddered and seemed to gather itself. The hands at her back held her firmly.

"Good God, no!" she screamed.

And sat up trembling in her bed.

She could still envision the nameless thing and the hands pinning her arms behind her back and she trembled, clutching her arms about herself until she was free of the dream.

Finally, urged by the burning of her bladder, she slid out from under the thin comforter and padded down the hall to use the bathroom. She splashed water on her face, then went across the hall to look in on her father.

He'd been sleeping late more often these days and she expected to find him still snoring softly, but his bed was empty. Puzzled, she checked the clock again, then went downstairs.

She found him at the kitchen table, a copy of the *Salt Lake Tribune* spread out beside his bowl of cereal. He'd put on a white shirt and a tie, the knot askew, but he hadn't changed out of his pajama bottoms.

She willed herself to smile, to inject cheer into her voice. "Morning, Daddy."

He glanced up at her, then raised the newspaper over his bran flakes and shook his head sadly. There was a headline about the heat wave, something about dying stock. "It's that nuclear testing. Ever since it started up again, the weather hasn't been right."

"Daddy!" she shook her head. It was equally chancy to agree or disagree with him. In the five years since her mother had died, he'd steadily declined, changing gradually from the strong, assured father she'd always revered to a cranky, eccentric stranger. More than a year ago she'd had to take over the day-to-day operation of the store.

"You think a drought like this is God's normal doings?" he continued, a bran flake stuck to his quivering chin.

"I don't think God has anything to do with it. I think he's over in Casper, at a cathouse." She wiped at his chin, but the bran flake held fast. It was best to try and keep things light.

"You'll wish you were in a cathouse when this place goes up in smoke." He regarded her dourly.

She poured a cup of the coffee he'd made. "It hasn't hurt business any, that much I know."

"What would stop a tourist from spending his money?" he grumbled.

"Why would you want him to stop?"

"I think you ought to reexamine your morals. Every time you sell a tent or a fishing pole, you're encouraging someone to die."

The coffee tasted as if he'd poured the whole can in the basket. She poured out half her cup, then filled it with water from the tap. Finally, she turned to him. "We've run that sporting goods store for thirty-two years. That's how we eat and live."

"That's before things changed. I wish they'd close that park, just shut her up tight. We have a fire up there, it'll be good night and little children."

"If I see Teddy Roosevelt, I'll tell him how you feel," she said, kissing him. "You've got cereal all over your chin."

He swiped at his face to no effect. "It's time we retired."

She laughed. "You *are* retired. I'm the one who works."

He looked at her, puzzled. "Where? Where do you work?" His face was an utter blank.

She felt her heart go heavy. No matter how often it happened, it tore at her every time. "Our store, Daddy. I work at our store."

"Oh," he said, meekly. "Didn't we sell that place?"

She felt her eyes begin to fill and bent to give him a hug. "I've got to go in this morning. But Anna's coming to look after you. I'll come home for lunch."

"That old bag?" he said. "Why don't you find a good-looking housekeeper?"

"She's a nurse, Daddy, not a housekeeper. Be nice to her."

"Have fun at college," he said, turning back to his paper.

She nodded, wiping at her eyes. He had slipped down another corridor somewhere and seemed oblivious to her presence. She felt an acrid taste in her mouth, and suddenly the memory of the dream was upon her again. She shuddered and moved through the screen door onto the back patio, desperate for fresh air.

It was just gathering light, the sun a vague hint above the tree-lined ridge behind the house. Though it was sure to be another scorching day, it was still cool out, and she felt gooseflesh gathering on her arms. She sipped at the bitter coffee, willing away the memory of the horrible sluglike thing that had trembled at her feet.

She'd seen a psychologist a few times her senior year in

107

college. In the space of three months, her mother had died, her father's illness had been diagnosed, and she'd had an abortion on her own. Though she told herself she felt fine, she'd found herself spending most of her time in movies, disinterested in studying, or eating, rarely sleeping. She forced herself into the counseling center after one of her professors had the courtesy to call and wonder why she hadn't been coming to class.

The psychologist liked to talk about her dreams more than anything else. She'd keep a diary of recollections and they'd spend their hour each week talking about the more interesting ones, with the doctor always prompting her to envision all the characters as aspects of her own personality instead of the things or people they seemed to represent. Her father was her dreamy side, the psychologist explained, her mother her authoritarian self, and so on. Her boyfriend wasn't really her boyfriend, the doctor suggested. Under the circumstances, it hardly seemed a revelation, but she dutifully tried to figure out what part of her he was anyway.

But a giant slug? That would have been a good one for the shrink. There was nothing she wanted to associate herself with in that monstrosity.

She grimaced and finished her coffee. It was so quiet outside with the sun still hiding. The nearby trees were vague shadows. There were no lights in the neighborhood. She found herself nodding. She knew where the psychologist would have led her. Of course she didn't want to own up to that thing. It was the awful part of her. The part no one would want to claim.

She smiled and shook her head. Early-morning Freud. She had no awful self. Last night, she'd thought about going to bed with Jack Fairchild, but that didn't seem awful. In fact, she suspected it would be rather gentle and altogether nice.

Dear God, that would be novelty enough, given the usual pickings in West Yellowstone.

Horny guys five years her junior and married men ten years older, that's where she'd been stuck. *"That's* awful," she said aloud, finishing her coffee.

There was a muffled stomping from the stables at the back of their lot, then a banging of horse muscle against stall as P-Dogie shook himself awake. The gelding had heard her and was asking for a ride.

She checked the clear morning sky, then glanced at her watch. She hadn't ridden in a week.

She moved in her stocking feet across the patio and onto the damp grass. Something caught her eye and she looked up at her father's bedroom window. The lace curtains fluttered outward, caught in an exhaling breath from the house. She hesitated, then moved toward the stables. He'd be all right. Mrs. Grant was due shortly. And she needed something to jolt her out of her gloomy thoughts.

She opened the door of the stables, reveling in the rich odor of hay, horse manure, and oiled leather. Inside it was cool. P-Dogie neighed his welcome. Delightful, his stable-mate, did not stir. She was twenty and had developed a resistance to excitement.

Larraine peeled off her nightshirt and groped in the darkness for the flannel shirt and jeans she kept on a peg by the door. She shook the garments to chase away any spiders, then worked into the jeans, guessing she'd put on a pound or two by the way the hips grabbed her. She slipped on the shirt, her nipples tingling against the soft cotton.

She remembered Jack Fairchild had put his hand to the small of her back last night, as if he'd guard her against the traffic outside the lounge. His hand had been warm, and she'd felt protected, at that. She found her hiking boots, turned them upside down and shook, then pulled them on, the old leather soft as stockings.

P-Dogie was stamping with impatience now. She smiled and lifted her saddle from the rack.

"Don't act jealous," she said. "He hasn't even kissed me."

The gelding nuzzled her over the top rail of his stall. She pushed his wet muzzle away and unlatched the door. The horse was ready to fly. She slipped his bridle on one-handed, then hefted the blanket and saddle to his back in one motion and elbowed him sharply in the ribs. P-Dogie lost the breath he'd been holding in a rush and she cinched him firmly.

"If all men were as easy as you, I might keep one," she said, and led him out.

There was a flat grassy meadow where the Little Murky spread itself, coming out of the canyon. In normal times it was soggy, but it had dried up in the drought and the footing was good, the grass spare enough to watch for gopher holes and other dangers. She loosened her hold on P-Dogie's bridle and goosed him in the ribs with her heels.

It was what he'd been waiting for. The horse burst across the clearing, throwing her back hard in the saddle. She rose in the stirrups and leaned forward. The horse felt her hesitation and surged even harder. She felt her boots popping loose in the stirrups and clenched her thighs tight at his heaving sides.

"Slow down," she shouted at his ear, laughing with excitement. The horse was lost in his sprint. Her sides ached, her eyes filled with tears from the wind. When the rugged upslope of the canyon loomed close, she had to stand to pull her horse in.

She got down and patted his steaming neck, then led him toward the streambed. "You're still a pistol," she told him, savoring the aftermath of her laughter. She hadn't lost herself like that in months. She shook her head in disapproval as she picked her way over the loose footing.

There wasn't much left of the stream. What was normally a wide, slow-moving pool full of catfish and suckers had become a moonlike sweep of dusty rock. Here and there were stale pockets of water spackled with scum and puddle bugs. They had to walk a hundred feet up the dry streambed, well into the growing canopy of pines, to find the last trace of running water. She let the horse go down for a drink and bent to splash water on her face and neck.

Abruptly she stopped, her attention drawn to something plastered to a rock nearby. She leaned closer and felt her breath catch. It was money. A bill. A hundred-dollar bill. For a moment, she thought it might be play money, or some jokester's advertisement, but when she touched the soggy paper she knew it was real. She stared at it for a moment, then turned to her horse and nudged him in the ribs.

"You're good for something," she told him. She glanced again at the bill, then shook her head and folded it into her jeans. She never found anything. Maybe it would be a good day after all.

P-Dogie would have gulped water until he burst, but she pulled him away and mounted, nudging him up the bank to a narrow trail. It led along the canyon a mile or so to a campground she'd always favored, a pleasant ride, shady, with a nice view of the stream and the cliffs opposite. It was park land over there, too rugged and pretty to do anything with but admire.

She let the horse find his own way along the path. He'd calmed down after his run and she was glad she'd taken him out. It had been too long. For her too. When was the last time she'd taken a day off? Here she was, living in the middle of God's own spit curl and all she did was drive from her house to her store and eat TV dinners.

Suddenly she remembered Jack Fairchild's hand at her back and the shy way he'd tried to sneak glances at her when he thought she was paying attention to Tom Clancy's TV set. All that talk about going partners. It was true, they could make some money. They could take half of Billy Bob Parks's guide business simply by staying sober and answering the telephone during business hours. But, there were these complicating feelings she had developed about her potential business associate.

A pine bough slapped across her face, and she ducked down to avoid another, heavier limb ahead. She noticed that P-Dogie had strayed from the path. Puzzled, she urged him back on track.

She'd have to face facts. She and Jack Fairchild were going to be either partners or lovers. If she decided it was partners, that's what it would be, for good; she'd have the satisfaction of seeing a good man doing what he ought. On the other hand, if they became lovers, assuming she was right and he was willing, they would have a brief but intensely satisfying affair, until their passion wore out or things got too intense for her comfort.

That'd be fun, but it would probably turn out too sour to build a business arrangement on. Besides, what if his wife came back? Though that wasn't likely. Fairchild's wife had been a square peg in these round parts from the beginning.

Suddenly Larraine felt hot and sticky. And her throat was scratchy as if she were coming down with a cold. Terrific. A summer cold. Just what she wanted. The store'd be a madhouse all weekend and they had inventory scheduled to begin Monday.

The horse stumbled and she looked down, but the path was clear. P-Dogie coughed, and stumbled again, his legs nearly going out from under him. Larraine swung down quickly, concerned. The horse was shaking his head back and forth drunkenly.

"Here, boy," she spoke soothingly, thinking a wasp or hornet might be tormenting him. Then she saw the blood dripping from his muzzle, and her throat went dry. *His lungs,* she thought, *something has happened to his lungs.* The same dreadful, gut-sapping fear she'd felt in her dream swept over her.

She was still holding the reins, trying to pull his head about, when he reared, tossing her back against a pine. She gasped, trying to regain her breath.

The horse was up, pawing the air wildly with his forelegs. She staggered forward, grasping for the reins, and the horse—her gentle, loving horse—attacked her, slashing down at her with his hooves.

She tried to twist away, but she felt groggy, disoriented. There was a burst of pain at her shoulder. She slammed into the dusty ground and felt the thudding of hooves near her head. As she rolled instinctively away, another hoof slammed into her side. Her breath left her in an explosion of pain.

She dug her elbows frantically into the dirt, trying to scramble into the heavy brush beside the path. P-Dogie neighed wildly above her, rearing, raking the ground about her again and again with his hooves. She grasped the root of a bush and pulled herself under its tangle of branches as the horse came down at her again. One of his hooves struck her solidly on the back of her thigh, and she screamed, feeling her flesh tear.

She dragged her numbed leg into safety and lay sobbing as the horse continued to batter the ground about the little pocket of brush, snorting and neighing wildly. Nearly as terrible as the pain was the shock. She had raised this horse from a colt. He'd never so much as nipped at her. And now, unaccountably, he was trying to kill her.

Abruptly, the horse's frenzy stopped. She struggled up on one elbow and peered out through the tangle of leaves and gnarled branches. P-Dogie stood lowering at her hiding place like a crazed bull. A bloody froth bubbled from his flaring nostrils and hung in long strings from his muzzle. His sides heaved erratically, his head wobbling as he tried to focus on her. Whatever she had known in this animal was gone. She was staring at a monster.

"Dear God," she sobbed. The horse stamped the ground. Even the vibrations racked her with pain. "Go away," she moaned, sinking back onto the mat of fallen leaves beneath her. "Please, go away."

In response, the horse moved forward and poked his bloody muzzle into the bush. There was a snapping of twigs as he tested the strength of her refuge. Skeins of bloody phlegm drooped across the branches above her. She could feel his breath, hot and rank, sweep across her face. In a moment he would lose his fear of the bushes and trample her to a pulp.

She put her hands to the ground at her sides and tried to push herself deeper into the undergrowth, but her foot lodged in the fork of a branch. It was the leg the horse had

114

stomped, and when she tried to twist it free, she nearly fainted from the pain that raced up from her ankle.

So this was how you died, she thought. Not like that poem she'd read in college, with a fly buzzing and everyone calmly waiting for the end. No. Your gentle, trusting horse goes crazy and smashes you into jelly in the forest and there's nobody there to hear.

She felt dizzy suddenly, and a wave of nausea swept through her. The bottom seemed to drop out of her stomach, and she clenched her buttocks tightly. She dug her hands into the soft humus beneath the brush, gritting her teeth as waves of sickness swept through her bowels. Her hand found a shallow root and she gripped it desperately as her body shook. The brittle wood snapped off in her hand as the last spasm swept through her.

She took a deep breath and was trying to pull herself up when the horse plunged its muzzle deep into the bushes and clamped his teeth onto her shoulder. The pain blanked her mind into a sheet of white, hot light. She jerked away, feeling her skin tear beneath the thin fabric of her shirt. He was trying to drag her out and kill her, she realized. Her stomach turned over again.

Instinctively, she struck out at the horse's muzzle, but her hand glanced harmlessly off the bony ridge above his nostrils. She stared at the broken shard of root she still held in her hand. It had sheared off at one end, forming a knifelike point. When the horse lunged at her again, she struck out with the stick, driving it into the soft flesh of his nose. The horse snorted, and backed off for a moment, then dove at her again. His muzzle slammed into her chest and drove her back into the ground. His teeth caught the flesh above her breast, but she jerked herself free.

His muzzle drove again into her ribs, and this time she

nearly blacked out with pain. She would not last much longer. She felt his hot, wretched breath at her cheek and
slashed out blindly, desperately, with her pathetic little stick.
It was not fair to die this way; it simply was not fair.

She felt the point of the stick sink into something soft
and yielding, and the horse uttered a terrible, shrieking
neigh. He burst backward from the tangle of brush as a sheet
of something warm and wet splashed over her face. The stick
was gone from her hand.

She struggled up to see the horse banging wildly from
tree to tree, frenzied. She stared, puzzled for a moment, until
she saw it: The gnarled hunk of root was impaled in his eye,
waving with the horse's erratic movements like some terrible
worm that was trying to burst free from the socket. Blood
gushed from the wound.

The same blood bathed her face and shirt. So much
blood. It seemed impossible, even for such a wound. The
horse, disoriented now, began to stagger away through the
trees in an erratic, sideways movement.

She sagged, trying to catch her breath, but it seemed as
if an iron band were wrapped about her lungs. Her ribs had
to be broken. She forced herself to take shallow, gulping
breaths, fighting against panic.

The thrashing of the horse was growing dimmer. There
was a far-off whine of a motor somewhere. She wanted to lie
down and sleep, for the pain to go away, for the world to right
itself again. Every shallow breath she took filled her with a
bolt of agony.

She bit her lip then and dragged herself out from the
bushes. It couldn't be more than a few hundred yards to the
road that skirted the boundary of the park. It was a holiday
weekend. There would be traffic. Someone to help.

She bit more fiercely into her lip, drawing blood, and

pulled herself up. Anything to block out the pain from her leg, and her ribs and her shoulder, she thought. Anything. She remembered that she'd found a hundred dollars. It almost made her smile.

"PULL OVER," Isaac Brigham Smith said. His voice was quiet, but firm. Nix Morin, his weekend partner, looked over from behind the wheel of the dump truck.

"Say what?" Morin said. He had one hand on the wheel, another around a Styrofoam cup of Short-Stop coffee.

Isaac pointed through the bug-spattered windshield at a screen of pines across the road. They were almost at the crest of the Little Murky draw, on a loop to the south entry station. Nix stared blankly out the window.

"Somebody's gone over," Isaac said in the same flat voice.

Nix cocked his head skeptically. "The hell you say." He steered the heavy truck onto the south shoulder and set the brake. The two got down from the idling truck and crossed the narrow road to a spot where heavy tracks cut the berm gravel. A small, shredded pine lay on its side at the shoulder, pointing off into space like a makeshift directional sign.

They stopped and stared down a ragged chute of torn and battered forest to the floor of the canyon. The end of a stainless steel tanker truck was just visible there, a red warning sign slashed across it like a wound: DANGER—CORROSIVE

118

CHEMICALS, it read. There was a happy-looking tiger logo painted just beneath. A ribbon of fog curled up from the general direction of the wreck.

"Jesus Christ," Morin said. "What was he *doing* up here?"

Isaac shook his head. "Who knows?" He was staring at something else, and pointed. "Why don't you ask him?"

Morin glanced uncertainly at Isaac, then turned. When he saw it, his half-full coffee cup tumbled from his hand and bounced down the steep slope.

There was a man lying on the rocks not twenty feet below them, unconscious, maybe dead. He'd nearly made it to the top, but had stopped where the natural slope gave way to the steeply pitched flank of the roadbed fill. One of his arms was flung about the base of a poplar, apparently to hold himself from sliding back to the bottom of the canyon. He was nearly bald and the top of his head was deeply bruised. *Like a rotten peach,* Isaac thought.

"Jesus Christ," Morin said again, but his voice had changed. Isaac heard him gulp, trying to hold his gorge down.

The man's other arm was upflung, as if he were trying to get what he held there to the top of the canyon. It was blue and curled, with a dark-stained knot at one end. It looked a little like a ruined crab, or maybe a huge spider with a bloody mouth. Actually, it was a severed hand.

Morin turned away now, puking. Isaac sighed, waiting until his partner was finished. He was thinking about when he had gone over the side with Sophia. How could you explain that they'd come out unscathed? Maybe they'd been saved for worse things. He nodded, staring down at the truck, wondering what was in it.

Finally, Morin stood up, gasping. There were tears in his yellowed eyes. He rubbed his grimy sleeve across his mouth.

"Let's go get him," Isaac said finally.

"Some fucking holiday," Morin said, and slid down the slope after him.

FAIRCHILD SWUNG THE pickup around the logging chain that barricaded the closed campground and chewed through a hundred feet of newly planted saplings meant to serve as a barrier. He felt a stab of pain in his bowels, and his vision blurred momentarily. He wiped a sheet of perspiration from his forehead and blinked rapidly until he could see clearly again.

He bounced the truck up from the graveled entrance onto the main road, holding out his hand to steady the little girl who lay unconscious on the seat beside him. She slumped into the fold of the seat, her thick tongue protruding from her mouth, the awful drool covering her chin. Her breathing was imperceptible.

He cut his eyes back to the road. The color of the sky seemed wrong somehow, as if he were looking through tinted glass. But tinted glass was not an option on Park Service trucks. Cheap bastards. Lena was right about that. He'd tell her when he got home.

Then he remembered that Lena wasn't at home any-more. He felt a momentary panic and looked quickly at the little girl. He couldn't tell if she was breathing.

He rubbed his hand heavily on his face, but the strange hue still draped the world. He turned back to the road in time

121

to see something big burst out of the underbrush and lumber onto the road in front of him.

He felt his foot lift from the accelerator and move for the brake, but it seemed as if he were moving through a thick syrupy ocean. His foot fell heavily on the pedal and the rear wheels broke free. They were skating, out of control, but it seemed a pleasing feeling, as if he'd kicked free of any responsibility for all this. The truck arrowed itself toward the thing, which had not broken stride.

A horse, he thought. A horse bathed in blood with something sticking out of its eye. He felt no panic, only a sadness for the little girl at his side. He'd meant to get her some help.

The truck slammed into the animal and a sheet of blood flashed up over the windshield. Fairchild felt them going over, into the bar ditch. His cheek cracked into the steering wheel, then his head rammed the roof of the pickup. His eyes closed. There were bright, intense bolts of light. He saw Lena's back, as she disappeared into the maw of the bus. He saw Larraine, sitting at Tom Clancy's bar, smiling at him. He saw huge jaws, full of yellow teeth, rushing up to swallow him. And then it was black.

"How'd you know there was a wreck, anyway?" Morin was slumped in the passenger seat now. He stared grimly ahead as Isaac steered the truck down the canyon. Sweat soaked Morin's uniform shirt, which had been rank enough to begin with. Isaac rolled down the window and caught a decent breath.

"Instinct," he said. There was a thumping sound from behind them as they swung down through a steep curve. Isaac glanced back through the rear window that opened onto the bed. The man had rolled over into the corner, but Isaac didn't suppose it would hurt him any worse than he already was.

"Forget it. That fucker's history."

Isaac glanced back at the road. "He's alive." His shirt was covered with the man's blood, but he'd felt a faint pulse in his neck.

"Right now, maybe." Morin rolled down his window and spat. "Sombitch he was holdin' hands with sure ain't."

"You're right, Morin." Isaac swung the wheel heavily into another curve. A Park Service sign signaled the Little Murky campground just ahead. There was a CLOSED sign slashed across its face. He figured they were twenty minutes from town.

"Fuckin' *hand.* You believe that?" Morin said.

Isaac wrestled the truck out of the curve and floored the accelerator as they passed the entrance to the campground. They had a half mile of straightaway. The wheel trembled in his hand. The truck was not exactly built for speed.

Abruptly, he hit the brakes. "I'd believe anything," he said, nodding at the sight rushing up before them.

Morin looked at Isaac, then followed his gaze out the windshield. "Well fuck me," Morin said. He gripped the window frame for support as the truck ground to a halt.

There was a horse lying dead in the middle of the road, a huge dark stain spread about it. Just beyond, in the bar ditch, lay a Park Service pickup on its side. Alongside the road were three bodies: someone in a ranger uniform, a woman, and a little girl. Isaac couldn't see their faces from where he sat, but he had a strange feeling in his gut.

"What the fuck is that?" Morin said, staring.

A dark shadow flashed across the scene in front of them, then was gone, chased by the abrupt roaring of an engine and clattering blades. A helicopter was rushing up the canyon, a hundred feet in the air. Isaac turned to his companion.

"Trouble," he said, climbing down from the truck.

Part
3

CONTAINMENT

Montserrat, B.W.I.

THE PHONE CALL came as Skanz was shifting his position above the woman. Her eyes flickered with surprise, but if she made a sound, it was muffled by the brightly colored scarf tied about her mouth. Skanz had been laboring toward orgasm, something he had not achieved in months. He tried to shut out the distraction, but the harsh continental ring cut at him until his thin excitement had evaporated.

He rolled off the woman and lunged at the phone, his hand still tight on the rope that looped about her neck and limbs, bowing her open in a provocative manner that she herself had suggested. Her eyes bulged momentarily as the pressure at her neck increased, but her expression did not betray fear. She was a professional. Nothing seemed out of order.

"I need you." It was Schreiber's voice. No one else could have found him.

"I am in the sun," Skanz said. His breathing was still ragged and he felt strangely light-headed.

"It cannot wait."

"You have a security staff," Skanz said. He thought of the spineless creature he had met in Schreiber's office, then, oddly, of the moment he'd seen his image overlaid upon that of the old man as he made his way into the building that day.

Skanz's breathing was heavier and he felt a sheen of sweat breaking fresh on his forehead. It was not normal. Neither his thoughts nor his body was supposed to surprise him.

There was a pause on Schreiber's end. On the ledge of the open window, a foot-long lizard worked its mating sac into a bright red bubble beneath its turquoise chin. Far below, the placid sea lapped at a beach of black volcanic sand. The woman cut her disinterested gaze at Skanz, then away.

Suddenly, Skanz saw all these things before him as if from a great distance, as if he were looking through the wrong end of a telescope. He felt the phone in his hand, but there was no longer any sound. He was cast in stone, a sculpture in time.

A wave of red swept over his eyes and he was somewhere else, running and sweating, his heart pounding, the heat of the Congo a wet glove that enveloped him. He saw himself holding a rifle before him to block the long, slashing grass as he ran, following after the billowing smoke from the exploding sheets of napalm. The planes roared as they ascended from their drops. A normal man might have been frightened, but the noise and the heat and the running effectively blocked his feelings.

Up ahead was a Katangan village the rebels had captured a week before. During the fighting, the rebels had slaughtered the white Belgian managers and the natives who labored there alike.

Skanz stumbled over an ox that had fallen in the brush, its side ripped away moments before, its entrails still steaming. He felt one icy jab of fear before he struggled away, out of the slippery mix of mud and entrails. He was rolling to his feet when he saw a strange thing: a clump of earth and grass at the edge of the clearing just ahead had moved, independent of all that surrounded it.

A tunnel, or a bunker, he thought, though he was young and inexperienced in such fighting as this. He hesitated, heard the crackle of automatic weapons on the far side of the clearing, then ran forward and pried the lid of the tunnel open enough to dump his grenades down the chute. He fell back as the explosions ripped the earth beneath him, then rose to his knees to shoot the survivors one by one as they struggled from their hiding place. When he had expended his ammunition, he stabbed to death the last ones who climbed out.

Other mercenaries found him there, surrounded by the corpses of the tribesmen and their wives and children, twenty-seven in all, above and below ground. The last he'd killed, a boy of twelve or so, was still sprawled at his feet. There'd been no rebels in the group. Not one.

Suddenly, Schreiber's voice interrupted his reverie. "My staff does one thing, you do another."

Skanz found himself back in the bed, dazed, the musty smell of the bedding mixed somehow with the imaginary stink of cordite and blood. He was holding the phone. He put his hand upon the woman's flesh. She was warm and real; the memory of the Congo battle disappeared as suddenly as it had come.

He took a breath, reorienting himself, forcing himself to concentrate on Schreiber's words. There was a job. A job that would be interesting. He nodded. He gave the rope a turn in his hand. The woman's eyes widened suddenly, and her cheeks darkened.

"I will be there," Skanz said, and hung up. He gazed down at the woman, and felt himself thickening again. The lizard leapt suddenly into the dense bougainvillea outside the window, its jaws cracking down upon some insect. A purple blossom fell from one of the thorny branches and drifted into the room. Skanz wound the rope tighter in his massive fist and, over her screams, went to work.

"THEY'VE FOUND IT, SIR."

Reisman stared wearily out the doorway of his office, holding the phone with his shoulder while he lit another cigarette. Allred sounded enthused. Reisman tried to remember what *enthused* felt like.

In contrast to the night before, the main area was full of activity. It had been for hours. His view of Allred's console was blocked by a pair of operators struggling with a coffee cart.

"I'm patching you in," Allred said.

"Do that," Reisman said. He hung up and turned to the computer terminal.

He was looking at an overview map that covered the northwestern corner of Wyoming, along with contiguous sections of Montana and Idaho. Abruptly, the master view shrank in size and became a blue reference insert in a detailed map of Yellowstone Park. A red dot pulsed at a spot in the southwest corner of the park, beside a secondary road that paralleled a stream. Seeing the stream, Reisman felt his stomach constrict.

A series of strange computer-generated characters glowed at the bottom of the screen. He tapped the appropri-

133

ate commands and the characters resolved themselves into readable text.

Bad as the news was, it didn't tell him everything he wanted to know. The phone rang again.

Reisman turned and saw the light on the emergency phone blinking. That line led only one place. He picked up the receiver and tapped out the code that would allow conversation with his employer to flow in intelligible sound.

"Reisman here."

"This is unfortunate, Alec."

"I'd call it worse than that."

"I've spoken to the research sponsor."

Reisman knew he was talking about the governmental agency through which their funds were channeled. "What did they have to say?"

"To clean it up, of course." The voice was calm, assured. "And to keep it quiet."

"Did they suggest how we keep a toxic spill in a national park quiet?"

There was a pause on Schreiber's end. When he continued, it was with aggrieved patience. "Alec, with the right friends and unlimited resources, anything can be managed."

Reisman shook his head, wishing he could share his employer's optimism. He glanced again at his computer screen. In the place where a code should have indicated the contents of the wreck, there was nothing.

"What was he carrying?" he asked Schreiber.

"One of the new ones, I'm afraid."

Reisman felt himself relax. "New" meant one of the binary agents: concoctions that, kept separated, were harmless. Once mixed together, however, they would create plaguelike diseases worthy of anybody's worst nightmare.

Schreiber's concern, so Reisman decided, was primarily political. Binary stockpiling had been instituted in order to circumvent verification stipulations in the new treaty Washington was trying to impose upon the other UN signatories. According to U.S. intelligence, neither the Soviets nor the Arab countries nor anyone else had developed binary technology.

In reality, the new treaty would force everyone else to destroy their stockpiles of chemical weapons, while allowing the U.S. to maintain business as usual, cranking out apparently harmless cultures and reagents that could be combined into chemicals capable of killing tens of millions of people at a moment's notice. Intelligence maintained that it would take years for the Soviets, the closest competitor, to catch up. Obviously, it would not do to have the U.S. plan made public.

"It's not so bad, then. Just a matter of keeping the lid on." Reisman thought he sounded confident, back in character for a director of internal security.

"It's bad, Alec. It seems there's been a problem with one of our scientists."

Reisman had no idea what he was talking about, but fear gnawed at him again.

"This man has met with an accident, but I have before me a rather unusual letter he directed to me sometime before his death."

Reisman tried to think. "He talked to someone?"

"No. I don't believe so. That's not my concern, in any case."

"Then what is it?" Reisman felt his hand going sweaty at the receiver.

"You're going to have to go up there, Alec. And you'll need some help."

"What kind of help? What's going on?"

"The government—" Schreiber interrupted himself and began again. "Our sponsor is extremely concerned. You'll understand once you arrive. Mr. Skanz will fill you in."

"Skanz?"

"We really shouldn't continue this, Alec. There wasn't time to consult with you. Just hurry up there. And cooperate with Mr. Skanz."

Reisman stared at the receiver, which had gone dead at his ear. There was a knock on his door. Allred stood there, gesturing at two stocky men who waited outside.

"There's a helicopter upstairs for you, sir."

Reisman looked at the two men, who stared impassively back. He flipped the switch on his computer and got up, feeling as bad as he had in years.

"Call my wife, will you, Allred?"

"Yes, sir."

Reisman shook his head bitterly. "Tell her we won't be going fishing."

REISMAN'S STOMACH LURCHED as the helicopter banked and turned above the crash site. The door on the helicopter had been removed and only a thin nylon safety belt prevented him from plunging a hundred feet into the narrow canyon below. Men in moon suits sprayed thick streams of foam about the ruins of the tanker. A huge tow truck was parked at the lip of the road and two more men in the protective suits struggled down the steep slope guiding its heavy towing cable.

Reisman held a sheaf of photographs in his hand. He'd flipped through them on the flight up the canyon. They showed a series of corpses, all of whom appeared to have been beaten until every pore leaked blood. The faces of the victims were ghastly blackened masks, dried blood congealed at every possible exit.

The copter righted itself finally, and he turned and handed the photographs to Owenby, one of the men seated behind him. Owenby was a research scientist from the Denver facility. The other man was Skanz.

"It's some super strain of hemorrhagic fever," Owenby shouted over the noise in the cabin. "If the truck had turned over in the desert, it would've just evaporated. Once it hit the water in that stream, it activated." He pointed down at the cleanup site. The men in the protective suits grew smaller as the copter rose and moved back down the canyon.

The Little Murky, Reisman thought, drained to the Yellowstone River. The Yellowstone curled across Montana to join the Missouri. And the Missouri, of course, became the Mississippi. If the Little Murky made its way into the Yellowstone, this concoction could end up sloshing into millions of homes, people drinking it, bathing in it, cooking their kids' meals with it. Christ, all their efforts would be like putting a Band-Aid on a brain hemorrhage.

Skanz leaned forward and grasped Reisman's shoulder with a hand that felt as if it could squeeze coal into diamonds.

"We're fortunate to have contained it as we did. Because of the drought, the stream had dried up entirely before it reached the main water supplies. There were less than fifty casualties. We're rounding up the casual contacts now."

Owenby glanced at Skanz, then cut in. "We've aligned our sources at the Centers for Disease Control. As far as anyone will know, there's been a severe outbreak of Rocky Mountain spotted fever, not unusual for the weather conditions. Spotted fever is a weird, constantly mutating disease bizarre enough to account for most of the initial symptoms. The story is that a regional medical task force is handling a quarantine process. All inquiries are being diverted to our channels."

Reisman nodded. "How about all *that?*" he shouted, pointing back at the activity surrounding the wreckage.

Owenby shook his head. "No problem. The media can't get within twenty miles of the area. They've been told an ammonia tanker went over the side, fumes're too toxic to let anyone in close. When we finally let them in, we'll show them a dead moose or two, tell them everything's copacetic."

Reisman turned away from the man's assured expression. It all sounded simple, but he refused to be placated. They were glossing it over. They had to be.

He swallowed uncomfortably, his throat sore from shouting above the sound of the helicopter. He glanced down at the forest rolling underneath them. He felt the big man's presence behind him. Skanz had boarded the helicopter just as they were lifting off, and introduced himself to the others as a consultant from the Public Health Service. Reisman had given him an odd look but said nothing. He assumed that Skanz was a watchdog from the government. That would explain Schreiber's insistence that Reisman kowtow to the man.

He glanced back at Skanz, who returned his gaze without emotion. Reisman felt as if he were staring at a machine. The helicopter lurched, and he cut his eyes away. They were climbing over a ridge to the north now. In the distance he caught the flash of the afternoon sun off windows in West Yellowstone, a dozen miles away.

Directly ahead of them was the clearing where they'd taken off. At one end was an L-shaped barracks building, with a number of vehicles nosed up to it. Several pieces of heavy equipment were working to enlarge the clearing. Another crew was erecting a tall chain link fence at the perimeter of the forest.

As the helicopter began its descent, Reisman turned back to Owenby. "Is all this necessary? We could airlift people straight to hospitals in Denver."

Owenby seemed uncomfortable with the question. He cut his glance to Skanz, who stared impassively at Reisman.

"We have a security situation here, Mr. Reisman," Skanz said.

"You have a lot of sick people. Is this the best place for them?" Reisman felt his distaste growing. He knew the position the company was in, but this man was the worst kind of bureaucratic thug. He glared at Skanz, who did not seem to register his question. The helicopter lowered itself to the ground in a great cloud of reddish brown dust. The moment they touched down, the roar of the engine dropped dramatically.

"Alec," Owenby cut in. "We don't know what this thing is going to do. On the books it was supposed to emulate the disease in a host, then die. But it was also supposed to require a very complex reagent to activate, not just water. The sonofabitch who was trying to blackmail us claims he concocted a plague. So the only thing to do is to isolate anybody we think's been exposed until we run some tests and find out what we're dealing with." He gestured at the barracks.

Reisman nodded reluctantly. He looked out of the helicopter door at the building, which had housed smoke jumpers during fire emergencies but was otherwise unused. It looked flimsy, a relic from the era of Audie Murphy war movies. It did not seem like a place where anybody could get serious medical attention.

Skanz unsnapped his seat belt and brushed past him out the helicopter door. Owenby got up to follow. He put a hand on Reisman's shoulder. "We have the entire medical staff on this, Alec. We're the ones who *make* the shit. Who else is better qualified to help them?"

Owenby gave him a reassuring smile and jumped down, his feet raising little puffs of dust in the dry ground. Reisman was undoing his seat belt, ready to follow, when Skanz leaned back through the doorway and pressed him firmly back into his seat. He regarded Reisman brutally before he spoke. The pilot had kept the engine at an idle and stared out into the distance through his mirrored sunglasses.

"Mr. Schreiber left instructions for you to go to the Idaho storage facility."

"I need to see your operation here. I have to certify security procedures."

Skanz kept him pinned in his seat. He signaled the pilot and the engines roared back into life. "I am in charge of procedures here, Mr. Reisman." He released his hold and stepped back.

Reisman felt the helicopter lurch into the air and scrambled wildly for a grip on his seat rails. His seat belt buckle clattered to the dusty floor.

"Take this thing down!" he shouted to the pilot, who shook his head and pointed helplessly to his headset, as if he couldn't hear.

They were fully airborne now, moving into a swirling turn. Reisman felt his stomach drop away and lunged for the buckle. By the time he got it snapped securely around him, they were a hundred feet in the air, arrowing west toward Idaho. He found himself shaking, drenched in cold sweat. He glanced back at the clearing, but Skanz and Owenby were already gone. The building lay in shadow, surrounded by the bright yellow graders, bulldozers, and front-end loaders that looked like toys at this distance.

As the fear drained away from him, Reisman felt his outrage return. It was unbelievable. He would get hold of Schreiber and straighten things out as soon as they got to Lost River. The helicopter bucked through a turbulent updraft and his hands clutched the seat rails again. When the ride became smoother he tapped the pilot on the shoulder.

"Your ass is grass too, buddy," Reisman shouted.

The pilot nodded, and smiled behind his mirrored glasses. "Pretty, isn't it?" he shouted in return, and swept a hand toward the horizon of green forest and granite peaks. "Prettiest country I ever saw."

From the *West Yellowstone Grizzly,* Holiday Edition

OUTBREAK CLOSES WEST YELLOWSTONE CAMPGROUND

(Local) A number of Pioneer Days visitors to the Tapeats Canyon area of Yellowstone Park have been admitted to the Gallatin County Health Clinic, suffering severe flu-like symptoms. Dr. Robert Lenzo, county medical officer and clinic director, confirmed that the clinic handled more than thirty admissions on Friday, a number of whom were termed "critical."

"We've closed the Tapeats Canyon area to camping and hiking until we find out what we're dealing with," Lenzo said. "Possibly there's a water contamination problem, or it could be a strain of spotted fever, but we just don't know."

Lenzo said that representatives of the Centers for Disease Control (CDC) had arrived to set up a quarantine center for those afflicted. Lenzo said that patients would be moved as soon as possible. Attempts to reach CDC representatives were still unsuccessful at press time.

Lenzo described the victims of the outbreak as suffering from high fever, difficulty in breathing, heavy mucus discharge, and severe hemorrhaging of capillaries in the facial area and extremities. Lenzo advised all park visitors and outdoorsmen to wear caps and long-sleeved shirts despite the continuing heat wave, to help protect against ticks. "Spotted fever is a serious, constantly mutating affliction," he said. "The hot dry weather has brought out the ticks, which could be causing what we're seeing here."

Anyone experiencing a sudden onset of high fever, dizziness, or constriction of the breathing passages should be brought directly to the clinic, Lenzo added.

"MR. SCHREIBER IS in conference," the secretary said. "I'll tell him you called."

"I'm at the Lost River number," Reisman added before she could hang up.

"I'll tell him," she said, her voice maddeningly polite. He listened to the hum of the broken connection for a moment before he put the receiver down. He reread the message typed and waiting for him upon his arrival at the Lost River storage facility:

> Coordinate research activity at LR. All personnel there responsible to you in matters of security. Sponsor liaison handling quarantine and mop-up in Wyoming. Know I can count on you.
>
> Schreiber

Reisman crumpled the message reflexively, then smoothed it out and fed it into the shredder. He was supposed to accept his place in these proceedings. Sit tight in a concrete block building square in the middle of four hundred thousand acres of stoutly fenced, abandoned government installation and stay out of the way of the important action a hundred miles away. Something's going down we can't trust you to know about, son. That's what Schreiber's message told him. For his own good.

He checked his watch, stood, and left the office. A block-long walk down a bright corridor to the briefing room. He met no one on the way. When he opened the door and entered, a dozen heads looked his way, registered his presence, then turned back to the front of the room where Riley, one of the chief scientists, stood at a lectern. Behind him was a wall map taped to a portable chalkboard. Riley gave him a nod and continued.

At 1000 hours, Riley explained, the detox team had begun blanketing the area of the spill with a neuro gas strong enough to short-circuit the functioning of a bull elk. Anything still breathing would have been immobilized by the gas until the cleanup team completed its sweep through the surrounding forest.

The animals they had found had been killed and incinerated. So far no additional humans had turned up. The thirty-four who'd initially been checked into the county clinic were the only immediate victims. Most of the humans with secondary contact—a couple of Bureau of Public Roads drivers, a passing motorist, two teenaged cross-country hikers who happened upon a pair from the moon-suited cleanup team—had been taken into the field hospital for observation. One BPR driver, an Indian named Isaac Brigham Smith, was still at large, but there were a number of men looking for him.

Reisman considered the Indian's name. Mormons, he thought. Always spreading the faith. So far, Riley hadn't mentioned anything he didn't know. Most of the others seemed bored as well.

Riley turned to a discussion of the spilled cargo. Some information on the contaminant had come from the lab back in Denver. It was a hemorrhagic fever derivative, distilled from the disease first brought to the attention of the medical community during the Korean War, when there had been one thousand cases in eight months among United Nations troops. The mortality rate among American soldiers was 37 percent.

Worse than the death rate, from a crisis-management point of view, was the panic brought on by the most apparent symptom of the disease, which caused all the surface capillaries to break down and eventually burst. Those who caught the disease and overlooked its initial flu-like symptoms might glance in the mirror to find their eyes full of blood, their fingernails suddenly black. In minutes, they'd be bleeding from every orifice: the ears, the nose, the mouth, the genitals, the anus, anywhere a great concentration of capillaries rose near the surface.

A particularly grim feature was a false recovery syndrome associated with the disease, a temporary euphoria that would get these "flu victims" up and out of bed, moving around and spreading the disease. Meanwhile, as they moved, the victims would add to the stress on their weakened blood vessels. After a certain period of time, these victims often literally exploded in spontaneous eruptions of blood.

Riley's face was deadpan as he spoke. His shirt pocket was filled with pens, and one had leaked, spreading a dark stain on his white shirt. Reisman tried to imagine Riley's face going black with blood.

Riley caught his gaze, glanced down at his chest, raised a disbelieving finger to the ink stain, and brought it away. Riley wiped his finger on his pantleg, wiped again, then cleared his throat and continued.

Intelligence reports claimed that Russian researchers in the Soviets' Amur Valley facility near the Chinese border had been able to reproduce symptoms of hemorrhagic fever in human subjects via the direct injection of urine or blood from an infected host. The field transmission agent was uncertain, though mosquitoes and trombiculid mites were suspected. Effective treatment: *none.* Give the poor bastards who caught it plenty of bed rest and hope for the best. Riley flashed what passed for a smile.

He was getting warmed up now. Hybrid strains of the disease had appeared spontaneously in the Amur research laboratories, each more deadly than the last. It was no surprise that the Department of Defense and its subcontractors had been attracted to the disease as a fine tactical weapon. With its initial symptoms readily confused with influenza, typhus, smallpox, and leptospirosis, it was a fine disease for military purposes. It would disable some soldiers immediately, but better yet, turn many of them into walking bags of blood. Watch your foxhole partner bleed to death in minutes and see how much fight you had left in you.

Riley gripped the sides of the lectern. Alas, those mites and mosquitoes. Such undependable little carriers, so difficult to mobilize, so dependent on climate and weather for their effectiveness. Lo, a PetroDyne researcher had come up with the perfect solution: a particularly virulent strain of the disease—estimated mortality rate 95 percent—and a synthetic microbe capable of dispersing said agent in water, and voilà: megadeath. You have an enemy who likes to hide in jungles where you can't bomb his ass to smithereens? No problem!

Reisman leaned back and stared at the ceiling, trying to draw a clean, clear breath. His chest felt tight, his throat constricted. He suspected his blood pressure was off the scale. He rocked forward in his chair. "So we just loosed a plague in Yellowstone Park? Is that what you're saying?"

Some of the others in the room turned around, their

faces pained, annoyed, as if Reisman had ripped an enormous fart. Riley seemed momentarily perplexed. "I think that's overwrought, Mr. Reisman," he said, glancing down at his notes.

"Overwrought?" Reisman repeated.

The scientist met his gaze. "We've safely contained those directly afflicted by the spill, after all. There's the one truck driver to be picked up, but there's no certainty that he's even been infected." He raised his hands in an amicable gesture of doubt, one man of reason to another. "We're not certain how this version of the disease operates in the field. It was never tested in terms of contagion. It's quite possible that the disease will expend itself within the primary hosts."

"Uh-huh," Reisman said. "And how *about* all those people you've got up there in that hospital?"

"We're going to watch them very carefully," Riley said. "We've got quite an unexpected research opportunity." There wasn't a trace of irony in his voice. "This is serendipity, Mr. Reisman."

Reisman stood up. Some of the assembled scientists stared at him, expectant. A few were taking notes. One, an Oriental man with hair down to his shoulders, had opened a book and was leafing through it.

"You fucking guys," Reisman said. He leaned over the row of chairs in front of his and flipped the book out of the Oriental man's hands. The scientist gawked at him.

"Is anybody worried? I mean, is this just a teeny tiny plague or something? Jesus Christ. You know how many people there are in that park this weekend?"

Riley stepped around his lectern. "We have things under control, Mr. Reisman." His voice was intended to be soothing. "The spill has been contained. And now there's an opportunity to observe. That's what scientists *do.*"

Someone handed the Oriental scientist his book back. The man shook his long hair and glared like a child whose bicycle had been pushed over.

Reisman took a breath. "Yeah, okay. You guys are happy, I'm happy for you." He turned, kicked a chair over, and walked out.

He made it back to his office, dropped into the massive leather chair, and stared out the window at a vast expanse of eastern Idaho desert. Even softened by twilight, it seemed the perfect place to store their products: not a tree, not a bird, not a goddamned living thing. He thought of something he'd read about British biological testing during World War II. There were islands off the coast of Scotland that were still uninhabitable, still palpitating with spores of God knows what, awaiting their chance.

The phone rang, startling him. He picked up on the second ring, still staring out at the steadily darkening landscape.

"Alec?" It was Schreiber's voice.

"We can't do a thing, can we?"

There was a pause. "We are doing quite a bit."

"You know what I mean. Those people in the hospital. They're dead meat, right? What am I doing over here in Buttfuck, Idaho?"

Schreiber's voice took on an edge. "We must find out if this disease *can* actually be retransmitted. Meantime, we must not have anyone gossiping, Alec. Put all that scientific talent to work. Let someone else worry about the cleaning up."

"Yeah, sure." He sighed. "I'll put them to work." He remembered Skanz's thick hand squeezing his shoulder. Then he thought of something else. It had struck him during

Riley's lecture and he'd meant to ask about it, before he disrupted their little powwow.

"Who's the guy who cooked up this disease, anyway?"

There was a brief pause on Schreiber's end. "He is no longer with the company."

"So? We'll haul him back. I want to talk to him."

"It is not possible, Alec."

"Anything's possible. You tell me where he went, I'll—" He broke off. Schreiber's tone had finally registered.

"For Christ's sake," he said, suddenly very tired.

"He was murdered in an elevator in New York, just last week. Shot and killed by a robber." Schreiber's voice was flat.

"Just a coincidence."

"You're sounding a bit strained, Alec."

"What did he tell you about this slime we dumped?"

Schreiber did not seem to hear him. "As soon as things are wrapped up, I want you to take some time off. You've been working hard."

Reisman bit his lip, thinking. He considered the tone in Schreiber's voice. He realized he was holding his breath and let it go in a rush. A rabbit had materialized on a hummock of scrub-strewn sand just outside his window, barely visible in the dying light. The thing cocked its head toward the sky, checking for predators, then scurried out of sight.

"He was one of our best," Schreiber said. "Bright, ambitious. He was ready to go off on his own, and look what happened." He clucked his tongue.

Reisman saw the dark shadow of a hawk slice through the view outside the window. He wondered how it could still see.

"Everything's in order up here," he said, finally.

"Good, Alec." There was a pause, then Schreiber continued in a softer voice. "I think we have caught this thing. I don't think we have to worry about it spreading."

"That's what they tell me."

"You're safer over there, anyway."

"Sure." He stared at the back of his hand, trying to imagine the nails blackened, peeling away like fruit rind.

"Keep me posted, Alec."

"I will," he said. A drop of perspiration fell from his chin and splattered on the shining surface of the desk. It seemed almost red in the dying light. Somewhere, he heard the connection break.

"I'M ROBERT LENZO," the thinly built man on the porch of the barracks shouted. *"Doctor* Lenzo, goddammit!"

Skanz stared impassively out at him through the window of the door. Another meddler, he thought. Well, there were ways to deal with meddlers. He held up his hand for the man to wait, disappeared into his office for a moment, then came back out, holding up a key for the man to see. He unlocked the deadbolt, then motioned to the fatigue-clad guard outside to let the man pass.

Lenzo burst through the door to confront him. Skanz held up a hand to cut him off. "I must warn you that this area is under quarantine," he said.

Lenzo glanced behind him at the guard, at the chain link fence that was going up around the perimeter of the barracks.

"I am the county medical officer," Lenzo said evenly. "I have allowed a number of my patients to be transferred to this place and I want to know what is happening with them."

"I am with the Public Health Service," Skanz said. He took Lenzo by the arm and squeezed, motioning him into a tiny office off the entryway.

He walked around a desk that nearly filled the room and sat in a creaking office chair, motioning Lenzo into a dusty seat against the wall. Lenzo's knees banged against the front of the metal desk when he sat.

"I drove up here because I wasn't making much headway on the phone," Lenzo said.

Skanz shrugged. "We have been extremely busy."

"I called Atlanta. They didn't seem to know much. They referred me back to you."

Skanz nodded again. He pursed his lips but did not speak. Lenzo was perspiring heavily now.

"So what do we have here, Doctor? You are a *doctor*, aren't you?"

Skanz allowed himself a thin smile. Lenzo's eyes were already bloodshot.

"What are we dealing with?" Lenzo repeated.

"It's altogether too early to tell."

"Why, hell, man. You must have a guess. That's what you people specialize in, isn't it?" Lenzo wiped at the perspiration on his forehead.

"I sent some pretty sick people up here," he continued. "Some of them are friends."

"Yes," Skanz said patiently.

"I'm responsible for what goes on, healthwise, in this county."

"And we will keep you informed, Doctor."

Lenzo seemed to be having trouble breathing. His eyes were watery as he rose from his chair.

"I came up here to get some information and you're fucking with me. I want to see my patients." He clutched the edge of Skanz's desk.

Skanz rose and nodded pleasantly. "I see no problem with that, Doctor."

"It's a goddamned good thing," Lenzo said, his voice no

more than a ragged whisper. He lurched away from the desk toward the open door. His legs were buckling.

On the third step, they gave way altogether. He pitched forward, his face falling toward the door frame. His cheek cracked against the grimy wood and broke open, spraying a crimson blur across the grimy floor.

Skanz stepped past him into the hallway and motioned for an attendant to bring a gurney forward. Lenzo's lips moved, but there was no sound.

"I think you can join your friends now," Skanz said as the man's eyes closed. "It's so good of you to care."

Part
4

VECTOR
ABERRATION

Skanz sat in the dusty office watching the moon inch above the line of mountains on the far side of the clearing. He had opened the window to savor the chill of the night air. No matter how hot it was during the day, at this altitude, it would always cool off at night.

The crisp air stirred something deep inside him. A rush of something like pleasure, though sadness came quickly behind. He stirred, uncomfortable with the emotions even though he was alone. He had spent his adult life purging himself of feelings, at least those that might kindle the seeds of doubt, uncertainty, hesitation. Pleasure was acceptable, given its proper context. And fear, fear was necessary to stay alive.

He took in another breath of the cool air and once again felt something waver inside himself. He'd been born in mountains not unlike these: a small village not far from Garmisch-Partenkirchen, now a bustling resort.

Oddly, he had found himself dreaming of the place more often these days. Typical Bavarian mountain homes, buried in snow all winter, overflowing with flowered window boxes in the brief summer. If he could, he'd go back, just to see. But his village no longer existed, or rather was preserved in a way all its own.

He was seven when it happened. He'd been sent to bring in the cow. He walked in a fine misting rain through the forest, perhaps twenty minutes across the face of the mountainside, found the animal munching on a neighbor's stack, felt a tremor in the earth, and returned home the way he had come.

When they emerged from the forest he thought at first he had taken a wrong turn, or that he was lost inside a dream. Where his village should have been, there was a vast tumble of broken trees and boulders, and a haze of dust rapidly clearing in the steady rain. Everything buried forever under the unfathomable weight of the earth.

He was the first to see it. When the others came, they found him sitting mute near the rubble, the arm of a child's doll cradled in his lap. And he had been taken away.

Skanz stared out the office window at a distant shadow of Wyoming mountainside. He took his gaze from the window and shook his head softly, as if to clear the vision. This would not do, he told himself. This would not do.

The phone purred softly on the desk and he brought the receiver to his ear.

"Yes," Skanz said. It could only be one person on this line.

"Everything is tied up." It was Schreiber's voice, steady, certain. "Your people are the last of them."

"And?"

"The research team would like to observe. We will simply let things take their natural course, at least for a few days. We have never had a chance to see how this agent operates— in the normal world."

"And if any survive?"

"Then you will see to them," Schreiber said. "We will

have the full team on site by midday tomorrow. Until then, keep things quiet."

"I am here," Skanz said, staring out the window into the dark sky. Outside, white pinpoints of light burned in the distance. Stars, he told himself. Only stars. And the connection broke.

Isaac was sitting in the High Country Cafe, a spoonful of chili poised in front of him. He had vague recollections of the time that had passed since he'd left Fairchild and the others at the hospital: being asked to leave a series of bars and roadhouses; several satisfying hours in Sophia's bed; and another melee with her brother, who'd tried to bludgeon Isaac with the new cast on his arm. But these were fleeting visions that shimmered briefly in his hung-over brain and were gone, merging one into the next without regard for chronology and certainly without regard for logic.

His head ached. His life was in disarray. Soon he was going to take that one fateful step on the far side of the line. And then what? He was still pondering the question when the moment arrived, and he realized that the shitstorm had finally sucked him in.

All the haze that had bunkered just behind his brow seemed to lift. His head was suddenly light, his vision clear, his breathing full and even.

The waitress had disappeared into the back. He heard the rear door of the cafe open and close, then everything turned quiet. He put his spoon down. He realized he'd been waiting for this ever since they'd found the shattered truck and the bald man all swollen up on the cliffside.

Someone entered the cafe behind him, sending the little entrance bell there into a dance. Isaac felt the man's presence as he took the stool beside him. Finally, he turned to see who had been sent.

"How you?" the man said affably. The voice sounded authentic. The jeans were properly faded, his snap-button shirt well worn. Dusty, pointy-toe boots; a weather-tanned face. He removed a silver-capped snuff can from his back pocket and took a pinch.

Isaac nodded and went back to his chili. He'd found what he was looking for in the man's eyes. Alert, of course, but somehow not alive.

Isaac chewed another mouthful of beans and spicy brisket. The chili had always been the feature of this restaurant, but tonight it tasted better than ever. Chili would never taste so good again, he decided. He crushed a package of saltines and dribbled the crumbs on the chili, then dumped in the little cup of onions the girl had brought him.

Isaac nodded and took another bite. He was thinking of his grandmother, long dead, who used to tell him the tragic stories of the Nez Perce while sitting on the porch of her little shack. She wore heavy, old-fashioned skirts and a full blouse, her hair knotted above her head in iron gray knots. She always told the same stories with the same endings and there was an angry flash in her dark eyes as if to say, "Do something about it, Isaac. Do something!"

He took note of the streamer of flypaper that twirled in the draft of the fan just behind the counter. He could smell the tang of the cleaner the girl had been using on the deserted tables behind him. He thought he could feel the weight of the air that pressed upon him and the tug of gravity at the bottom of his boots.

"How's that soup?" the man beside him said.

Isaac nodded. He heard the man's tone properly. This was when it began.

"Here," he said, turning to the man. He lifted the bowl in one hand. "Try some."

He slammed the heavy china bowl into the man's face, driving him off the stool and into a heap on the floor. Car doors were slamming on the street outside. Isaac vaulted over the counter, flipped off the lights, and ducked aside as someone burst into the dining area from the kitchen.

Isaac lifted one of the glass water pitchers and brought it down over the intruder's head. There was a satisfying thud that tore the handle clean off in his hand and a crash as the rest of the pitcher shattered on the floor. The man he'd hit with it crumpled across the counter.

Then the front door slammed back, and a flash of light erupted, nearly blinding him. He heard a soft whir and a thump as something struck the wall close to where he stood.

He ducked down and scrambled into the kitchen beneath the half-door divider. More thumps ripped into the flapping doors and one of the silenced shots took out the long fluorescent fixture on the kitchen ceiling, throwing everything into darkness. Isaac scrambled toward the back door, slipping in something wet.

He rolled over, hesitated, then kicked the back door open. When he heard nothing, he rolled on outside, ducking behind the dumpster that was always parked there. The south end of the alley looked clear. He turned the other way in time to see a dark shape sprinting around the corner of the building toward him. Isaac ducked back and ran south, the dumpster hiding his movements.

As he reached the cross street at the end of the alley, he heard the back door of the cafe fly open and the muffled calls of his pursuers. He slipped around the corner and ran silently along the quiet, deserted street toward the cover of the forest, no more than a few hundred feet ahead.

He felt light on his feet, as if he were flying. He thought that his grandmother could see him. The footsteps of the others were a dim thunder behind him. He ran and ran. He had never felt so alive.

Saturday, July 23

When Fairchild awoke, he felt no pain at all, not at first.

He heard a child's voice somewhere, a cry of distress: "No, Mommy. Not funny. Not funny, Mommy. *Mommy!*" And then it broke off abruptly.

He thought he was dreaming, drifting on a raft atop gentle waters, weightless, free. But the child's voice. Where had it come from? Something brushed the raft upon which he lay and he dreamed that it was two men in a fishing boat, but they were wearing the white jackets of hospital orderlies. They glanced at him, then were gone. "Shut that fucking kid up," he heard someone say.

Fairchild nodded, smiling dreamily. He would be left alone now, and it would be quiet. Those men, those strangely dressed fishermen, had gone to comfort the crying child and he could rest, listening to the waves.

But then he slid down a tunnel of darkness and came out into another world, a brightly lit kitchen in the little house that the Park Service had provided him, where he and Lena lived, a million years ago. He was drinking a cup of coffee before leaving for work and he was watching the terrible stiffness of her back as she moved over the stove, working at breakfast. And he was miserable.

Then, abruptly, the memory vanished and pain fell upon

him like a sheet of icy water. Everything, every millimeter of his flesh, pulsed and burned, every organ seemed to throb. Even his eyelids raked him painfully as he fought to bring his vision into focus. And someone was shaking him.

He opened his mouth to cry out, but a hand fell over his mouth, sending a new burst of pain through him. His eyes rolled back and jagged blue bolts zigzagged across the backs of his lids.

"Be quiet," a voice hissed. "They're coming back."

The hands left him then, and mercifully, the pain abated. He blinked again, and this time tears flooded his eyes and cleared his sight.

He was in a long narrow room with metal cots lined up along both walls. Indistinct shapes occupied the beds. An occasional moan wafted through the stuffy air.

Fairchild struggled to raise himself, but could not. It was as if a huge hand gripped his frame, and he gasped softly with the pain. He tilted his chin gingerly down to his chest and saw he had been strapped into the bed.

From far down the other end of the room came muffled voices, and a soft thudding sound as something had hit the floor. He caught movement from the corner of his eye and turned his head to the right. In the next cot a slightly built older man, his face heavily shadowed with bruises, was rearranging the heavy straps across his own bedclothing.

"Lie down," the man hissed. "Pretend you're asleep." It was the same voice that had awakened him.

Footsteps echoed from the far end of the room. Fairchild eased back onto his pillow.

He held his chin near his chest, ignoring the waves of pain. Through half-closed eyes he watched a pair of men in orderly's whites moving down the aisle, struggling to carry something heavy.

As they approached, he saw it was a man, or had been. The two orderlies had the body slung between them, the lead man holding the feet, the one in back grasping his burden under the shoulders. The dead man's face was dark and bloated, his feet swollen and nearly black. The trailing orderly lost his grip suddenly and the dead man's head listed sideways against the metal railing at the foot of Fairchild's bed. There was a soft wet thud, like a melon dropping to the pavement, and a sickening tremor that Fairchild felt to the pit of his stomach. He clamped his eyes shut, fighting to stay calm.

"Fucking A," the orderly hissed. Fairchild felt the bed jiggle again as the two struggled with the body.

"I'm glad this ain't dynamite," his partner said. "You want some handles to put on him?"

"Fuck you," the first orderly said. In a few moments there came the soft sound of a door closing and the room was quiet.

Fairchild opened his eyes to find the slightly built man back, looming over him.

"Do you understand me?" the man asked.

Fairchild stared. He had seen the man before, but where? He looked as if he'd been kicked in the face by a horse. His eyes were blackened and swollen and crusts of blood lined his nostrils.

"You look good," the man said, casting a glance at the cots about them. "In comparison." He glanced back down at Fairchild, waiting for some sign. Fairchild managed a nod. He'd never felt worse in his life.

The man returned his nod and moved to busy himself with the thick straps at Fairchild's chest and legs. In moments, he felt a great pressure lift and he raised himself on his elbow. Abruptly, the pain swept over him and he caught

171

his breath, watching the lightning dance across his eyelids once again.

"That happens right at first. It'll ease up once you start moving." The man appraised him as Fairchild's eyes blinked open. "It's painful, isn't it?"

"I could live without it," Fairchild said. His voice sounded like something cranked from rusty gears. Even talking hurt. He swallowed, choosing his words carefully. "What is this place?"

"Well, it's not the Mayo Clinic," the man said. He glanced about, then turned back to Fairchild. "I'm Robert Lenzo. The county medical officer."

Fairchild stared. Of course. He'd seen the man a dozen times, only never with his face beaten to mush. *A horse,* he found himself thinking—and then he remembered: the bloodied creature bursting out of the woods, the crash, the world turning over and over, and then darkness.

"The little girl," he said, sitting up, ignoring the fresh wave of pain that accompanied his movements.

"Keep your voice down," Lenzo hissed, grasping his wrist. It felt as if a band of fire had been placed there. It hurt too much to struggle.

Somewhere outside a truck motor kicked into life. "She's down there," Lenzo said, indicating the far end of the ward.

He seemed distracted by the sounds outside and leaned close to Fairchild.

"I want you to see something," he said.

He urged Fairchild to his feet, then stood up on his own cot, gesturing for Fairchild to do the same. They could just see over the sill of the high windows. Through the accumulated grime the front of the place was visible in the first light of dawn. They were in a barrackslike building with a

SPILL

swath of forest cleared away before it. The room was part of
a wing that angled down from the main entrance of the place.
Outside, a pair of bulldozers glowed faintly yellow, parked at
the fringe of the trees. A canvas-topped dump truck with its
tailgate down was butted up to the entryway, its heavy exhaust drifting into the still morning air.

In a moment, the two orderlies emerged, carrying a body
bag between them. They struggled down to the second step
of the entrance, nodded to one another, and slung their
burden up into the back of the truck. One of them turned
and spat into the dust by the steps while the other moved to
raise the truck's tailgate. He gave a sign to the driver and the
truck dropped into gear and groaned away, little puffs of dust
rising in its wake.

Fairchild realized his legs were trembling and he eased
himself down to sit. The pain was less this time, though it felt
as though his skin had shrunk, as though a sudden move
could send his elbow popping out through the flesh.

"You're Fairchild?" he heard the doctor's voice say.

He nodded. "How'd you know?"

"I checked you into the clinic on Friday. They brought
you in with the little girl and some others."

Fairchild considered things for a moment. Orderly
thought seemed a long-forgotten skill. "What's wrong? What
do we have?"

The doctor shook his head. "I wish I knew. Early Friday
we started carrying people down from Tapeats Canyon, a
number of them dead, a number of them swollen up like
ticks." He glanced at Fairchild. "You were one of the ones
who seemed better off."

There was a sound from the far end of the ward and the
doctor paused. After a moment he continued, his voice just
above a whisper. "I'd never seen anything like it. When I

173

reported what was happening to the Centers for Disease Control, I was told that it was a form of spotted fever, that there had been several outbreaks in the region. Before long we were ordered to transfer all the cases up here. Things didn't seem right to me and I came up here, looking for answers." He shrugged. "The next thing I knew, I woke up in this ward."

Fairchild shook his head. "Well, let's get somebody in here. Let them tell us what's going on."

Lenzo put a hand on his arm and nodded upward at the window. "I don't know if we want to do that. I don't much care for the bedside manner around this place."

Fairchild hesitated. He imagined the sound the body must have made when it hit the bed of the dump truck. He felt dizzy and gripped the side of the bed for support.

"They've carried four bodies out since I've been awake," Lenzo continued. "I haven't seen any evidence of medical attention—except for that." He nodded at a tray containing a number of syringes beside Fairchild's cot. "Demerol," the doctor said. "They're keeping everyone sedated."

"Until they die?" Fairchild heard the disbelief in his own voice.

The doctor shrugged.

"But I don't get it. I'm achy as hell, but I'm not going to die. And you seem all right. Why would they—?" He broke off at the sound of footsteps approaching the ward door. Lenzo stood up and pushed Fairchild back into his bed, then scrambled beneath his sheets and motioned wildly for Fairchild to do the same.

Fairchild hesitated, then thought of the body bag flying through the air into the dump truck. He swept the sheet up over his legs just as the door swung open, sending a shaft of

174

light across his bunk. *The straps,* he thought wildly. *The fucking straps.* But it was too late.

He lay as still as he could, fighting to control his breathing, afraid for his life. It was an effort just to move his tongue. What could he do if the two thugs dressed up in hospital clothes decided to give him a ride to the dump in a Hefty bag?

But there were three of them this time. And they weren't paying any attention to him. The new one was a brutal-looking man in a long white lab coat. He was carrying a large hypodermic and was moving with a purpose toward the far end of the room, the two orderlies following grimly behind him.

The three walked to the far end of the ward and stopped before a door. The big man nodded and one of the underlings found a key and swung the door open. A shaft of light spilled out from a tiny room. Fairchild rose up as the three men went inside. He could make out the foot of a cot inside the small room.

Someone shouted and one of the orderlies staggered back across the door opening. There was a crash of glass, and the cot in there bucked wildly off the floor.

Then Lenzo was beside him, urging him up. By the time he swung his feet to the floor, Lenzo was halfway down the ward, moving in a frantic, crablike scuttle. The doctor clutched a handful of the Demerol syringes in his hand.

Fairchild started after him, then froze before one of the cots. He felt as if someone had struck him at the base of his skull. Larraine lay unconscious before him, her mouth slack, her eyes sunken and bruised. He gripped the foot of her cot with his hands, astonishment slowly turning to rage that burned away the numbness in his brain.

"Hurry!" Lenzo hissed from down the ward.

Fairchild leaned close enough to be sure she was still breathing, then turned and hurried after the doctor, who had drawn himself up outside the doorway to the inner room. Inside, the big man flashed across the open doorway, his huge hypodermic pointing upward and squirting clear fluid toward the ceiling.

By the time Fairchild joined the doctor, the big man was leaning awkwardly across the fallen cot, struggling to jam the needle into a man pinned to the floor by one of the orderlies. Abruptly the orderly screamed and fell back, holding his hand up as if it had been burned.

"He *bit* me," the orderly cried.

The big man swept him aside and moved in on their prey, a bald, burly man nearly his equal in size. The balding man turned his face toward the door and Fairchild winced. His face was one huge bruise, his eyes deep pools of blood, his lips swollen, his nose still leaking thin trails of red. Even the top of his head was shadowed blue. As the big man with the needle dove at him, the bald man kicked for his groin.

The big man grunted and sank to one knee. The orderly with the bitten hand sucked wildly at his wound. The second orderly was advancing, a metal chair aimed at the wild man on the floor. Abruptly he stopped, his gaze drifting out the open doorway to lock with Fairchild's.

"What the fuck?" the orderly said. He started out toward Fairchild. Lenzo stepped forward into the doorway and swung. The man gasped and staggered backward, clutching at a pair of hypodermics that the doctor had plunged into his cheek. Within moments, the orderly had collapsed.

The man with the bitten hand glanced up in time to catch Fairchild's foot under his chin. He took the blow solidly and flew back into the wreckage of the cot.

The big man with the needle had shaken off the blow

to his groin and rose toward Fairchild with a growl. The bald man who'd kneed him lunged forward, knocking the huge hypodermic to the floor. The big man backhanded him savagely, dodging a swing of Fairchild's at the same time.

The big man advanced on Fairchild and grabbed him by the front of his gown. He drew him in a close embrace, ignoring the blows Fairchild showered on him. He began to squeeze and Fairchild's breath flew from him in a groan. The big man jerked his arms again and Fairchild heard himself scream. He was being crushed to death.

Fairchild tried to get his feet under him to kick, run, anything, but the big man had him lifted from the floor. His breath was long gone, red and gold spirals of light flashed across his vision . . . and suddenly Fairchild felt the pressure ease. The big man staggered, his eyes suddenly losing their focus.

Fairchild felt the big man's grip loosen and his own feet fall back onto the floor. He pried himself away, then watched the big man do an awkward sideways dance away from him, crash against the door frame, and slide down. His eyes found Fairchild's and stared wonderingly for a moment, then closed. At last he slumped forward, his massive head fallen across one knee, the other leg still tucked beneath him.

From the back of his leathery neck hung three hypodermic syringes, buried to the hilt. Lenzo stood by the doorway, gasping, trying to catch his breath. He looked at Fairchild and shrugged.

"I was a vet when I started in this business." He glanced down and prodded the fallen man with his foot. "He wasn't any worse than a bull."

"Is he dead?" Fairchild asked.

The doctor glanced at him. "You ever try to kill a bull?"

Behind them, the bald man with the ruined face was

177

dragging himself to a sitting position against the door frame. "Fucker came in to kill *me*," he rasped.

After a moment he pulled himself to his feet and approached the doctor, pointing to his throat as if it pained him to speak. He indicated the full syringe the doctor still held in one hand, then pointed at the orderly whom Fairchild had kicked. The man was stirring, making soft mewling sounds amid the wreckage of the cot. Lenzo registered his request and started toward the orderly, but the bald man stopped him. He gently took the needle from the doctor's hand.

The bald man dragged the orderly from the tangle of bedclothes. He bent down, jammed the needle deep into the orderly's ear, and squeezed the shot off. The orderly bucked once and lay still. The bald man looked up, gurgling, his mouth gaping open, his eyes grotesque red slits. After a moment, Fairchild realized it was supposed to be a smile.

"I'D CALL IT very good news, sir." The scientist smiled and leaned across the conference table to slide Reisman a report. The scientist wore a lab coat atop a pair of jeans and an Izod shirt. He was tanned, lean, and radiated cheer. Reisman thought he should be on a tennis court a thousand miles away from this desert.

"Just hit the high points for us, okay?" Reisman slid the report across the table to a hard-boned man in an expensive suit.

The young scientist hesitated. Reisman gave him a reassuring nod. "It's all right, Corey. This is Mr. Birk, our research sponsor liaison."

Corey Rasmussen peered across the table at Birk. "Are you a scientist?"

Birk glanced up, disbelieving.

Reisman cut in. "Mr. Birk, this is Corey Rasmussen. *Doctor* Rasmussen," he added.

Birk nodded without taking his eyes off the young man. Rasmussen's cheeriness wilted under the gaze, as if he were some bird just noticing the awful place he'd lit. Finally, Birk spoke. "Let's just say I'm a policy advisor, son. And you're here to tell us what you know." There was no mistaking the command.

Rasmussen nodded docilely and cleared his throat twice before he found his voice. "Well, what it says there is that the inorganic water-soluble coupler breaks down inside of twenty-four hours. Without the artificial carrier component functioning, the water's about as safe as club soda." He reached in his pocket and held out a vial of clear liquid, as if offering Reisman a drink.

Reisman felt his throat constrict. The young scientist glanced at him and continued. "With that stream dried up, you can consider the spill itself contained. The only conceivable way this thing could spread now is by direct human contact."

"*Is* it contagious?" Birk asked.

The scientist paused. "We're still working on that. With all the original research records missing, we're going to be a little bit in the dark until the guys in the rat lab are finished." He shrugged as if to apologize. "That takes time." He glanced at Reisman again. "Isn't everyone who was afflicted under quarantine?"

Reisman gave them a grim nod.

"What about all the birds and the bees?" Birk said.

The scientist shook his head. "Unlikely. This thing only affects warm-blooded species and it would have knocked them flat right away. The cleanup team was in there within a few hours and incinerated what carcasses they found. Any animal they missed would have broken down on its own very shortly after death." The scientist paused. "I mean, if you chased down an infected deer and tore out its heart and ate it, maybe you'd stand a fair chance of getting sick, but otherwise—" He stopped short, realizing he'd gotten carried away.

Birk looked at Reisman. "Do people hunt in there?"

Reisman shook his head absently. He was thinking of

some crazed caveman, crashing through the forest after a steadily weakening doe.

"It's against the law," the scientist said.

Birk had apparently heard all he needed. He gathered the report up, turned to Reisman, and cleared his throat. Reisman blinked away the image of the caveman gobbling up a pulsating heart.

"That'll be all, Corey," Reisman said. The scientist nodded and scurried out of the cavernous office. Reisman sat back in his chair and stared out at the scrubby landscape stretching away from the huge windows. If Rasmussen's report were accurate, the company was in good shape. Once those people in the barracks died, all their problems would be solved. He took a deep breath. He couldn't remember ever feeling so tired.

"We'd never be able to claim defensive research on this one, would we?"

Birk glanced at him. "I don't know what you're talking about."

"If it leaked out what we've been brewing up. We'd never be able to square this stuff with the treaty. That's all we're worried about now, isn't it?"

Birk dropped Rasmussen's report into his briefcase and snapped it shut. He rose with a thin smile. "Just hope it never comes up, Mr. Reisman."

Reisman turned back to the desert as Birk let himself out. There were buzzards circling the updrafts far out over the dusty horizon. There probably wasn't anything dead below them, he told himself. That was just a myth created by old cowboy movies. No, they were just having fun in the sky. Circling around. Killing time. Waiting for him to come out and play.

"WHAT IS IT, JACK? What's happened to us?" Larraine stared at him plaintively. She sat at the edge of her cot, cradling the still-unconscious little girl to her breast.

Fairchild knelt down before them and covered Larraine's hand with his. It hadn't taken the doctor more than a few minutes to revive her. A good sign, he hoped. He felt the shallow, rapid breath of the little girl. Larraine's face was sunken, her eyes circled with dark shadows, as if she'd taken a blow that had broken her nose.

"I don't know," he said, squeezing her hand. "But I know we've got to leave here." He regarded her carefully. "Are you sure you can move?"

She nodded. "Everything's sore, but I'm okay."

"Good." He gave her a smile and turned to regard the big man they'd overpowered in the fight. He was still unconscious, tied up in sheeting like a mummy. He turned back to her. "We're going to get out of this, you hear me?" He stared at her until she finally managed a thin smile.

The badly swollen man they'd rescued—Ripley, he'd said his name was—came out of his little room, jamming his shirt into a baggy pair of Forest Service greens. They'd found some of their clothes along with a cache of the musty government-issue garments in a locker just off the entrance to the place.

Ripley stopped to look at the big man on the floor, shook his head, then gave him a solid kick in the groin. The big man groaned softly in his sleep.

"Stop it," Larraine cried.

Ripley stared at her, then turned to Fairchild as if to explain. "He would have killed me," Ripley said. Fairchild turned away from his ruined face.

One of the earth-moving machines roared close to the building and Fairchild looked up at the bank of windows that faced the east. The sun was still behind the mountain, but it wouldn't be long before it came up, bringing with it the heat and whatever load of bad shit the day had in store. He glanced down the rows of cots where the silent forms lay. Every last one of them was dead.

"And you'd have been next," Ripley added in his phlegmy voice.

As he spoke, the doctor hurried back from the office area, stuffing a sheaf of papers into a pocket of his pants. He was still wearing the street clothes they'd strapped him into bed with, but he'd thrown one of the dark green shirts over his white one for better cover.

The doctor turned to Fairchild. "I grabbed everything I could find." He shook his head. "I don't know if it will tell us anything. We can look at it later."

Fairchild nodded. Along with the clothing, they'd found a few tinned rations, a revolver, and a few shells in the office desk and some topographical maps left behind by the smoke jumpers.

Fairchild looked their group over briefly: Ripley appeared as if a sprint to the door would finish him; the doctor was unmarked, lean, healthy—no problem there. He glanced at Larraine. He didn't know what they would do about the little girl.

There was a lull in the motors' roaring outside, and abruptly the phone in the distant office began to ring.

"It's time," Fairchild said.

"Oh my God," Larraine cried softly.

The men turned as one. Her eyes were full of tears as she clutched the child fiercely to her.

"She's not breathing," Larraine said. "She's not breathing."

The doctor hurried to examine the girl, then glanced up at Fairchild and shook his head.

Fairchild motioned him away and knelt beside Larraine. "I'm sorry," he said softly.

He nodded to the doctor and Ripley, who moved toward either end of the trussed-up big man. The two picked him up and struggled away toward the front of the barracks.

"I'm sorry," Fairchild repeated, wrapping his arms around Larraine's shoulders. And then it was time to go.

ARTHUR BIGGS HAD been picked up from his normal post guarding company perimeters in a vast swampy tract of south Georgia and transported without explanation to the West Yellowstone forest overnight. So when he glanced up from his position and saw a body crashing through the window of the barracks, he immediately clamped hand to automatic rifle and fired a full clip into the air. Where he came from, it was an instinctive way to call for help.

He'd just happened to be looking that way when it happened. There was a flash of white inside the office windows, then abruptly the glass exploded in a glittering shower, and then there was someone bound up in bandages twisting through the air like a human torpedo, turning over once, twice, and finally slamming to the ground with an impact that raised a heavy cloud of red dust in the dry morning air.

At the sound of the gunfire, his companion, an older man who claimed to have Special Forces experience, came running from his post just down the road. The two other perimeter guards did not show up, never having heard the shots. One had stepped into some bushes to relieve himself and the other was asleep on his feet, gazing idly as one of the bulldozers gathered itself for a charge at a stubborn pine.

That left Biggs and his backup man alone, warily moving

185

in on the figure in the bandages, their weapons at the ready.

Thus, no one saw the door at the north end of the barracks fly open or the rush of people across the narrow strip of cleared land separating them from the forest: three men and a woman who crashed wildly into the underbrush and were gone.

They moved frantically uphill for a half hour or so. Except for the steep grade, the going was relatively easy, over a thick carpet of needles beneath the shade of the pines. The sun was up now, and the heat grew steadily as they climbed. Though they'd heard the sound of the heavy machinery shut down soon after they reached the cover of the forest, there had been no sign of pursuit so far.

Fairchild felt a fire growing in his lungs and came to a halt, leaning against the trunk of a huge pine. The others were strung out behind him, with Ripley far in the rear. The doctor helped Larraine, who was still moving in a daze, to a seat on a fallen log. Ripley finally joined them and collapsed onto a pile of needles, gasping for air. Fairchild took out one of the silk topo maps to study.

"We'll clear Mack's Ridge in an hour or so," he told them finally. "We could work our way down the canyon on the other side, which would bring us out a mile or so from town."

The doctor gave him a look. "I don't know."

"Anything that's downhill," Ripley wheezed.

"I'm not sure we'd be safe there," the doctor continued. He held up the sheaf of papers from the office. "There are news bulletins, Park Service announcements, even a piece in the *Grizzly*. There's no mention of this, this hospital. Or us."

"Maybe there wasn't time," Fairchild said, trying to ignore the chill inside him. "Maybe they didn't want to start a panic, until they saw what they were dealing with."

"And just what is that, Doc?" It was Ripley, wheezing from his place on the ground. "Those papers tell you what we got, what killed all those other people?"

The doctor glanced at him and finally shook his head. "There are some possibilities."

"Such as?" Fairchild broke in.

The doctor spread his hands. "I'm not sure. It would take lab tests. Anything I'd say now would be a pure guess."

"But we're okay now, right, Doc?" Ripley struggled to one elbow, still panting. His face was so bloated it seemed ready to explode.

"Do you feel okay?" the doctor asked him.

"Great. A little winded, that's all."

The doctor nodded, then turned to Fairchild, who shrugged. "Larraine?" the doctor called, but she did not answer.

"Larraine?" Fairchild asked, taking her hand. She glanced at him, but did not speak. Her eyes still carried the forlorn emptiness they'd had when he pried the child's body from her. He gave her hand a squeeze and put it back in her lap. He stared hard at the doctor, who met his gaze steadily. Finally, he cleared his throat.

"Okay, let's figure they've got things sewed up around West Yellowstone." Fairchild spread the map out on the ground before them and pointed at a spot in the middle of a dark band of green.

"We're here." He traced his finger up the map over a series of ever-tightening gray circles that indicated the high country. He stopped, pointing at another broad area of green

187

quartered by two intersecting roads. "This is the center of the park. There's a hundred thousand people milling around in that area on any given day."

The doctor nodded thoughtfully. Ripley leaned between them and measured the distance with his fingers. He looked up doubtfully at Fairchild. "How far is that?" he asked.

"Two days, maybe. More or less."

"You done it?" Ripley asked.

"No," Fairchild said.

"Well, shit," Ripley said.

"But I know what it'll take."

Ripley shook his head and lay back. "I hope I got whatever that is," he wheezed.

Fairchild turned back to the doctor. "What do you say, Doc?"

The doctor nodded. "We should avoid the town," he said.

"Then let's hit it," Fairchild said, getting up. "We'll cross the last of the fire trails about a mile up. Once we're past that, the only way they can come after us is on foot."

He helped Ripley to his feet and watched as the doctor urged Larraine ahead. He watched them all struggle off, shaking his head. It was going to take a miracle, he thought, and fell in behind.

They moved that way for another half hour, long enough to have reached the fire trail, Fairchild was thinking. But then he always overestimated how fast others could walk out here, always figuring on the basis of Fairchild time. He stopped to lean against a pine, resting, savoring the bark's tang of vanilla in the clean dry air.

Lena had never liked to hike with him for that very

reason. He always had her gasping, on the ropes after an hour or two on the trail. And the funny thing was, he never meant to do it that way. He'd promise her an easy hike, a short climb to a little high-country lake, but then he'd get out of the truck and put his pack on and all his instincts would take over and he'd be pounding up the trail as fast as he could.

He swung his eyes to the forest above and saw that the others had all climbed out of sight, even Ripley. He listened, but could hear no sound of their movements. He had no idea how long he'd been daydreaming.

He pushed himself away from the tree and hurried up the incline. He caught sight of open sky through the screen of trees ahead and knew he was nearing the crest of the ridge, but there was still no sign of the others.

He reached the embankment that marked the fire trail, worn and rutted by many seasons of runoff. The road, never used in all the time he'd been working, had nearly faded back into wilderness. To his right, it curled around an outcropping of rock; eventually, he knew, it would peter out atop Mack's Ridge that loomed just over his head. It was the beginning of the real wilderness.

There were scuff marks leading up the road, indicating the others had climbed that way. He glanced down the faded path and paused. Something had caught his eye. He took a cautious step down the road and saw it again, a glint of metal behind some brush.

He slipped quickly across the trail and into the forest on the uphill side, moving in a looping circle away from the road, then back down the rugged hillside toward what he had seen. In moments he had a clear view of it: a dusty jeep with a fresh dent in one side where someone had scraped it up against a tree.

The vehicle seemed empty. He scanned the nearby forest

but saw no one. He slipped from pine to pine until he could step out past a clump of brush where the driver had meant to hide the jeep. He placed his hand on the hood. It was cold and still bore a faint sheen of morning dew.

He heard what sounded like a cough from higher up the mountain and glanced toward the ridgeline. He started back toward the road and began to climb hurriedly, fighting panic, his lungs burning in the thin air.

He reached the point where he'd crossed the fire trail and paused, listening. A jay cried out, jumping from branch to branch high above him. A breeze sighed through the pine tops. He glanced up the trail. It curved through the trees, an inviting tunnel, the easiest way to the top. He shook his head and turned away from the trail, then began the steep ascent directly up the ridge, pulling himself along with the help of scrub and low sweeping limbs.

As he neared the top he slowed, taking each difficult step as silently as he could. He lowered himself to the ground and levered himself the last few feet up to the ridgetop on his elbows and toes.

At first he saw nothing on the flat table of land; but then he heard a voice, followed by a groan. He drew himself up and pulled quickly back into the screen of trees, then began to edge toward the sounds.

Abruptly, he stopped. Across the narrow clearing there was a break in the forest where the road builders had cut out a turnaround and dumped a pile of boulders. It formed a shallow bowl a few feet below the level of the clearing, and that was what had hidden them from his sight until now.

They were all lying facedown, hands clasped behind their heads: Larraine, Ripley, the doctor. A man with an Uzi hovered above them, a nervous-looking type whose gaze roamed constantly over the backs of his prisoners. He had a battery-operated phone slung on his back and lifted the microphone to his lips with one hand, the automatic held ready with the other.

"Goddammit," he barked into the microphone. "Goddammit, come in!"

Fairchild heard a burst of static in response. Ripley was struggling to rearrange himself on the rocky ground, and the man stepped forward to kick him in the ribs with his heavy hiking boot. Ripley gasped and sagged against the ground.

The man tried the radio again, with the same result. He glanced about in frustration. Fairchild quickly pulled back, praying he hadn't been seen. When he looked again, the man was backing slowly up the side of the little bowl, jiggling at the antenna of his radio, his Uzi still trained on the others. Fairchild realized the man was moving toward him, trying to find a spot where the radio signals would come in.

When the man reached the ridgetop he stopped. Fairchild tried to calculate the distance between his hiding place and the spot where the man stood. At least fifty feet, nothing for cover, and loose talus to rattle under every step. Still, once that radio call was made, they were finished.

He crouched down and slipped quietly from his cover out into the open. The man punched the key on his microphone.

"Elkherd?" he called. "Elkherd? This is Crowpoint."

There was a burst of static and then a dim voice. "We read you, Crowpoint. Go ahead." Fairchild thought of the calls from astronauts he'd listened to on TV—people listening in, wanting to know how it was out there in terra incognita. People who'd never find themselves a million miles from home with their asses hanging over a big, deep crack. He'd always counted himself among them.

He rose to make his charge. His boot tip plowed through

191

a skiff of loose rock and sent it clattering ahead of his path. The man with the radio spun, dropping his microphone. He swung his Uzi up to meet Fairchild's assault. The loose microphone dangled over the short barrel of the weapon. The man flicked it away and set himself to fire. Fairchild knew he would come up a step or two short.

Suddenly, the man's expression changed from hatred to surprise. Then as he pitched forward, his finger tightened instinctively on his weapon and a burst of fire cut a path a foot in front of Fairchild's boots, sending sharp fragments of rock against him.

Fairchild danced aside, stunned. A fountain of blood poured from the man's mouth as he staggered past, his eyes blank. He took one last spinning step, dropped his gun, and collapsed.

Fairchild stared down. Buried in the back of the man's skull was a sharp wedge of rock lashed into a split stick the thickness of a hammer's handle.

He heard someone running toward him and spun about. He froze, disbelieving. Isaac, huge Indian Isaac, his chest bare, his hair pulled back in a ponytail, trotting easily and soundlessly across the gravel-strewn clearing like something out of a dream.

The Indian came to a stop by the fallen man, nudged him with a bare foot, then turned to Fairchild. He pointed down at the crude weapon that was lodged in the man's head.

"We used to make those things when we were kids," he said. He looked up at Fairchild. "Old Indian stuff."

"Old Indian stuff," Fairchild repeated. He was still shaking. The others scrambled to their feet, staring up at them in astonishment.

"Come in, Crowpoint," a scratchy voice called. "Come in!"

SPILL

Isaac stomped on the radio and the forest was suddenly quiet. Fairchild thought of those astronauts again. He looked about the faces of their group: uncertainty, fear, surprise, anger, desperation. Ordinary human beings transformed to something else. About what you'd expect in a bunch of people kicked loose from the orbit of the earth.

Part 5

DETOXIFICATION

IT WAS NEARLY one o'clock when Fairchild stopped to check his map again. He stared down at the steadily tightening lines of elevation that mirrored the increasing pitch of their climb. They were nearing nine thousand feet. Another three or four hours would put them near tree line. Then they'd have several miles of exposed traverse along treeless Alpine meadows and outcroppings of rock until they descended back into the forest. That was a crossing they'd have to make in the dark.

He glanced up as the others trudged by him: Isaac, Larraine, the doctor, and, after a minute or so, Ripley, still the picture of ruin, still wheezing along. Larraine had yet to say a word, though he'd caught her staring at him from time to time. The doctor turned back and gave him a silent nod of encouragement. Everyone was moving more slowly by the step. It would only get worse as they climbed and the air thinned further.

Ripley, despite his appearance, had not seemed to weaken, but everyone was drawn, even Isaac. Fairchild glanced up. There was a solid cover of pines. He called after the methodically plodding Indian for a rest. Isaac nodded and sank to his haunches near a stand of poplars. The others fell to the ground, and Fairchild broke out some of their rations. They'd picked up a few provisions, including a canteen, from the man Isaac had killed. The Uzi would have come in handy, but its clip had been emptied.

"We should've just taken that fucker's jeep," Ripley wheezed, his face still swollen, his eyes closed tight. He was on his back, his chest heaving. Fairchild wondered where the man's energy was coming from.

"Where would you drive it to?" Fairchild said. "You heard what Isaac said." They'd listened to Isaac's account of the incident at the cafe, his description of the men he'd seen combing the town since the day they'd all been found in the canyon. All of it had confirmed the doctor's fears.

"No one in the town knows what's been happening," Isaac repeated. "Except for the ones who want us."

After he'd escaped from his pursuers, he'd gone directly to the field hospital and kept watch.

When he saw them loading the bodies, he had decided to run, to hike through the forest toward his relatives' place north of Jackson. He'd been about to leave when he saw the others make their break. He had followed them up through the forest until they'd been rounded up by the man with the Uzi.

The Indian rocked back on his heels and met Ripley's plaintive gaze. "We got to get far away from here, my man. Far away."

Ripley stared behind them, down a chute through the trees that gave a view of the vast forest below. "These bastards must have a lot of suck," he said mournfully. He didn't turn around.

"About as much suck as there is." Isaac nodded.

Fairchild glanced at Ripley, then at the doctor, who stared down at the dirt between his knees. Fairchild was trying to make sense of it. He'd found some people, sick and dying, up the Little Murky canyon. Larraine had been riding in that same canyon. The two of them had turned up sick in that barracks. But that didn't account for the doctor. And what about Ripley?

"What kind of world is it?" Fairchild turned, startled. It was Larraine's voice, the first words she had spoken since he'd taken the little girl's body from her.

She looked at Fairchild as if he were somehow responsible. "I've been thinking about it all the way up this mountain," she said, "and I still can't understand. Who are these people? How can they just come in and take over a town, a national park?"

"I did it."

They all turned to stare at Ripley, who had struggled up to a sitting position. He looked around at them, then dropped his gaze. "It was my truck. I went over the side and dumped the load in a stream down there." He waved vaguely down the chute at the green folds of mountainside. No one spoke. He glanced up at their faces.

"I drive for PetroDyne. They make chemical fertilizers, pool additives, shit like that. In Denver, and other places around the West." He looked around for a sign of recognition.

Fairchild felt another chill run through him even though the heat was intense. "So? You spilled pool chemicals in the Little Murky and twenty people swell up like blood sausage and die?"

Ripley shook his head bitterly. "It wasn't no pool chemicals. They make it, but it's just a cover-up. They got contracts with the government for the real money-makers."

Fairchild glanced at the doctor, who wouldn't meet his gaze. Ripley began to cough violently. It sounded as if a huge bucket of gears and bones were being stirred inside his chest. Finally, he got his breath.

"Germ warfare shit. Stuff turn you every which color, grow you two or three assholes. That's what they make." He struggled to clear his throat. "That's what I was hauling."

"What exactly was it?" Fairchild said.

Ripley shook his head. "I dunno. I'm not supposed to know. They tell you it's caustic chemicals, which is bad enough." He shrugged. "I just haul what they give me over to Idaho. There's a big storage yard in the desert. Used to be for the Atomic Energy or something."

"What were you doing on the Tapeats road?" Fairchild asked.

Ripley shrugged. "I got lost."

Fairchild studied him for a moment, then turned to the doctor. "What do you say?"

The doctor shrugged, staring at a pile of pine needles he'd raked up between his boots. Finally he looked up. "I called the Centers for Disease Control. They said it was a strain of spotted fever."

"They got everybody working with them, Doc. They're in bed with the damn Feds, for Chrissakes." Ripley hacked and spat into the dust.

Fairchild searched the doctor's face. "Is it possible he dumped something, like he says?"

Lenzo threw up his hands. "It's possible. We all know what happened at Dugway." He glanced up at Larraine. "You were all in that stream."

"No," Larraine protested, "I just wiped my face."

"That could have been enough," the doctor said. "If the agent were skin-permeable." He looked around at the others. "And Fairchild gave mouth-to-mouth to the little girl."

"Then it could be contagious." It was Isaac, his voice matter-of-fact. He rocked on his toes, staring thoughtfully.

"It could be," the doctor agreed. "But you were exposed

two days ago. That's a good sign." His eyes met Isaac's. Isaac nodded, without expression.

"Well, why is he so swollen and we're not?" It was Larraine, pointing at Ripley.

"I don't know." The doctor shrugged. "I just don't know."

"Why do they want to kill us?" she asked.

"I can't answer that either," the doctor said. "Maybe they think we could spread the disease to others."

"Or maybe they just want to cover the whole thing up," Fairchild said. "It doesn't really matter, now. We need to get out of the park, go somewhere we can get help, then we'll worry about *how* and *why*."

He turned to Ripley, who had begun to cough his horrible cough again. Fairchild felt his own gut clench at the wracking sound.

When he was able to breathe again, Ripley stared up at them through his ghastly red-rimmed eyes, shaking his head. "We can't get out of this. There isn't anyplace to go. They're everywhere, just waiting." His eyes were dancing. "They got the phones, they got the newspapers, they got everything."

He broke off, his eyes desperate.

Fairchild shook his head. "It's hard to believe."

Isaac nodded, waving his hand at the forest below. "It's your tax dollars in action," he said. "Your own Uncle Sam chasin' after us."

Ripley groaned and sagged back against the trunk of a pine. After a moment the doctor rose and peeled back the man's eyelids, glanced at the dark masses there, then stood and raised his brows doubtfully at Fairchild. Larraine moved to get him a drink from the canteen.

Fairchild followed the doctor away and finally took his arm. "Are you holding out on us, Doc?"

Lenzo's eyes flashed. "What the hell do you expect from me, a lab analysis? I've got plenty of guesses, but they aren't much use without—"

He broke off. A sound had materialized from somewhere, a mechanical buzz that swelled almost instantly into a roar, doom itself sweeping down from the sky. They all flinched involuntarily as the terrible clatter passed over them, dragging its shadow after itself, a black thing that flittered through the trees like a monster from a bad dream.

A *helicopter*, Fairchild realized, though the roar had subsided before he had finished the thought.

"Oh, Jesus," Larraine moaned.

The doctor stared up at the trees, dumbstruck. Only Ripley seemed unaffected. He sucked the canteen dry and tossed it aside. He glanced up at Fairchild. "I guess it's over, then." His swollen features arranged themselves into a forlorn grin.

"Fuck that," Fairchild said, jerking him to his feet. He shoved the man roughly up the hillside and turned to wave the others on after him. "Let's go, let's hit it!" he cried over the receding echoes of the helicopter.

Ripley turned and stared at him for a moment, hesitating. Finally, he gave a mirthless laugh and moved off. He mumbled something that was lost to Fairchild.

"What did he say?" Larraine asked.

Isaac turned to her. "Custer's last stand," he said. He grinned and helped her along.

"LET ME GUESS," the young woman in the first-class seat beside him said. "Advertising."

Reisman glanced at her. A leather blouse, three buttons undone, a matching skirt hiked to within an inch of her crotch. Black hair that cascaded to her shoulders. Her pupils were pinpoints. She rubbed the back of her hand vigorously across her reddened nose. She wasn't pretty, but it didn't seem to matter.

He smiled and shook his head. "Fight promoter." He downed the rest of his vodka rocks. He'd had two in the Clipper Lounge of the Salt Lake airport before he boarded and two more as they sat on the ground, delayed, waiting to take off for Denver. He was on his way to have it out with Schreiber. He was either going to be in charge of all security or he'd be gone.

The woman shifted in her seat, giving him a better look at the triangle of dark panties barely shadowed by her skirt.

"That sounds interesting," she said. "What are you doing in Utah? I thought all boxers were Negroes."

He signaled the stewardess for another drink; this woman was insane, but he didn't care. The plane had finally begun to taxi.

"That's a misconception," he said. "There's this Mormon kid down in Provo. He's an animal. The great white hope. Killer box office."

The stewardess brushed by and Reisman caught her arm. "Bring something for the lady."

"That's okay. I don't drink."

The stewardess pulled away from Reisman and gave him an uncertain look. The girl in leather rubbed her nose again as the stewardess went back toward the galley. She leaned toward Reisman, her breast pushing heavily into his arm. "Screws up my buzz, you know?"

Reisman nodded and gunned his drink. He'd flown for twenty years. Twenty years of fat guys and mean old ladies and kids traveling to see their divorced parents. This was the payoff. A frequent-flier bonus. He felt out of control. He would fuck this woman in the john, or right here in the seat if it came to it.

"So, is there a lot of money in fights?"

"Huh?" he said.

"Money. In fights."

He glanced down the front of her blouse. "It's absolutely amazing," he said. "What do you do?"

She shrugged. "Typist. I work Vegas the weekends, though. Free-lance."

Reisman was figuring it out when the captain's voice cut through the Muzak on the intercom. "I'm sorry, ladies and gentlemen, but we're going to have to return to the gate."

There was a chorus of groans from the other passengers.

"Just a few moments and we'll be back in line for take-off," the captain said, and the Muzak sprang back to life.

"Free-lance?" Reisman repeated. The girl was digging for something in her purse.

"Mr. Reisman?" the stewardess said, leaning across the

204

seat to hand him a note. Reisman looked up at her blearily, glanced at the note, then swung his glance out the window, toward the terminal. A black limo was drawn up on the macadam near the gangway, a driver at the ready. The rear window had been drawn partway down and he caught sight of a familiar shock of iron gray hair.

"Jeez, what's going on?" the girl beside him said. She bent her nose to her cupped hand and sniffed. She shook her fist, still hiding what was in it, and brought her other nostril down.

Reisman gave her a forlorn look. "The guy died," he said finally. "That boxer. He was jumping rope. Just keeled over and died."

"Wow," she breathed. She fell back against the seat cushion, smiling beatifically.

"You bet your ass," Reisman said, and stood to get his bag.

"We must find these people and bring them back, whatever it takes. I don't have to explain the stakes, do I, Alec?"

Schreiber stared calmly across the little table that took up most of the tail space in the private jet. They were cutting the air north, back toward Idaho, toward the compound Reisman had never intended to see again.

"No, you don't," Reisman told him. He still felt the drinks. He wanted to tell Schreiber to go fuck himself, wanted to tell him he'd been on his way to Denver to deliver his resignation. But now, staring face to face at the man, the words stuck in his throat. He felt impotent in Schreiber's presence.

Though the man was at least seventy, he looked fifteen

years younger. His face was lined but firm, no fleshiness at the neck, no folds about his eyes, those cool blue eyes that took in everything.

"I know I've kept you out of some things on this," Schreiber said soothingly. "But it's best. You've been very helpful," he added. "Very loyal. Believe me, I appreciate what you've done."

He knows, Reisman thought. He looks in my eyes and knows everything in my mind. He glanced up at the open cockpit door. One pilot, one copilot. He could strangle this imperturbable man before they knew what was happening. He could explain why he'd done it, maybe become a national hero. Sure.

He turned back to Schreiber, who reached to pat his hand softly. "We're reassembling the support team at Lost River and you'll be in charge there, just as before. As soon as we have everything under control again, you can go home, take some time off."

Reisman glanced down. They were skirting the forested mountains north of Boise. There were broad swaths cut through the pines that in winter would become the ski slopes of Sun Valley. Beyond the manicured slopes, fold after fold of densely forested mountainscape stretched into the distance. How could you find anyone who wanted to hide in such country?

He turned back to Schreiber. "What do you need me for? Anybody could handle the desk."

"I want my best people there," Schreiber said, staring closely at him. Reisman felt the man probing, reading, evaluating. He felt helpless. A little bird frozen in front of a snake, waiting. Whatever made him think he could quit?

"What's wrong, Alec?" he asked finally. His concern seemed sincere.

"Nothing," he said, averting his eyes. "I'm just tired." He took a deep breath. "These people. We don't know if they're carriers, do we?"

"It's not the sort of thing you gamble on."

Reisman nodded. "But they could just keel over out there, on their own."

"Anything is possible." Schreiber's voice was reassuring.

As the plane began a broad swinging turn to the east, back over the high desert, he cut a glance at Schreiber. The man would never have been drawn here if he weren't worried out of his skin.

"But if they *did* make it out of there, if they *were* carriers." Reisman trailed off, watching Schreiber. *Just admit it,* he thought. *Tell me that you're worried. Tell me that you're human.*

Schreiber hadn't taken his eyes from him. He smiled. "Don't worry, Alec. We'll find them." Then he shrugged and gazed back down upon the desert. Reisman thought he saw the first hint of worry in the man's eyes. "It would be terrible if we didn't."

THE HELICOPTER HAD not returned. They had moved steadily for what seemed hours, keeping in heavy cover, though that meant a gradual tacking movement as the mountain grew steeper and the trees began to thin.

In other circumstances, Fairchild would have felt exhilaration. He'd be yearning for that first break out from the forest. That was the payoff, the carrot that drew him steadily up the mountainside and never mind if your pack was heavy, or there was a thunderhead moving in, or it was hot and dry and your nose and throat were full of red mountain dust.

Never mind, for when you finally came out of the trees and turned and saw the whole world laid out below you and sucked in those gulps of clear, thin air, you knew you had done something worth doing. You got a look at something most people would never see, and you hadn't taken one goddamn thing out of the world in the process.

He heard muttering curses down the slope behind him and the noise of someone thrashing through brush. He glanced ahead, at Isaac's back receding into the pines, then turned around in the direction of the labored sounds.

He'd put Isaac on the point, with Larraine and the doctor in between. He had wanted to keep back, close to Ripley.

After a bit of searching he found Ripley tangled in a clump of vines and briars. The ground fell away steeply there and Ripley had lost his footing. He lay out nearly parallel to the mountainside, wrapped up in green tendrils like a huge bug in a spider's trap.

Fairchild circled the tangle of brush and came up from under the big man, working to get his arms and legs free of the clutching vines and brambles.

"How'd you get in here?" he asked, trying to avoid the blasts of rank breath that Ripley gave out as he struggled.

"Walking backward," Ripley said. "I thought I heard something," Ripley wheezed. "So I turned around. Then it just seemed easier to walk that way."

Fairchild dragged Ripley clear, finally, and sat down beside him, catching his breath. He thought of the huge, wheezing Ripley tottering backward up the slope, suddenly losing his footing and windmilling into the underbrush, and he felt himself start to laugh. He couldn't remember the last time he'd laughed and he couldn't stop himself now. In moments, he and Ripley were howling, beating the ground, their eyes filled with tears. It might have gone on longer, but finally Ripley's laugh turned to involuntary grunts, and then broke into the miserable, wracking cough that made Fairchild's own ribs ache.

When he was able to breathe again, Ripley crawled up on one elbow, wiping his grotesquely swollen lips on his sleeve. A trail of pink traced across the fabric. Fairchild turned his head away. He felt he was watching someone disintegrate.

"I had me a sweet deal, Ranger." He started to cough again, but managed to cut it off. "Some little fucker used to work for PetroDyne," he wheezed. "Whatever was in those tanks, he knew they'd shit diamonds to get it back."

Fairchild turned to face him. "So he paid you to dump it?"

Ripley shook his head. "Wasn't supposed to do that. Just hide the rig and walk away. I got fifty grand."

"And what was going to happen when they found you?"

"Shit. If they ever did, I'd just say we was hijacked."

Fairchild stared at him. "Who was this man?"

Ripley shook his head. "Just some little prick with a hard-on." He looked off sorrowfully. "Still owes me money, too."

After a moment he turned to Fairchild. "What do you think about all that?"

Fairchild studied him. He ought to feel *something*, but curiously he didn't. He ought to want to kill him, this greedy redneck moron who'd put them all here, but what good would it do? Would it save them?

He glanced at Ripley's ruined face. So now he understood how this had started. It wasn't just some chemical company in Denver that could mount all that down below. The government was involved. That much was clear. It was a big-stakes game.

"I think you made a mistake," Fairchild said finally.

"I expect you're right," Ripley said. "But somebody puts fifty grand in your hand, you get brand-new emotions."

Fairchild nodded and got to his feet. "Let's go," he said. He grasped Ripley's hand to help him up. The big man's face glowed with the effort, and Fairchild felt that if he squeezed hard enough, the man's features would explode like a ruptured balloon.

"Where's Larraine? Where's my daughter, mister?" Bud Keller stared up from the wooden office chair that everyone in the shop knew as his, even after he'd retired.

The man stared back at him with eyes as flat as a snake's. He'd said whom he worked for, but Bud had already forgotten. "We're looking, Mr. Keller. We've got a lot of men out there looking."

"In the park, right? You said maybe she was in the park."

The man nodded impatiently. "It might help if you could remember where she said she was going."

Bud looked embarrassed. "I can't," he muttered. He felt miserable. Maybe she had told him. But he just couldn't remember. She'd leaned over while he was eating his cereal and kissed him on the cheek, and he'd thought he was a boy again. And Larraine was his mother. How could he forget that? She'd smiled and bent down and kissed him on the cheek. It was the nicest moment he could remember. But if she'd said anything, he couldn't think of it.

"Has your daughter seemed depressed lately? Acted strangely, anything like that?" The man moved so as to be in Bud's line of sight.

Bud glared up at him. He couldn't remember a lot of

things but he could still spot a sonofabitch when he saw one. "She worries about me, mister, but who the hell wouldn't? Now get out of here and go find her."

His voice had risen, and a salesman guiding a tourist through the sleeping bag display glanced up at the loft office at their confrontation.

"We're doing everything we can, Mr. Keller." He turned and started out, his highly polished boots thudding against the wooden floor.

"Do you have a—one of those things with your name on it?" Bud called after him. He got up from his desk and hurried to the railing that looked down over the store.

"One of those *things*," he repeated. But the man didn't stop. He went right out the door of the shop without looking up.

As the door closed, Bud found himself standing at the railing, wondering what he was doing there. He glanced down at the clerk, who was struggling to unroll a sleeping bag. "What the hell are you doing?" he demanded. The clerk looked up, alarmed. "Don't you dare send that man out in the woods," Bud shouted. Then he turned and found his way back to his chair.

"A *card*," he muttered. "Sonofabitch didn't even have a card!"

Tom Clancy polished glasses, lined up bottles, dabbed at invisible spots on the mirror behind his bar. It was the slowest part of his day; the attitude-adjustment hour was still two hours away. He'd been watching the Indians and the Yankees, courtesy of his new satellite dish, but rain had swept in off Lake Erie in the bottom of the third, leaving a view of soggy canvas and Phil Rizzuto and Mickey Mantle making small talk. He switched the set off.

Now he was listening to the conversation going on at the far end of the bar, which was considerably more interesting.

"So you think you've got it whipped?" It was Russ Richards, editor of the *Grizzly,* his pad laid out in front of him, finishing his drink as he waited for an answer from the stolid man in the Western-cut suit. The man gestured for Clancy to refill Richards's drink.

It wasn't a complicated operation. A splash of vodka, no rocks, and a chunk of lemon on the side. Richards nodded his thanks but didn't look his way. His nose and cheeks might be red enough to start a fire, but his breath was clear. The man waited for Clancy to move back down the bar before he answered the newspaperman.

"We've transferred a few cases to Denver, and the rest are in Atlanta." The man shrugged. "People don't want to believe it, but spotted fever is a very serious matter. It's constantly mutating, and, clearly, it can be deadly."

Clancy leaned against the huge brass cash register, staring up idly at the vaulted ceiling. Funny thing, acoustics. He'd seen a demonstration once, in the Mormon Tabernacle: the androidlike teenager who took them around left their group at the back of the hall, then went up front and dropped a pin to the hardwood floor. It was a *bobby* pin, but sure enough, they could hear it, a hundred feet away.

"I'd like to get a look at that field hospital up the mountain," Richards said.

The man shook his head. "Nothing to see. We've moved everything out, shut it down." He glanced down the bar at Clancy. "Besides, it could be dangerous."

213

"I thought the whole area had been fogged." Richards stared at him over his drink.

"No point in taking chances, is there?" The man smiled tolerantly. The editor nodded and took a hasty sip of his drink. He bent to make a note.

"What about the families?"

"We're keeping them informed. As soon as a patient can be moved, they'll know about it."

"Right." Richards scrawled rapidly. "So what are you doing to keep this from happening again?"

The man stiffened. Richards looked up innocently from his pad. "So people can feel secure, make them stop worrying, you know."

The man nodded finally. "Just tell them it's over with."

Richards shrugged and wrote something down. He pointed at a business card on the bar between them. "And this agency is a part of the Centers for Disease Control, right?"

"It's a kind of liaison between the public and the private sectors," the man said, nodding. He signaled for the check.

Clancy took his time getting there. The man gave him a twenty and motioned for him to keep it. Clancy nodded his thanks and watched the two get down and start toward the door.

"Take it easy, Russ," he said. Richards gave him a wave but didn't turn. "Say," Clancy added. "Why don't you give Jack Fairchild a call, see what the Park Service has to say?"

Richards paused at the doorway. "Tom, do I tell you how to mix drinks?"

"You drink straight vodka. I'd have to be pretty stupid."

The newspaperman ignored the remark. He gestured at the man in the suit. "We don't want to start a panic. This whole matter's been coordinated."

The man in the suit stared thoughtfully at Clancy. "Besides," the editor said, waving his hand about the bar, "panic'd be bad for business, wouldn't it?" He gave Clancy his heartiest laugh and followed the man in the suit out into the street.

"I wanna see Doc Lenzo," Joss Humphries repeated. He stood in the reception area of the Gallatin County Health Clinic, turning his Proust cap in his hands. For some reason, he found himself thinking of the rabid cat he'd shot at in front of Fairchild, how so many things had gone weird, recently. He cleared his throat and pointed out the clinic window toward his pickup.

The man sitting behind the reception desk glanced idly in the direction Joss was pointing. There was a pile of dead goats in the back of the truck.

"Looks like you need a vet," the man said.

Humphries glared at him. "We could work it where you was to need the vet."

The man shrugged. He picked up the phone and turned it around. "Here. Call him up." He scribbled a number on a pad and pushed it across at Joss. "He's in Denver, assisting with the analysis of a very serious outbreak of spotted fever. But I'm sure he'll be more than happy to take time out to speak with you about your sheep."

Joss studied the number uncertainly, then tossed the pad back down in front of the man. "They're goats," he said. He looked about the empty clinic building. "Where's Dora, anyway?"

"Sick," the man said, bored.

"How about if I made a local call?" Joss grumbled.

The man nodded. Joss thumbed through the directory,

found the Park Service number, and dialed. There was a long series of clacks and squeaks that sounded like line trouble. Finally a distant female voice answered.

"I'd like to speak to Jack Fairchild," he said.

"Just a moment," the voice said. There was a pause. Joss glowered at the man behind the desk, who was holding his hand up to the the light, inspecting his cuticles.

"I'm sorry," the distant voice said. "He's assisting a search party in the park. I'd be glad to take a message."

"Thanks," Joss growled, and slammed down the phone. "A hell of a lot of assisting going on around here."

The man leaned back in his chair, his heels up on a rung, his knees bent, his legs spread wide like wings. He lifted a hand to his mouth and nipped at a hangnail. He spit the bit of skin over his shoulder and turned back to Joss. "Are you through with the phone?"

"Yeah, sure," Joss said. He tossed it abruptly at the man, whose eyes grew wide as he tried frantically to untangle his heels from the chair rungs. He was still trying to clamp his legs together when the phone slammed into his crotch.

He went over backward, moaning. Joss didn't waste time checking on him. He was making plenty of noise. Besides, Joss could hear the operator asking if *she* could help.

He went outside and glanced up at the waning sun. There was a vet down near Jackson Hole he trusted, but it was getting late. He put his hand on the bed of his truck and shook his head sorrowfully. He had the feeling there was no one around he could count on. And he would dearly love to find someone who could explain to him about his goats.

"Not very pretty, is it?"

Larraine sat on a lichen-streaked boulder with her hiking boots undone, one of her feet propped on her lap. Fairchild stepped off the ancient deer trail they'd been following and pulled himself up to join her. She twisted her leg a bit so that he could see the broken blister on her heel.

"I like your toes," he said.

She shook her head. "I tell customers these boots are blister-proof, too." She grimaced and pulled her sock back on.

He sat down on the rock beside her. "You see Ripley?"

She shook her head. "Not for a while."

He knew he should feel concern, but it was hard to muster the energy. He felt bone-tired, incapable of considering another serious thought.

He stared down at his own boots, a pair of Vasques he'd had for years, soled and resoled. "I bought these at your place," he said, pointing. "And I went right over to the Little Murky, laced them up, and walked through the water all the way to the campground."

She smiled at him. "And you never had a blister since, have you?"

217

He was drifting off, thinking. "It was your old man told me to do it."

She laughed. "I didn't know anybody ever took him up on it."

"It worked." He heard the huffiness in his own voice.

"Well, I'm glad," she said. They sat in silence for a bit. Finally, she turned to him. "What do you think?" she said.

"About what?" He knew what she wanted.

"You think Ripley is right? We don't have a chance?"

He took a deep, sighing breath. "The first year I was with the service, I was just a summer intern, we spent ten weeks looking for an airplane, some rock star and his family went down in a private jet." He turned to her. "We haven't found it yet."

She nodded. "I keep thinking about that Cooper guy who hijacked the plane and bailed out. They never found him either."

"Umm-hmm," he said, checking the angle of the sun. It seemed about half an hour yet above the peaks to the west. "He might be dead, too."

"You're a hopeful sort," she said.

He shrugged. "There's a good side to it. He might have wandered around for a long time, hurt and trying to be found. And still everybody missed him."

She studied him for a moment. "That's supposed to make me feel better, I guess."

He nodded. "It's big country, that's all. That helicopter flew right over us and didn't see a thing. And it isn't like these people can make a circus out of looking for us." He doubted she really believed him, but she seemed happy for the tone of his voice.

"Every year there's two or three hunters or fishermen who disappear and we never find a trace," he added. He

218

found a blade of grass by his feet, snapped it off, and sucked on it a moment before he continued.

"Sometimes I think they walk away on purpose. Something's wrong back home and so they arrange a little trip into the mountains and fix it to get lost, then they walk out to the highway, stick out their thumb, and start life all over again."

She smiled, and it seemed genuine. "A new life, just like that."

"Yep." He nodded. "I thought about it, a time or two."

"Really?" she said. "What was so bad about your old life?"

"Nothing you don't already know about," he said. He'd actually wanted to do it just to spite Lena, just for the look it would have put on her face, but that didn't seem like something noble enough to tell.

"Oh, Jack," she said, and the sudden sorrow in her voice surprised him. He turned and put his arm around her shoulders. He brushed her hair with his lips and held her tight.

"Ever been up to Glacier Park?" he asked. He felt her quiet sobbing against his chest. She shook her head. "It's real pretty," he said. "We'll go up there sometime."

He felt her nod agreement. "We'll do it," he continued. He believed it, too. He began to think about it, him and Larraine, two people in a normal world holding hands at Tom Clancy's, or fishing a high-country lake at sunset, not even having to talk things felt so good. He looked down at her, amazed at the warmth that had spread through him. He'd forgotten you could feel like this about someone. He smiled. Her sobbing had softened. He kept a hopeful eye on the sinking sun.

RIPLEY STOOD BY the trunk of a huge pine, his hands on his hips, listening hard. There was nothing but the steady hum of a silent forest, cut occasionally by the buzz of a fly that had been trailing him for the last fifteen minutes. He waved his hands aimlessly around his head.

"Beat it," he growled, and realized he was losing his balance again. He staggered into the tree, his cheek dragging against the rough, sweet-scented bark, and clutched the trunk, holding himself upright until his legs seemed steady.

It was the heat, he assured himself. He eased away from the tree. There was a bright splash of blood on the trunk where his cheek had struck it, as if it had been marked for chopping. He brought his hand to his cheek and felt a ragged edge of skin, an oozing wetness. He hastily took his hand away and pressed the sleeve of his shirt against the wound.

He scanned the forest below him again, fighting a surge of panic. He'd come up against a steep shelf of rock that shut off upward movement. He'd have to make a long swing to his left or right to get around the barrier, but he'd gotten ahead of the others and now he wasn't sure which way to go.

He could just sit down and wait for them to catch up with him, of course, but he'd already been standing around for what seemed like forever. What if he'd gotten way off course somehow? What if they'd already passed him by? They could be miles away before they missed him. The thoughts made him dizzy, made his bowels ache, made him want to urinate.

He unzipped his fly and let go a stream into the dusty pine needles at his feet. He thought he was finished, when he felt a fresh surge and let go again. Abruptly, he felt his knees give way. He was pissing a bright red stream of blood, splashing the needles as if he were emptying a bladder of paint.

He lurched back against the big pine and vomited. He didn't dare to check that for blood. He wiped his mouth, zipped up his fly, and staggered into the forest, following the foot of the rocky shelf to the west.

Before long he found himself edging along a narrow trail. He looked down at the tops of pines that minutes ago had hidden him from view. Directly across from him was a rising upslope of mountains blanketed with more pines. He stared across the narrow valley, his head hammering.

He fought to calm himself. Slowly he brought his breathing under control. He had read about that technique in *Argosy* a long time ago. A story about a guy and his buddies who got lost on a fishing trip up in the Maine woods. The other guys panicked. The guy who had lived to write the piece hadn't, although he carefully explained how he had to fight the urge to blow all his energy into a headlong rush out of those endless woods. Which would have turned into a crazy, endless circle. Like it had with all the other guys, who died.

Ripley turned his face against the shelf of rock at his back and pressed his forehead against its cool darkness. He had taken the wrong direction. He just had to retrace his steps to the tree, then turn the other way, and he'd find the others. It was very simple.

But something was hurting him, stinging, stinging his brow, his forehead.

He jerked away from the rock, swatting at his head and eyes where something was crawling and biting. *Ants.* They were swarming on his hands as he brought them away from his face. Big, red ants with fiery stings, on his cheeks and eyelids and fingers. He brushed his hands frantically on his shirt, then smashed at his face, and clawed, staggering backward, and suddenly he was off the ledge, over backward, falling.

He slammed onto the talus slope on his back and shot downward as if he were gliding on ball bearings. His shoulder cracked against a jutting boulder and threw him sideways. He began to roll then, and even though he flung out his arms to stop himself, he only picked up speed.

He hit another shelf of rock and was launched out into space again. *It's all over at last,* he thought. But he tumbled over only once, and then thudded onto his side, abruptly motionless.

He blinked, staring out into space, afraid even to move his eyes. He had landed on a narrow ledge of a sheer cliff. Beneath him was a drop of at least five hundred feet to the ground. He sensed he was an inch away from falling again. He took a careful breath, grateful that no pain blossomed in his lungs. His ribs were all right, then.

As the clatter of rocks died away beneath him, he tried wriggling his fingers, then his toes. Finally, he lifted himself up carefully on one shoulder.

A rock skidded out from under his hand and flipped into space. It spun out of sight into the pine limbs that kissed the side of the cliff and landed with a crash far below. He felt sick and edged gingerly back from the lip of the rock.

He'd seen enough: there was no way down from where

he'd landed. He craned his neck and looked glumly up the sheer side of the cliff above him. He was trapped. It was like having the dry heaves—just when you figure the worst is over, there's another jerk on the string. He wanted to cry. He fell back against the cavity of rock behind him, closed his eyes, and bit his lip, instantly drawing blood.

He felt something stinging the soft flesh between his thumb and forefinger and looked down, incredulous, to see an ant still clamped on there, wriggling, struggling to work its pincers deeper. He stared at the thing a moment, letting the pain work his despair into fury. Finally, he bent and caught the creature between his teeth and ground it to shreds. He was only sorry that ants couldn't scream. He swallowed the fragments, which tasted like peanut skins salted with his own blood, and he felt better.

There was a cool breeze blowing at his back, which soothed him. And he could be dead instead of just trapped—where he could die slowly. God had a great sense of humor. He bit idly at a fingernail he'd torn in his fall and felt it lift away entirely like a scab. He looked at his hands. All his nails were black, as if he'd beaten them with a hammer.

Then it struck him. A *breeze?* He turned gingerly, dislodging more gravel out into space. And found himself peering into a sizable black crevice that gushed cool air and the scent of damp earth against his burning cheeks. A *cave?* he thought. A *way out?*

He ventured a hand into the darkness. The breeze was steady, flowing from somewhere, another entrance. He rolled onto his side and began to laugh. Just when you think you're finished, you get another shot. He pulled himself up on his hands and knees and edged carefully into the mouth of the cave.

He'd moved a dozen feet or so when he felt his knee

223

crack against something dry and brittle. Sticks? He fumbled in his pockets, found matches, and struck one, carefully shielding the flame from the draft.

Sticks, all right. Sticks and brush. Piled up and hollowed out in the middle as if something slept there. A little bolt of fear ran through him. What kind of something?

He glanced back toward the entrance to the cave where the light shone, where someone might find him and lift him from the ledge. Maybe that would be better.

But he was just being silly, he told himself. Wild animals were more afraid of humans than the other way round. He'd read that in *Argosy* too.

His match was burning his fingers now and he dropped it, shaking his fingers against the pain. He was panting with fear now, he realized, his breathing so harsh he could hear it echoing off the walls all about him. He fought to control the fear, clamped his mouth shut, held his breath. But could still hear the harsh, ragged panting. Impossible, but still it was there, filling the tiny chamber of the cave with its ragged rhythms.

Ripley let out his own breath in a burst and lit another match, slashing frantically at the cover until it caught. He had an instant of clear vision then, of the thing wobbling toward him, its breath rasping ever closer, its eyes as red as his own, its yellow teeth draped with skeins of saliva, a huge cat that crouched, sprung, its awful jaws opening wide, his scream echoing with the beast's, and then there was only darkness.

"No sign of him," Fairchild said, struggling down from a ledge in the fading light. "He could be anywhere."

The doctor stared about the gloom beneath the trees. "Whatever you think." He looked exhausted.

Fairchild hesitated, then took a breath. "All right, let's get back to camp." He hated the sound of his own voice. He scanned the forest one last time before he turned back uphill to lead the way.

It was another ten minutes until they reached the spot Isaac had chosen for them. Larraine lay motionless in the gloom, atop a mound of pine needles. She looked like something arranged for a sacrifice, but she rose up on her elbows when they arrived.

"No good?" she asked Fairchild. He shook his head.

She indicated the upslope of the mountain with a movement of her head. "Isaac went on ahead, just in case he slipped past everyone."

Fairchild nodded as he sank down beside her and took out his map. The sheen of the silk was barely visible in the shadows.

"Heart Mountain," he said, pointing. Larraine looked at him questioningly as he traced his finger along the map. "This looks like the shortest route to where we're going, but

225

if we tried to keep going up, we'd come out just east of the peak." He shook his head. "The north face is too steep. We'd never get down it without gear."

Dr. Lenzo joined them. He squatted and examined the map. "How about this?" He pointed to a dark green band on the map east of their position. The band curled about the foot of the mountain and seemed to lead directly to the center of the park.

Fairchild nodded. "Falls River Canyon."

"Couldn't we just follow that?" the doctor asked. "It'd keep us from having to cross open country."

Fairchild studied the map, but shook his head.

"Be hell even getting down there, now. We'd have to drop back two, maybe three thousand feet. Then, the canyon deadheads at the falls. It'd take us forever to climb that."

"How about the plateau on the other side?" Larraine broke in. "Maybe we ought to cross the canyon and go north from there. It's forest all the way."

"That'd be all right," he told her. "Except I don't know of a way to get up the far side of the canyon. Like I said, it'd be hard enough getting down from this side."

"Well then," the doctor said. "Sounds like we're headed the only way we could be."

Fairchild glanced up at him. "That's about the size of it."

"Then anybody else with good sense knows it too."

Fairchild shrugged. "Only if they're sure we're headed north. And it's still a lot of ground to cover. We could be crossing the divide anyplace along fifteen miles of rough country."

"So we rest and make our crossing just before daylight?" It was Larraine.

"Unless somebody's got a better idea," Fairchild said. He waited, but they were silent.

They heard soft footfalls in the forest above them and turned as Isaac approached. He had removed his dark Forest Service shirt and his bare skin flashed as he moved through the shadowy trees. He shook his head curtly before anyone could speak.

"No trace of him. But I found these," he said, nodding at the bundle he'd made of his shirt. He knelt down and untied the cloth, exposing a cache of dark berries. "Go on," he said. "They're safe. Indians been eating them for centuries."

Fairchild gave him a look, then took one and bit into it. It was sour, and mostly seed, but the taste cut the dustiness in his throat. He gnawed the rest of the fruit from the seed and took a handful of the berries. The others joined him.

Isaac nodded as he ate. "You can tell when something you've been tracking gets into these," he said. "Turns their shit black."

Larraine paused in the middle of a bite, then shook her head and went on eating.

When they had finished the berries, they shared a can of tinned meat and passed around the last of the canteens. "We better hit water pretty soon," the doctor said.

"There's plenty on the north slope," Fairchild said. "We can be there before the sun's full up." He turned to Isaac, who was on his back, staring into the night sky. "You know a way up the other side of the canyon over there?"

"Falls River?" Isaac considered it, but finally shook his head. "We used to run deer up there, to box 'em in."

Fairchild nodded. It was nothing to think about, then. They'd just have to take their chances up ahead.

"I'll keep watch for a while," he said. "Maybe Ripley'll turn up yet."

"Maybe," Isaac said. "Wake me when you want a rest." The Indian closed his eyes. He seemed to be asleep at once.

Fairchild turned to Larraine, but she was out too, her mouth slack, a little dark stain of berry at the corner of her mouth. He suppressed a chill. For a moment she looked to him like someone who had gone to sleep on a funeral pyre.

THE SENTRY STOPPED SUDDENLY, his gray eyes narrowed. He moved his hand slowly inside the Park Service vest he wore because of the growing chill. It might have been hot down below, but he was at ten thousand feet, and the sun had dropped behind the mountains.

He'd heard something, or more properly *sensed* something, moving nearby. His hand folded over the grip of the pistol he carried in the sling holster, and he waited. His eyes swept over the canopy of forest that spread dramatically below. He'd taken his position on a brush-covered ledge that jutted from the mountainside. He knew this was only one of a million ways they could come, but there was always someone who would win a lottery.

He scanned the forest carefully, sure that he was concealed by the scrub and his dusky clothing. But he saw nothing. And there was no further sound.

Still, there had been *some*thing. He had felt it. And he had lived long in this business by heeding those nudges.

He turned and craned his neck to inspect the sheer rock wall at his back. Nothing. And no place for anyone to hide. He turned back to the silent forest below.

Maybe it *was* nerves. He'd prefer to be collecting on bad drug debts in Little Haiti. It was too empty out here in God's country. Like the six months he'd spent policing an oil-drilling outpost in Saudi Arabia. Listen to the wind blow till your brain went all white and as hollow as the sound of whistling sand.

He waited until the light was nearly gone before he moved. It was getting colder by the minute. He was going to freeze his *cajones* off tonight.

Another stream of cold air washed over him and he shivered. Then stopped. He was rigid. He'd sensed it again. And now he knew what it was.

He moved back a step and felt the cool stream of air at his neck. Moved forward again and was out of the airstream. Back one step and it was there again.

He did not turn to search the rocks at his back, but began to move casually down the narrow trail again, as if he intended to leave. When he reached a switchback, he ducked quickly behind a screen of brush and scanned the rocks above, where he'd felt the wash of cool air. Though the light was dying, it didn't take him long to find the cleft in the rock just above the trail where he'd been.

A cave, he thought. The source of the draft. And the source of the feeling that had come upon him: *someone was in there watching.*

He scanned the cliff for possible lateral approaches to the cave. Nothing on the far side, for just beyond the spot where he'd been keeping watch, the rock fell away sharply. You'd need climbing gear for that.

But here, just above where he stood, was a series of fissures that crazed the dark face of the cliff. He'd have to climb a bit above the level of the cave and work his way back down to its ledge, but he could make it.

He edged back around an outcropping of rock, reached up above his head, and found a grip. He dug in his toes and began to climb. It was as easy as ringing a bell. He was up twenty feet and even with the maw of the cave before he found himself having to search for handholds.

In seconds he was standing steady on a ledge. Unless he'd lost his bearings in the bad light, what he was on would take him around one last jut of rock onto the shelf where he'd spotted the cave.

He moved forward, to his last cover, and waited a moment, listening. There was nothing. He slipped his hand inside his vest and withdrew the pistol. It came out with a soft *zith* on the nylon lining, a sound that he felt more than heard. He took a steady breath, braced himself, and moved in front of the mouth of the cave.

He felt foolish there, his legs spread wide, the pistol raised in classic firing position, with nothing but a flapping bush to shoot at. In this light, the thing *looked* like a bushy buffalo's head, though. It hung out incongruously from the cliffside just above the cave entrance, the only living thing tenacious enough to keep a place on the sheer slope. Maybe he'd caught a glimpse of it from down below, or maybe he'd heard it scrape against the rock in a momentary breeze.

He turned and looked out over the forest behind him. He felt the heavy rifle at his back. If anyone came that way, they'd be dead meat. He smiled and sat down, trying to make himself comfortable on the rocks, staring out into the night. It seemed the perfect place to wait.

WHEN HE HEARD the footsteps, Fairchild thought for a moment it was Isaac. It was well after midnight, but he hadn't felt tired. He'd found a rocky platform that looked back down over miles of mountainside. The corpse of a lodgepole pine, stunted and finally strangled by the altitude, gave him cover.

The evening breeze down the slopes had long since stilled, and there had been nothing much to listen to save the occasional hoot of a canyon owl and the skitter of ground squirrels through the scree. The moon had risen and lay blood red on its back, a quarter full, its horns pointed up. Mars was a bright dot about an inch away.

Fairchild felt oddly peaceful sitting there, staring over the quiet forest. He didn't expect anyone to look for them after dark. There wasn't much percentage in that kind of a search. Only distraught parents or drunk college kids looking for a buddy would have you out wasting your time once the sun went down. Funny how all the frustration and heartache of the unsuccessful searches he'd been in on had been transformed into reassurance.

He stared down through the trees toward the footsteps, expecting to see the big Indian, but it was Larraine. She was fifty feet or so away, hidden occasionally by the dark trunks of pines. He saw her stop finally and stretch luxuriously in a shaft of moonlight. Then she dropped her hands to her sides and undid her pants.

He was vaguely ashamed but wouldn't take his eyes away. In a moment she rose. He caught only a glimpse of her flesh, the long length of her thighs vaguely silver in the moonlight, and then she was clothed again.

She was about to go back when she hesitated, as if she'd heard something. She turned and stared up the steep hillside, directly at his perch. He felt his face burn under her gaze. He hadn't moved, but he knew she saw him.

He heard her laughter drift up from the trees. He smiled, the reluctant voyeur, willing her to come his way. When he heard her footsteps approaching, he felt something give inside his heart.

"I couldn't sleep anymore," she said, sitting beside him. He sat with his knees drawn up, watching her. He couldn't think of a thing to say. She put her hand to his knee and pressed her cheek there.

"It's pretty," she said, staring out over the quiet forest. He felt the warmth of her cheek on his leg. He put his hand on her back.

"I had a cousin who was always trying to catch me in the bathroom," she said. "One time I was sitting there and saw a mirror come sliding under the crack in the door."

"Poor cousin," he said.

"Yeah. He's a cop in Boise now." Her hand traced down the inside of his thigh.

"I'd have let you know I was there, but I didn't have the heart."

"I can feel that," she said.

He thought he might come under her touch. He moved aside and took her in his arms. She rose up to meet his lips,

233

pushing him until he lay with his back against the rocky shelf.

He felt her hands at his belt and guided his own to the front of her jeans. Though his eyes were closed, he had a clear picture of her long white thighs, which seemed at once cool and burning under his touch.

They were kicking gravel over the side, trying to get loose of clothes, struggling to press skin on skin. He felt a sharp rock stab one of his buttocks but ignored it. He would have danced on knife points for this.

She finally got a foot kicked free of her boot and tangled pantleg and lowered herself upon him. "Dear God," she breathed, and bit into his shoulder.

He thrust deeply into her. It was as though he'd entered pleasant fire. His eyes were open now. He smelled the faint musk of her hair and the dust they'd kicked up and the tang of pine that was always in the air. Their rocking took him out of time. The moon grew huge and bright and seemed to fill up the sky. She rose up gasping as she came, her back arched, her face thrust open to the sky. He drove himself hard off the ground, lifting her, watching the moon shatter into fragments across the night.

Finally, he fell back and she dropped down with him, her cheek on his heaving chest. "Oh my," she said breathlessly. He thought for a moment she was crying, but then he looked down and realized she was laughing softly. It warmed him.

"I'm going to take that as a compliment," he said finally.

"Well, you should," she said. She sat up, still holding him inside her. She stared thoughtfully at him for a moment. "Is this what people do when other people are trying to hunt them down?"

He saw a shadow cross the moon behind her, an owl on the hunt, or maybe a crow heading home. "I don't know what they do," he said finally. "I never practiced for this."

She sighed and turned her face back to the stars. "Me either." After a moment she nestled down in his arms, her legs still tight astride him.

"What a pretty night," she said.

"Yes," he said, "it is," and kissed her. He thought about nothing but how it felt to be inside her, to have her cheek warm at his throat, her fingers tangled in his hair. They went to sleep that way.

It was Isaac who woke him, bending at his shoulder. "Time to move," he said. His face was expressionless.

Fairchild nodded. Larraine stirred and the Indian turned away as they rose and dressed in the cool darkness. Fairchild watched her brush sandy dirt from her knees and felt an ache rise in his throat. They deserved to be eighteen, caught bare-assed in the woods by somebody's dad. Not this. She glanced up at him, her expression uncertain.

"That was real nice," he said softly.

"We didn't use it up, either," she said.

"I'll hold you to that." Just let them get out of this, he prayed. Let them be all right. He had never wanted anything, anyone so badly.

"I'm counting on it." She said it firmly, and snapped up her pants.

Isaac cleared his throat behind them. "It'll be a good day," he said. "I have a feeling."

SKANZ FOUND HIMSELF in a tiny room, the light blinding, the walls smooth stainless steel and studded everywhere with numbered buttons. He held a baseball bat in his hands and could feel the grain of the smooth bleached handle under his fingers. There was a panic-stricken little man trying to get away from him, pounding desperately at one of the walls, which was split by the seam where two sliding doors met. The doors didn't budge.

Skanz strode forward, the man turned, his mouth gaping, and then the bat struck home. There was a crack, the sound of a ball striking the meat of the bat, and the light in the shining room went red. An unseen crowd roared its approval.

The blood-slick doors of the elevator slid open, and Skanz stepped through into a long narrow room full of cots where faceless creatures struggled against heavy straps that bound them in. Some had enormous, shaggy heads that flopped atop their shoulders like huge flowers too heavy for their stems. They gave out piteous, mewling cries, which pleased him and made the bat at his shoulder swell.

He stopped at the first bed and clucked his tongue. The creature there peered up at him finally, its eyes two specks of red in what had once been a face. Skanz grunted and swung

236

from the heels. He had never felt so strong. His blows produced a shocked rush of breath, an agony beyond the register of screams.

He moved methodically down the rows and when he finished every bed was silent, every snowy sheet was stained dark crimson, and he could rest at last. Except for some thought nagging at him, something he had forgotten, a detail overlooked, a moment of carelessness.

They all lay quiet now, yet something was wrong. Nothing moved. And then came the sound behind him. An inhuman gurgling. He did not want to turn. Sweat washed over him. Sounds of padding footsteps, their pace increasing to a run. He turned just as the thing rushed upon him, its foul maw yawning, each huge yellow fang as tall as a man. He screamed as the rank, rotted breath swept over him and the jaws snapped down.

He jerked awake, banging his head on the roof of the Land Rover. He sat quietly for a moment, staring out through the windshield into the darkness as the thudding of his pulse receded and his breathing calmed. He thought he heard the rustling of some animal scurrying away across distant talus, but he couldn't be sure.

He turned to the passenger seat, but his companion was gone. He glanced outside, but the moon was down, making it impossible to see.

"Hammer?" The radio below the dash crackled. "Come in, Hammer." It was his code, the voice calling for a report on his position. Skanz ignored the call. His position had become a private matter.

He opened the door and stepped out into the cool night. The sheen of sweat on his face evaporated instantly.

He had parked the vehicle at the terminus of a narrow jeep trail. He had come up from the center of the park with

237

another man, someone sent by their "sponsor," as Schreiber liked to say. They had driven upward toward the peak of Heart Mountain, until the land rose abruptly in a series of shelves too steep for vehicles. At first light they were to move on by foot.

He had studied the maps well. There were other routes his prey might have taken, but he had discounted them and ordered others to cover those routes. *This* was the way they would come. He felt it in his blood. And he would be there to greet them. Himself. It had been a mistake to bring a companion. He would not be needed. He could only get in the way.

There was already a faint coloring of light in the east. It would not be long. He heard a shuffling noise from the path that led into the woods and turned as the man he'd brought emerged from the cover of the trees, a pistol drawn. Skanz waved it aside, and the man holstered the weapon.

"What the hell was all that hollering?" the man asked.

Skanz stared at him.

"I could hear you all the way up to the ridge." The man regarded Skanz with some concern. "You okay?"

Skanz stared at him. "You heard nothing."

The man met his gaze for a moment, then turned away. "Whatever you say."

Skanz studied him. He knew what the man was thinking—he'd mention the incident in his report. It was required. Beyond that, it was a matter of self-preservation. No one wanted to find himself in a difficult situation with a partner whose nerves could be questioned.

The man lit a cigarette and Skanz tapped his shoulder, signaling for one. The man handed him the pack and Skanz lit up. It was mild, like everything else packaged for consumption in this country full of mild, inoffensive creatures.

The man glanced at the steadily brightening sky and gestured toward the path. "It's a good spot up there, just a mile or so. The ground falls away and you can see all along the main ridge all the way east to the river canyon."

"Good," Skanz said, exhaling smoke.

"We ought to just set up there and wait to see if they come across that way," the man said. "We go tramping around, we might walk right past 'em. I don't see there's much point going any further."

"Yes," Skanz said. "There is no point." He remembered their hands on him. Felt himself spat upon, tied, humiliated.

The man looked at him strangely. Finally, he went around to the back of the Rover and came back with the rifles. He handed Skanz one of the elaborately scoped weapons. "You ready to go on up?"

"I am ready, yes," Skanz said, and allowed him to lead the way.

The sky had begun to glow behind the distant line of mountains when they broke out of the trees. The man was right. Their climb ended in a breathtaking drop to the east, which allowed an unobstructed view of the forest that stretched for miles below, all the way to the river canyon. To the southeast the land rose up from beneath the pines, forming a series of sparsely covered ridges cut by jagged outcroppings of rock.

If the fugitives came out anywhere along those ten miles of ragged landscape, one of Skanz's security people would spot them. There were other men out there, watching. And if their quarry came within half a mile of this post, he could drop them one by one with the sophisticated sniper's weapon in his hands. But that was not the intimate meeting he had in mind.

Skanz lifted the rifle by its stock and brought the barrel down savagely across a boulder. The heavy scope flew off into the underbrush. He smashed it down again, shearing metal from wood.

"What the fuck!" his companion said, bursting from the underbrush. When he saw the shattered rifle in Skanz's grip, he clawed for his sidearm. "What's the matter with you?"

Skanz spun and caught the man just above the breast-bone with the heavy slab of the stock. The man staggered backward, his hands clutching at his smashed throat; he was already strangling in his own blood. He toppled back into a clump of bushes, his mouth moving in silent, hopeless gasps for air.

Skanz turned away and lifted his face to the breeze that wafted down from the sparsely covered mountains, his hands flexing like strong claws at his sides. *They* had done this to him. He breathed in deeply, as if he might catch the scent of their blood. They were out there somewhere, miles to the east, but he would find them. He would drive them out.

The radio in the vehicle below had come to life again, the inane request repeating itself over and over, echoing through the forest. The man at his feet was thrashing galvani-cally now. It was nearly over. Skanz reached down and lifted the small submachine gun that the man had slung over his shoulder, then unsnapped a heavy brush-cutting knife at his belt. These were weapons more appropriate for close-quarters work. He stepped carefully around the man and moved back down the path. He would go to fix the radio. He would fix everything. And then he would see about his prey.

Sunday, July 24

"WE GOT SUN," Isaac said matter-of-factly.

Fairchild glanced behind him at the eastern horizon. There was the barest hint of light behind the line of mountains, but that was enough: in minutes they'd be sitting ducks for anyone watching from the surrounding cliffs. He stared down the slope that stretched out ahead of them: one last quarter mile of open country before the forest would take them up again.

The doctor was seated, his knees drawn up, his head hanging. Larraine was flat on her back, her eyes closed, her chest heaving. Fairchild's own legs were quaking involuntarily and his head was splitting. They'd been struggling to the top of this ridge for the past two hours.

"We've got to move," Fairchild said. No one but Isaac met his gaze.

"I need a minute, Jack," Larraine gasped.

"We don't have a minute," he barked.

She opened her eyes and stared at him strangely. He turned to the others. "Let's go. It's downhill all the way."

He heard them struggling to their feet as he moved out to lead the way down the steeply sloping meadow, holding it to a trot, fighting the urge to panic. As he began to run, he

243

felt as if they'd all turned into little targets in some vast arcade game that had just had its power turned on.

His legs quickly turned to jelly, and he knew that with the slightest lifting of his will he could simply let go, run wildly with gravity until his muscles gave out and sent him crashing down the rocky slope. But the forest was looming closer with every step. Another minute, another hundred strides.

He felt someone hurtle past him then and turned to see the doctor staggering out of control. In the next instant, his foot caught a rock and he went down.

As the doctor crashed down the slope, Fairchild felt his own feet go out from under him. He launched out over a hidden foot-high ledge and followed the doctor tumbling out of control.

By the time they'd stopped rolling, they were in the shadow of the trees. Fairchild struggled to his feet and ran to check on the doctor, but Lenzo was already up and scuttling on toward cover.

In moments the others had joined them under the trees. Fairchild collapsed at the foot of a gnarled spruce. The doctor pulled himself up against a fir that rose from the smaller trees at the fringe of the forest. Fairchild stared after him, still marveling that neither one of them had been hurt.

"That's it. I'll never run again." Larraine sagged to the ground, her back against a boulder.

Isaac stood staring back the way they had come, gently shaking his head as if he couldn't believe they'd made it. The sun was now a clear line of fire at the horizon.

"Doc's lucky his neck's not broke," Isaac said.

"There are worse things."

Fairchild turned, struck by the tone in the doctor's

voice. Larraine followed his gaze. The doctor was facing them now. Fairchild felt his stomach turn over.

The doctor's face was a dark, swollen mass. His eyes had turned red, his pupils barely visible in the soft light beneath the trees.

"Jesus God," Larraine whispered.

The doctor nodded.

Isaac turned. "It's back," he said softly.

The doctor took a rasping breath. "I'd been hoping all along that what was in the truck was chemical in nature." He turned to Fairchild, steadying himself against a pine. "That would've explained why you and Larraine suffered such slight symptoms: something toxic enough to make you sick but that, if you didn't drink too much, you'd survive." He coughed then, a deep, gurgling cough that sounded as if all his organs were colliding inside him. "That would have been best," he added when he'd caught his breath.

Fairchild stood up and moved toward the doctor, who warned him off with a gesture.

"I wouldn't get too close," he said, backing toward the clearing. His voice was halting, intense. "I don't know. I can't be sure. But I think we're talking about something that is biological in nature. A disease, a virus." He hesitated, glancing at Larraine. "They may have injected me with it or I could have caught it from one of you at the outset, I can't be sure."

He swung his head back and forth in slow wonder. "In any case, I've relapsed. I could reinfect you." He backed another step away.

"What are you talking about?" It was Larraine, her voice cracking.

"Tell us what you know, Doc." Isaac stretched his hand out, but the doctor shook his head.

"If it were chemical . . ." He drifted a moment, then came back. "*This* wouldn't have happened." He jerked his hands up to show them his nails, each one swollen black.

He paused, as though forcing himself to think. "It must be some form of biological agent. There are a lot of things it could be, but the important thing is"—he broke off to gesture at his ruined face—"look what it can do."

Larraine shook her head. "But how about us? Jack and me. We're okay. We're better. Aren't we?"

The doctor shrugged. "I thought *I* was getting better." He coughed, another horrible, wracking cough. Fairchild thought of sand and gravel being stirred in a bucket full of Jell-O. "There are some exotic diseases, they do strange things." He raised his hand to touch his swollen cheek absently.

"So you think it'll happen to us, too?" Larraine asked, her voice barely above a whisper.

"Possibly," the doctor wheezed.

"Bullshit," Fairchild said. "Don't even think like that."

"Then how else do you explain it?" she said.

The doctor stifled a cough. After a moment, he seemed to gather strength. "It depends. Maybe the two of you got a light dose of this thing. If so, it's possible your immune systems had time to respond before things got out of control." He shrugged. "Or you could have built up antibodies in the everyday course of life." He raised his blackened palms. "Different people respond to disease in different ways."

"But what you really think is that we're going to swell up like ticks all of a sudden and burst, is that right?" Fairchild had the feeling that the doctor had become their enemy. It wasn't possible, what he was suggesting. He wouldn't let himself think it. It was loser talk. It would undermine his strength.

"You're screwed up, Doc. That stuff's in your brain."

"Jack!" Larraine cautioned him.

"It's all right," the doctor said. "You're not going to hurt my feelings." He turned to Fairchild. "It's impossible to tell what's going on inside you without lab tests. Meantime, we can't go into the center of the park, not until we know."

"Know what?" Fairchild said. He felt an unreasoning anger building inside him.

"You could be contagious. There's a hundred thousand people jammed together in there." He waved his arm weakly toward the north. "You could start a plague."

Fairchild shook his head. "I know you're upset, Doc, but the only thing to do is to get out and find help. You know people. You can take us somewhere to get checked out."

The doctor shook his head insistently. "If this *is* a weapon, it could have been bred to lay dormant for a period after the initial symptoms have subsided." Even in their awful state, his eyes were pleading. "You could have a host up and about, hosts like us, mingling with a population, spreading the thing like wildfire."

"*Doc,*" Fairchild said. "We can't just turn ourselves in. We're going to get out of here. Then we'll worry about who's a Typhoid Mary."

"I'm just saying we'll have to be careful," the doctor said, taking an uncertain step toward the clearing. As he moved, he passed into a shaft of sunlight. He looked up, surprised by its brightness, then turned back to them. He opened his mouth to say something else, when suddenly there was an explosion from far above, and the face that had been Dr. Lenzo's disappeared in a spray of red.

THE SENTRY SAW the wisp of smoke leap from the back of the man's head and watched with satisfaction as his body bucked and tumbled to the ground. He jacked another round into his rifle and scanned the area inside the forest with his scope. He could make out someone's leg jutting from behind a boulder. The woman, he thought. He considered putting a round into her thigh, then getting her as she flew up, but it was a tricky shot. He'd wait for someone to make a break.

He saw a glint of her hair near the top of the boulder and brought his finger to the trigger.

"That's it, sweetheart," he whispered. "Come to poppa." She was edging up, trying to get a look. Another two or three inches, he was thinking. And then he heard the sounds behind him.

A soft scuffling noise. Feet padding across rock. A terrible smell, ranker and more rotten than any he'd ever known. He was trying to comprehend, was rolling over, clawing wildly for his sidearm, wondering who on earth could have outflanked him all the way up the side of a cliff, when he caught sight of it.

"Jesus Christ, fuck, shit," he said raising his pistol.

"The thing hurtled through the air as he tried to swing his weapon into line. It was a huge cat, its eyes encrusted, leaking pus, long skeins of saliva at its jaws. The horrible odor enveloped him. He felt the foul breath hot at his throat and an instantaneous wetness there.

He squeezed the trigger finally, and an aimless round coughed upward. In an instant, he fell over backward with the weight of the thing.

There was a terrible grinding of teeth in the flesh at his throat, and a momentary jerking before the tendons snapped and he was dead.

It took them an hour or more to find the man who'd killed Lenzo, much of it spent finding a way up to the narrow ledge where the cave entrance was tucked.

Isaac had joined Fairchild on the cliff face while Larraine waited on the shelf below. Fairchild turned the body over with the toe of his boot and grimaced. He wished he could feel some satisfaction in the way the man had been mauled, but instead he turned away, fighting the urge to vomit.

"Mountain lion," Isaac said quietly as he scavenged through the man's pack. "He'd have to be sick to come out here to attack, but it's the only thing that could do something like this." He produced a few rations, a knife, and a long coil of nylon rope.

Fairchild turned and studied the entrance to the cave. Bloody tracks smeared the sand-strewn rocks there. He remembered Joss Humphries raising his rifle to shoot at that creature wobbling under the cover of the forest, remembered pushing Joss's arm aside. It had happened some distance from here, but it was possible. If that were so, and Fairchild had saved the thing's life, he'd done well. "If there's any justice," he mumbled.

"What's that?" Isaac asked.

"I said this sonofabitch got what he deserved." Fairchild let the ruined face roll back against the rocks.

He studied the vast canopy of forest to the north. "Figure he came that way?" he said to Isaac.

Isaac nodded glumly. "Only way *to* come."

"There'll be plenty more after him."

"Yeah," Isaac said, following his gaze. In the far distance, a geyser sent a plume of steam high into the air. He nudged Fairchild with his elbow. "You remember that time those bikers came back, was gonna kick our ass?"

Fairchild nodded. He remembered all right. A score or more that time—the three he and Isaac had put in the hospital plus over a dozen of their buddies. They'd caught Fairchild and Isaac in the parking lot outside the Buckaroo, at closing time. They'd carried bats. Chains. A knife or two.

"Remember what we did?"

Fairchild was blank for a moment. All he could recall was the initial paralytic, pants-pissing terror. He shook his head. "No, Isaac, what'd we do?"

Isaac laughed. "We ran like hell," he said, and pointed them back the way they'd come.

"I DON'T WANT anybody blaming *me* for this," the driver said. He glanced at Reisman, then quickly back at the road. The Wagoneer thundered over an eroded section of jeep trail and Reisman had to brace himself to keep his skull from pounding the headliner.

"Nobody said anything about you coming up here," the driver continued.

"I'm security director of this company," Reisman said, as the road smoothed and the rattling of the chassis dropped off.

"Right now, maybe."

Reisman glanced at him, then looked back at the trail. He checked his watch. They'd been traveling for over an hour, ever since he'd shown up at the field hospital and commandeered this vehicle. Schreiber was long gone, back to Denver. Skanz was directing the "rescue" team, but he wasn't responding to radio calls.

He glanced at the driver. "You sure this is the right road?"

The driver shrugged. "I don't drive it a lot."

Reisman studied him for a moment, then abruptly reached out and yanked the wheel savagely. The Wagoneer's rear end broke loose from the gravel, and the vehicle began to broadside down the trail. A lodgepole pine was hurtling toward the driver's door. Reisman let go of the wheel and the driver wrestled madly to straighten them out of the slide. They came to a stop about a foot from the looming pine. A great cloud of dust washed through the open windows.

The driver stared at Reisman, his face white. Then he saw the pistol that was pointed at his navel.

"What's your name?" Reisman asked.

A smile began to form on the driver's face. "You must be crazy."

Reisman pulled the trigger. The vent window exploded into fragments at the driver's shoulder.

"Jesus Christ!" the man wailed, brushing glass from the front of his shirt.

"No," Reisman said. "You don't look a thing like him."

"Frazoni," the driver said. "Earl Frazoni."

"Good," Reisman said. "Now, Earl, I'm going to assume that we agree on who's in charge."

Frazoni nodded, his eyes on the pistol. He had regained some of his surliness.

"I want to find Skanz, is that clear?"

"It's clear, but I don't know what you think you're doing."

"It's simple enough, Earl. This is a security operation, isn't it? Therefore, I'm in charge of it."

Frazoni shook his head. "It's not the same thing."

"Explain that to me, Earl."

"We're a contract team, right? We come in, do a job, we clear out." He nodded at the pistol. "It'd be better for you if you just went on home now."

Reisman thought about that for a moment. "I don't doubt it," he said, and made a gesture with the gun. "Now, let's find Mr. Skanz."

Frazoni rolled his eyes and turned back to the wheel. He threw the truck in reverse and spun them around the way they had come. They backtracked for about ten minutes to a place where a narrow jeep trail cut straight up the mountainside through choking brush.

Frazoni gave him another look but Reisman waved the gun at him. The driver shook his head and gunned the Wagoneer forward. Even in four-wheel drive it took them twenty minutes to cover the mile or so of trail, wallowing through impossible ruts, boring through scrub that tore at the sides of the vehicle.

Reisman caught the acrid smell even before Skanz's vehicle came into view. He looked over at the driver and knew he'd also recognized the scent of burning rubber. Still, it was a shock when they rounded a curve where the trail flattened and petered out at the foot of a cliff.

The Rover was still smoldering. All the windows had blown, and the interior was gutted. Only one tire still carried air and that gave the skeleton of the vehicle the look of a drunk about to keel over.

Frazoni brought the Wagoneer to an abrupt halt. "Well kiss my ass," he said. He turned, but Reisman was already outside.

There was a steady breeze moving up the mountainside, and high atop the ridge above them Reisman could see thin white smoke rising into the early-morning sky. He pointed up as Frazoni joined him near the burned-out car.

"There's fire up there," Reisman said, pointing at a series of charred clumps of brush studding the cliffside nearby. "It jumped right up the rocks."

There was an explosion then as the last tire on the Rover blew. Frazoni backed away. "We ought to move out. The gas tank could go."

Reisman didn't move. "What do you think got the fire going in the first place?" He waved his pistol at the open fuel port. A length of charred rag still dangled there, twisting in the breeze.

Frazoni stared. "Shit." His hand moved automatically to his sidearm. "You figure the assholes made it this far already?" He scanned the nearby forest uncertainly.

Reisman raised the pistol so that it pointed just below Frazoni's throat. The man took his hand away from his holster. Reisman nodded. "Is that what you'd do if people were looking for you? Burn up a jeep so everybody'd know where to look?"

Frazoni slowly digested it. "So who the fuck did it?"

Reisman looked up at the thickening plume of smoke. The forest around them seemed tinder dry. It would surely be a bad one. He turned abruptly back to the driver.

"You know how long it's been since Skanz had a psychological?"

"It hasn't been on my mind," Frazoni said.

"I had one of the computer operators call up some files for me last night," Reisman continued. "He butchered a target in New York. And a hooker in the West Indies, it looks like. Took them apart. He's looney tunes. Out of control."

"So what?"

"His jeep," Reisman said, pointing at the charred rag sticking in the gas tank. "*He* burnt it. He's defoliating."

Frazoni stared up at the ridge, where smoke now boiled in black, angry knots.

"The hell with the wilderness," Reisman said. "He's burning off their cover, trying to smoke those poor bastards out, and when he finds them—" He broke off, shaking his head. "Of course, none of this particularly bothers you, does it, Earl?"

255

Frazoni looked at him, his surly frown back in place. "It's not what I get paid for."

Reisman nodded, staring off in the forest. He wasn't sure any longer what he'd intended to accomplish by coming out here. Was he going to have a reasonable chat with this lunatic Skanz? Shoot him and take over the search himself? It didn't matter much now. Skanz was on the loose. He turned back to the driver and gestured with the pistol.

"Let's get back," he said wearily. "We need to report a fire."

THEY HAD REACHED the canyon's edge, an abrupt falling away of the forest that in other circumstances would have been breathtaking. Larraine rested, propped against a tree. Fairchild stared down into the chasm, wishing to God he were just a sightseer.

Two hundred feet below was the river that had cut the canyon bit by bit over the past million years. Despite the lack of rain, it was running almost full, carrying the last of the runoff from the highest peaks in the north. You'd expect a river to look blue at such a distance, but this one was almost all white water, the riverbed dropping fifty feet a mile.

Across the chasm lay the Buxton Plateau. There were a dozen or more fire trails that led down through that wilderness toward safety. If they could only get up the other side.

He saw Larraine steal a glance at his watch. Isaac had gone north, looking for a better route to the bottom. He had promised twenty minutes but he was already late.

Larraine gave him a questioning look. Fairchild put a comforting hand at her shoulder. "He'll be back, Larraine." She nodded, but wouldn't look at him.

The muted roar of the water drifted up the cliffside to where they waited, and Fairchild felt almost hypnotized. He remembered walking the halls of a museum, thirteen years

257

old, separated from his classmates who were doing their best to find an unsupervised exit and duck out of their field trip; but he was entranced, wandering from room to room, gaping at huge landscapes that the little notices on the walls identified as part of a "Hudson River school."

He had always pictured the Hudson River as a polluted estuary that surrounded the Statue of Liberty. Now he found himself lost in one great sweep of chasm, storm, and mountaintop after another.

After that afternoon in the Cleveland Museum, he'd never wanted more than to be part of what he'd been looking at. And he had found a way: he was taking care of the wilderness; he helped other people find that same mysterious charge he got just from living in the middle of it. The only problem was that someone was trying to kill him for doing that simple thing.

They heard the popping of helicopter blades in the distance then, and hurriedly withdrew into deeper cover until the sounds of the machine died away and the roar of the rushing water had returned.

They got up, brushing dust and needles away, and approached the canyon rim again. Larraine pointed across at the thick forest falling away to the south. "We'll get out that way." She said it with certainty. Fairchild nodded. It was important to think so.

He gazed down the sheer canyon wall. After the first fifty feet or so of rimrock, the cliff appeared to break up; from there it angled more gently to the bottom. And there was a ledge down there. He hefted the length of nylon rope they'd taken from the sniper.

He eyed the distance below, then tossed the rope over the side and watched it dole itself out in dizzying loops until it was nothing but a thin blue line that swung back against the cliffside, brushing away little puffs of sand and dust with each slap into the rocks. He leaned out as far as he dared.

"How short is it?"

He edged back from the cliff and smiled at her. "How did you know?"

She shrugged. "I wouldn't expect anything different."

He nodded. "Maybe five feet."

"We can handle it."

Fairchild stared at her. If force of will counted, they were home free. He tied the rope off on a pine and began drawing it back up the cliff.

"I had to steal a little bit. It'll be more like a ten-foot drop to the ledge."

"No problem," Larraine said.

He stared at her. This was a woman to love.

He turned then and began fashioning a sling at the end of the rope. When he was finished, he checked his watch again and glanced in the direction Isaac had taken. The drone of the helicopter was barely audible in the distance.

"I'll go first," he told her. He gestured at the tree where the rope was looped. "We'll leave this tied off for Isaac."

"Sure," she said. He thought that her voice had lost some of its authority.

He stepped into the sling and fed a loop of the tied-off rope into an eyelet he'd fashioned. He drew the loose rope through the eyelet, back through his crotch, and over his shoulder, leaving only enough slack to allow him to step to the edge. He held up his hands to demonstrate to Larraine. "You hold tight and just feed a little bit at a time," he said. "You can walk yourself right down the wall. It's going to hurt a little because we don't have everything we need, but you can do it."

"A piece of cake," she said, her voice steady.

He smiled and backed toward the edge. "Holler if I fall?"

She stared at him, deadpan. "What if you pull the tree out of the ground?"

He liked that, he thought. No. He loved that. He met her glance. "That'd be against park regulations."

She nodded. "Just checking."

There was a far-off rumble. Thunder, he thought, but the sky was as clear as it had been for the last two months. Maybe they were shelling the forest.

He leaned back, testing the pull of the rope. He was hanging in space now, and he cast his gaze from Larraine to the dizzying sky and pine tops above. *This* was the moment where Isaac was to appear and tell them he'd found a handy trail that cut the rimrock. Sure. Or maybe an escalator. And a Ramada Inn with a pool and a bridal suite down there ready for them.

He took a step backward and launched himself out into the thin dry air. He heard Larraine gasp as he disappeared over the edge. The sound coincided with the emptiness that sprung up in his own gut when his feet left contact with the earth.

There was only an instant of weightlessness, but it seemed to last forever. *The earth. That's where I get my strength,* he thought, his hands burning with the terrible pull of the slick cord. And then his boots banged back into the rock wall.

He let his knees flex to absorb the impact, but he was late. His soles bounced, hit again, slid sideways, and finally dragged him to a stop.

He eased his fingers inside the coils of rope, steadied himself, then focused his gaze firmly on the rock face a few feet away, trying to wipe out the picture of the jagged boulders rushing up from below. He twisted in the sling, easing the bite of the rope across his shoulders.

His gaze drifted to the ledge below and a wave of fear swept over him. He closed his eyes tightly. If he didn't begin to move that very instant, he was going to freeze up forever.

"Go," he told himself, and forced his legs to flex and propel him away from the rock face. There was another sickening plunge through space, but this time he was thinking how much closer to the ledge it would bring him. When his boots met the rock again he was ready and steadied himself quickly.

After the second push it became automatic, just like in training school, with a safety line and instructors there to talk you through every step. In another minute he found himself out of rope, his boot tips nearly touching the ledge below.

He could have untied the sling and slid cleanly to the bottom, but he didn't want to rely on talking Larraine through redoing it. He looped the cord around his hand and hoisted himself out of the makeshift harness, then dropped to the rocks.

Finally, he let himself look back up the cliff. She was leaning out there, staring down, her expression softening as he gave her the sign to hoist the rope.

She pulled back, out of sight, and the rope began to snake its way up the cliff. He turned to survey their next step, another drop of twenty feet or so to the next ledge, which he hadn't been able to see from atop the rim. He shook his head. This country kept fooling you.

He felt a dusting of sand and tiny rocks across his shoulders, and turned to steady the bundle that contained their remaining provisions. Larraine was lying flat at the rim, her head and shoulders visible, playing the rope out from her hands. He quickly undid the bundle and she pulled the sling back up.

He heard the distant rumble again and looked south along the canyon rim. Maybe there was a thunderstorm building up just over the peaks, but it was still impossible to be sure.

He turned upward then, and caught his breath as he saw Larraine poised, the rope looped over her shoulder as it should have been. If she would just move slowly, calmly, she would make it. She was carrying maybe half his weight. She could ease herself down without ever leaving the rock face.

As she took the first step over the side, he realized that his palms were sweating again. He was far more frightened for her than he had been for himself. He'd been scared, dangling up there, but this was different. He was helpless now.

Abruptly, she bent her knees, leaned into the cliff, and pushed. She soared out into space in a graceful arc, and when she came back to the cliff, her boots met the wall in a soft kiss. Fairchild stared up, dumbstruck.

She looked down at him, gave him a high sign, then launched herself back out, repeating the graceful movement again and again until she was dangling a few feet above his head.

She smiled down at him. "Not bad, huh?"

He shook his head. "Why didn't you tell me you knew what you were doing?"

"You didn't ask." She shrugged. "Besides, I haven't been climbing in—"

She broke off and swiveled her glance back up the cliff-side. "Hey!" she said, and then she fell.

She crashed into the rocks, screaming as her leg twisted awkwardly under her. Fairchild lunged and caught her by the shirt before she could go over the ledge.

He saw the frayed end of the sling she'd been holding slither over the edge of the ledge and vanish.

He turned back to Larraine, who was biting her lips, her face white. "Shit," she said, grimacing. "My ankle."

"The goddamned sling broke," he muttered.

She stared out over the edge, then glanced up at the spot where the other end of the line dangled, sawed in half against a jutting rock.

"Now what?" she said.

Fairchild shook his head helplessly, staring at the drop below. On either side, the ledge fell away to nothing. They were stranded. "Wait for Isaac, I guess." He fell back against the rock wall and sighed.

"Every time I think we're in deep shit, it gets a little closer to my chin," he said.

"We could be dead like those other people in the hospital," she said. He glanced at her. There were the tiniest shadows in the hollows of her eyes, but otherwise there were no traces of the disease, whatever it had been. She held his shoulder and tried her ankle gingerly.

"I don't think it's broken," she said. She sat down and loosened the laces of her boot. She peeled down her sock and shook her head at the angry swelling that had begun there.

He bent and probed at her ankle softly until he heard her sharp intake of breath. "Better lace it up while you still can," he said.

She nodded and took his hand. "We'll figure something out," she said.

"Right," he said dryly. "You're absolutely right. I just lost my head there for a minute."

He stood up, wanting to believe her. He knew it was the right way to think. He turned and kicked a rock out over the edge. He doubted it would ever hit bottom.

263

Isaac had found no better trail down the canyon. The further north he traveled, the deeper the sheer slope of the rimrock grew. But he hadn't really expected to find a way down. He had begun to catch the scent of smoke on an occasional gust of wind and he suspected that a fire had sprung up in the north. With the wind coming from that direction and the forest as dry as it was, there'd soon be another problem for them to deal with.

But he had more immediate concerns. He glanced down at his fingertips where the nails were beginning to show a bluish tinge. He brushed away the perspiration on his forehead and finished tying off the limber branch.

So the disease had come upon him, too. He'd felt its stirrings even as Dr. Lenzo tried to explain it to them earlier that day. He could remember wiping Ripley's blood from his hands after loading him in the truck and assumed that's where it had come from. But it didn't really matter *how*, did it?

He thought of the doctor again, almost envied him, at peace, his spirit moving wherever white people's spirits go. He wondered how long it would take to run its course with him, how long before he turned into a walking bag of blood like Ripley, like a tick gorged up on an old hound's throat.

264

He tested the point of the stake he'd lashed into a crook of the branch. It was sleek green wood, strong enough to pierce an animal's hide, pliant enough not to shatter if it struck bone. It would only deflect and drive deeper.

He carefully drew the branch back to the spot where he would set the trap, stepped aside, and let go. The deadly point rushed past him at stomach level, sweeping across the sweet spot of the narrow trail faster than his eye could follow. He nodded with satisfaction and set the trap in place.

That would have to be the last of it. He'd buried all the punji stakes along the rugged paths, used up all the choker vine setting the spring traps in the brush, and there was no time to ready more. He heard the dim hint of the men's voices more clearly now, drifting up the shallow draw below him.

Fairchild and Larraine would be worried about him, of course, but if they had any sense at all, they would have given up on him by now. He would take care of these men and help them on their way. He closed his eyes and fixed the vision of their escape in his mind, willing it to become a part of the fabric of this life. Then he turned, and went after the men.

SKANZ LEANED AGAINST the trunk of a huge pine, resting, listening to the careless thrashing of the two men through the nearby forest. They were his own men, and they had no idea he'd been following them. Their stupidity disgusted him. If their prey were anywhere within miles, those two would have long since warned them away.

He felt rage flush through him, his face glowing with heat, the power coursing through his shoulders and down his arms to his fingertips, which felt like spots of molten fire. He raised his hand and stared at it as if it were no longer a part of his body. This was a weapon that could crush, bore, pulverize any living thing. Its capacity to cause pain was unlimited.

Finally, the wave cooled, and he brought his hand down to curl about the handle of the heavy blade. He took a deep breath. He was going to discipline these men, and then he would find the ones they were looking for.

Their voices had faded again and he knew he should begin to move. But he felt strangely tired, as though the force of his hatred had drained him. The thought that he was somehow losing control flashed through him, but he denied it instantly. He had *always* ruled himself. He could will himself to ignore pain, he was impervious to emotion, he could squeeze sickness out of his body by merely focusing on it until it fled from him in fear. Weakness was for others. He thought of the day in the elevator, the look in the scientist's eyes, and smiled. It seemed such a long time ago.

He closed his eyes momentarily, gathering strength, then pushed himself away from the tree. He hadn't taken a dozen steps before he felt his foot catch something stretched taut across the trail. There was a soft rushing sound that came from a bush just ahead and he flung up his arm instinctively, to protect himself.

At first there was no pain, just a sudden impact against the flesh of his upraised arm. Then it became agony. He staggered back, confused, thinking for a moment he'd been struck by a snake. But the thing had burrowed into him, holding him fast, shooting fresh waves of pain as he tried to pull free.

He slashed out with the heavy blade and abruptly, with one fresh, fiery jolt, he was loose. Still, the pain remained and he finally saw it, the needle-sharp shaft of wood that had plunged through the flesh of his raised upper arm as if it were soft butter. The point emerged from his biceps and stopped an inch from his throat, still dripping with his own blood.

His mind was red flame. He lowered his arm and fell back against a tree, grappling with the pain, containing it, pushing it into a bright glowing ball that gathered at the spot where the stake had pierced him. Slowly, he envisioned it coursing out from him, into the air, until it was gone and there was only numbness.

A miserable, primitive jungle trap. He shook his head to clear the fog that still drifted at the corners of his consciousness. *Idiot,* he cursed himself. He was worse than the fools he'd been tracking.

Tendrils of smoke drifted through the forest near him, but he had forgotten its source, was even unaware of the danger that it posed. He bit down savagely on his lip, drawing his attention to *that* pain, slowly forcing his breath back to evenness. He felt the solid weight of the machete in his good hand and he hefted it, swinging it back and forth in a smooth pendulum stroke until the rhythm had calmed him.

His left arm still ached, but the pain was under control now. In fact, it only helped fuel the fire. He glanced down at the heavy knife. It felt so very pleasant there, glowing dully in the refracted light beneath the trees. The trap was actually a good sign, he thought, as he began to walk. He was coming closer to them with every step. The bloody point of the stick jutted out from his arm like a compass needle showing him the way.

THE TWO SCIENTISTS stood before a double plate-glass viewing port, intent on the sight before them. They were underground in a steel-reinforced bunker, part of a series of interconnected laboratories and associated facilities that honeycombed several acres beneath the Idaho desert like an enormous rabbit warren. It was a lonely place to work, but it was secure, and they could work without restriction and without distraction.

They wore their curling gray-black hair in similar disarray. Barbering was not high on their list of priorities. Both wore standard white laboratory coats, and the gold-rimmed glasses that had been popular on college campuses in the late sixties. They looked like the forty-five-year-old identical twins that they in fact were.

They had attended Yale undergraduate school, finishing a combined physics/biological sciences program in two years. They had graduated from the Harvard School of Medicine with distinction. They had gone on to postdoctoral fellowships in medical physics at Johns Hopkins and had become perhaps the most knowledgeable individuals in the Western world concerning the mechanics of disease transmission. Neither of the brothers had ever married.

They turned to one another before the viewing port, one

brother frowning, the other smiling. Ten feet away, on the other side of the glass, an ordinary white rat rocked back on his haunches and pawed at the air. The rat was one of thousands raised by Nordie Jensen, a farmer from the Cache Valley of Utah. Jensen sold the rats to a blind subsidiary of PetroDyne for an unknown purpose at a rate of profit that had turned out to be significantly greater than that of maintaining his father's dairy enterprise. Jensen couldn't have cared less about what happened to the rats. They were squealing, disgusting, four-legged pieces of coin to him, and he wouldn't have seen one thing worth writing home about concerning the rat that was the focus of the Drs. Brock.

"He's happy as a barn owl," the smiling Brock said.

His frowning brother nodded glumly. The cage where the rat sat was littered with the bodies of rodents apparently similar to the one who was now placidly preening himself. The only thing that distinguished them were the tiny clots of blood that marked their eyes, the bluish swelling that had taken over the normal pink of the nose, the footpads, the tail.

"He ought to be happy," the frowning brother said. "He's alive."

"Four days since we shot him up, and continuous exposure to the others as well," his brother said, shaking his head. He seemed proud of the rat.

"Wouldn't you think," the unhappy one mused, "that just once we could come up with something that was absolutely, positively, one hundred percent fatal?"

His brother shrugged. "Nobody's perfect." He nodded at the rat, who would raise his tiny pink paw to his mouth, lick it furiously, then swipe it about his face and body. "Want to take him apart, see what's inside?"

The unhappy one thought about it, finally nodding his head in agreement. "But we won't find anything. He was just

lucky, that's all. Same as people. *Most* would die, though."
And he reached to push a button that filled the chamber with
a colorless, odorless gas. He turned back to his brother,
shaking his head. "One of these days, we're going to get it
right."

His brother laughed and clapped him on the shoulder.
"Life's a bitch, isn't it?"

The unhappy one was not amused. He turned and began
to guide a pair of mechanical hands toward the cage, where
the rat now lay motionless on its side.

THE TERRAIN HAD turned rocky under Isaac's feet; the trees started to thin as he approached an area where a series of geysers brewed. He heard the frustration in the voices of the men, their complaint at the heat, now compounded by the warm, sulfurous drafts that rose up from the very earth at their feet.

In places, deep fissures cracked the dry earth, venting steam and choking gases that sent them tacking back and forth through the ever-worsening heat. The men were moving ever more carelessly, dragging their feet, snapping back low-hanging branches.

He stopped to finger the sap still oozing from a broken pine bough and stared at a low hummock no more than a hundred feet ahead. He listened carefully to the sound of their voices and knew that they had stopped. He nodded and began to move forward carefully.

He thought of his grandmother's stories of the calamities visited upon their people by the whites: the whiskey, the disease, and, worst of all, their disloyalty toward the earth that nurtured all things.

She'd had no use for white people and did her best to instill her disdain in him. But it had never fully taken hold. He had a few white friends, Fairchild the closest. The rest he

272

viewed as misguided spirits, most of them simply dumb, except for those willing to take advantage of their own kind.

He reached the crest of the low hill and hesitated. He could let these men go. They would not find Fairchild or Larraine. These men were of the foolish sort, simply led by the evil ones. He pondered it, and thought of the doctor's face exploding into jelly before his eyes. He looked down at his fingertips, swollen nearly black now, and moved on.

He crept to the top of the ridge and found the two sitting perhaps twenty feet below him, wearing the familiar green uniforms of park rangers but with a submachine gun slung incongruously across one man's back. He had tilted his cap back and was lighting a cigarette. The other man had removed the ball cap with its Park Service insignia and was scratching at the sweaty indentation in his thinning hair. He'd already pulled off his boots. They were thickly built, hard-eyed men. The one with the cigarette had wrists so thick they made his hands seem small.

They sat with their legs dangling over a precipice in front of them, a dozen feet or so above the bubbling mass of a large mud pot that burped and splatted, sending up great clouds of odorous steam. Most of the trees that overhung the area had withered and died long ago, their branches poking through the foggy air like skeletal creatures.

"This place is fucked," the one with the cigarette said.

"Beats the shit out of the jungle," his partner said. He'd removed one of his socks and was inspecting a callus on his big toe.

The smoker spat over the edge into the mud pot. When he looked up, his gaze locked suddenly on Isaac's.

"Fucking A," he said, tearing at his shoulder for the Uzi.

Isaac rose from his crouch and dove down the hill at them. He heard the chuffing sound of the automatic weapon and felt something burn his shoulder. He hit the ground, rolled, and came up in front of the man with the Uzi.

Isaac saw the weapon swivel down upon him and slashed at it with his palm as he came off the ground. The flimsy weapon flew high into the air and came down with a splash in the mud pot below. The man was still trying to spit his cigarette out of his mouth as he charged. Isaac swung and hit him full in the face, smashing lips and cigarette into a bloody-black paste.

As he went down, his partner clambered up from his knees, jerking a knife from his ankle holster. Isaac kicked him just under the point of the chin, lifting him cleanly off the ledge.

He caught a brief glimpse of the man's terrorized face before he went over the edge, his arms windmilling. He screamed as he hit the boiling, superheated mud, thrashed briefly, and went under. He came up once, covered with the lavalike mud, his mouth moving silently like a statue trying to come to life. Then he was gone.

The first man came off the ground and wrapped his forearm about Isaac's throat, then slammed the butt of his free hand into the base of his skull. Isaac staggered forward, lifting the man off his feet. This man, the one with the thick wrists, was terribly strong.

Isaac bent forward, reaching back for a wad of his attacker's shirt. He twisted hard, flinging the man over onto the rocky ledge, driving his breath from him in a rush.

He moved in to finish him, but the man rolled aside, still gasping for air, and took Isaac's legs out. Isaac came down on the shoulder where the bullet had entered and nearly fainted with the wave of pain. The man wedged himself against a boulder and pushed Isaac inexorably toward the edge with his boots.

Isaac clawed at the sandy surface of the rock, but it was like trying to get a grip on a dance floor. His gaze was locked on the man's, who seemed to know he'd won. He felt his buttocks moving out into the warm air that rose up from the mud pot, felt steam crawling over the flesh at the back of his neck.

Abruptly, Isaac felt his fingers catch a fissure in the rock. The man's expression shifted. He saw Isaac's hand digging in to the rock and lifted one of his heavy boots to smash it loose.

He never got to bring his foot down. With his free hand, Isaac found the knife he'd taken from the sniper and drove it into the leg that was still pushing him toward the edge. He felt the heavy blade shatter bone and grind all the way through to the rock.

The man screamed and clutched at his ruined leg. Isaac pulled him by his shirtfront and flung him out over the edge. The man's scream echoed again as he hit the boiling muck.

Isaac rose to his knees, still panting. This one did not come back to the surface.

His shoulder ached terribly, but the bullet had only grazed him, tearing out a blackened furrow of flesh above his collarbone. It would be all right, he thought. For an instant, he had forgotten about the sickness. There was a peal of thunder and a shadow fell across his face. At last, the rain was going to come.

A drop hit the ground in front of his nose, and he thought that it was rain. Then another drop splashed on his hand, which still held its grip in the fissure, and he saw instead that it was blood.

He looked up then and realized there were no clouds. A man was standing there. He had cast the shadow. There was a bloody spike ripped through one arm, one of *his* spikes,

275

Isaac thought. It was the last moment of satisfaction he would know.

A tendril of smoke drifted past, a black fragment of ash fluttering in its current like a mutant butterfly. The big man held a huge blade poised high above him, its steel glinting. And then it descended, cutting squarely through the orb of Isaac's sun.

ANOTHER BLAST OF thunder sounded as Fairchild crawled out on the ledge, playing out the last of the slack in their make-shift rope. Larraine was on the other end of the two shirts they'd braided together, dangling against the face of the cliff below him, frantically searching for some kind of purchase with her boot tips.

She was still a dozen feet shy of the next landing. Below that, the ground at last began to angle away toward the bottom. It was steep, but looked passable, fifty feet or so of loose talus slide to the bottom where a thick border of pine and scrub crowded between the cliff bottom and the river.

There was another peal of thunder and he glanced at the swiftly moving water, which had gained force visibly in the past minutes. The sky looked dark to the north and the occasional sounds of thunder had become almost constant. Evidently it was raining high up on the plateau, and the river was swollen with the runoff. He grimaced, straining to hold Larraine, wondering how on earth they'd get across a flood-swollen canyon.

Her face was angled up at him, taut with effort. "A little more slack. Another foot."

He shook his head. "You'll pull us both over the side." He could already feel his weight ready to shift.

"I can see something, a little crevice," she insisted. "Come on."

"Forget it," he said. "I'm going to pull you back up. We'll tie this thing off and I'll drop down first. Then I can catch you."

She opened her mouth to protest, then froze. Her eyes were locked on to something high above him. He saw her expression shift rapidly from confusion into terror.

"Oh my God. Jack . . ."

He turned to follow her gaze, then caught his breath. High atop the cliff where they'd made their descent was a man—the same phony doctor from the field hospital, he realized—with an automatic weapon in one hand, something else in the other, something he was holding aloft for them to see.

"Isaac," Fairchild said, feeling his stomach turn.

The big man atop the cliff released his grip on the thing he'd been holding and it hurtled down toward them, growing huge, its hair flying straight back as it turned slowly in its own rush of air. It struck the cliff above them and came to rest on the ledge a dozen feet away.

A human head. Fairchild recognized Isaac's hacked, swollen features, the ragged flap of skin where the neck had been chopped in two. Then Larraine screamed again.

A shot echoed above them and rock fragments exploded a foot from his shoulder. He began to pull frantically on the makeshift rope. Larraine swayed out into the air and the fabric slid along the rough edge, jerking him along with it. He was sure they were going over when the knot holding the two shirts together lodged against a sharp finger of rock.

Another shot blasted the rocks at his opposite shoulder. Fragments showered his face and he felt a trickle on his forehead. He could already feel the next bullet taking him squarely in the back. He jerked frantically to free the rope and there was a horrible rending sound.

"Jack!" she cried.

The cloth was limp in his hand. A third shot struck the ledge and blew a storm of burning rock fragments into his face. He tried to open his eyes, but all he could see was a haze of red.

"You sonofabitch," he screamed. He stumbled blindly to his feet and heard another shot and felt a rush of air at his face. He went over backward then, off the ledge and out into space, weightless, floating, oddly unafraid, thinking, *You can't hear the shot that takes you out.* And then he lost his breath as something heavy slammed into his back and then his side. And then it was mercifully black.

SKANZ WATCHED THE ranger's body crash into the pines and disappear. He was sorry to have killed him at long range. He would have preferred to use his hands. He would have liked to carve a trophy or two from the ranger and from the woman as well.

He was also sorry he had dropped the head of the Indian. Why had he done that? On purpose? But why? He needed something to show them when he returned. To prove to them all what he was capable of. He would have to be more careful.

He waited at the edge of the cliff, staring down at the silent canopy of pines where the two had fallen. He flipped the mechanism on the submachine gun to automatic and sprayed the trees with a random burst of fire until the clip had emptied. Nothing moved.

There was angry thunder from the plateau behind him. He turned back to the forest. A haze drifted through the ranks of the pines now, unmistakable smoke from the fire he had set. The effect was ghostly, as if spirits might materialize from behind the trunks at any moment. He wished they would. They would surely be the sort of creatures who would lend a hand.

He watched the smoke drift in layers, waiting patiently

for the slightest sign of life below. Not until the sunlight had disappeared and gloom had settled on the forest for good did he feel satisfied.

He could smell the acrid odor of burning brush as he counted the prey off in his mind. Three were dead now. Three more still out there somewhere? He wasn't sure, but he would find out. He tossed aside his Uzi and began to move toward that place where the fire would eventually drive anything still living, the long knife slapping time at his side.

In Fairchild's dream, they all sit about a dazzling blue pool—he, Dr. Lenzo, Isaac, and Ripley—all dressed in white linen slacks and Hawaiian shirts, all enjoying drinks in tall thin glasses painted with flamingos. They are appreciative of Larraine's trim figure, as she poises at the end of the low board, wearing a sleek black suit. Fairchild is happy—blissfully, unreasonably happy to be with this woman.

Then, everything changes: she is about to leap into the water, which Fairchild sees has turned a vile, bilious color and roils with unseen creatures.

He has hardly opened his mouth to warn her, when the scene changes again, and the two of them are walking hand in hand down the streets of a strange European city. The sun is dying and they are searching intently for something. He has no idea what it is, but he is content to have Larraine guide the way.

He follows after her, watching the soft flounce of her unpinned amber hair, feeling the heat from the warm flesh of her arm sometimes brushing his. They reach a deserted fountain square, with the sunlight nearly gone, and she turns to draw him near, her expression relieved, as if they have at last found what they have been searching for.

He is about to step toward her, take her in his arms, when, without warning, there is a brilliant flash of white light that obliterates the scene and a thunderclap of noise that is the engine of an enormous machine hurtling toward them on the heels of the light.

And then he awoke, blinking, his face pressed into swampy mud. It was dusk, and the aftershock of thunder was still reverberating above the roar of the swollen river. He could smell ozone as he pushed himself to a sitting position. The lightning strike must have been right on top of him. He raised his hand to his head, where a cut had congealed to a crust of blood. On the spongy ground nearby he found their shirts, wound together into a rope, and finally, sickeningly, he remembered.

There was a throbbing pain in his side where it felt as if he had broken some ribs. But he could still move. He pushed himself up slowly and began to search the thicket floor for Larraine. Though it was nearly dark under the dense cover, he could see well enough. And there was no trace of her. He felt panic welling in him. *She has tumbled into the river, it has swept her away,* he thought.

Then he heard a moan. He glanced about in confusion. The sound came again, seemingly at his back. He spun around. Still no one. Then a shower of needles drifted down from the trees. He swung his gaze upward and found her.

She had fallen into the heavy canopy of pines and undergrowth and lay caught in a tangle of interlaced boughs a few feet above his head. He struggled to reach one of the limbs and pulled it down until he could get his hands beneath her shoulders and ease her to the spongy ground. He cupped water from a tiny pool and rubbed her face and wrists with it.

He wasn't sure how long he sat cradling her, urging her awake with whispers, with prayers. When her eyelids began to flutter, he felt such gratitude as he had never felt.

He cast an instinctive glance upward, toward the canyon rim, but no one was there. The man was long gone, surely considering them dead. This should have pleased him, but even as Larraine began to stir in his arms, something nagged at him, something he couldn't put his finger on.

The sky above the canyon was cloaked in a heavy pall of smoke, making it seem later than it actually was. Ashes drifted down from the rim toward the river. And still no rain had fallen. Only fire up there. A bad one.

Larraine moaned again and he turned back to sponge water on her face with the shirts. After a moment she opened her eyes and lay staring at him before she spoke.

"I thought I was dying," she said finally.

He shook his head. She was alive. Talking to him. For a moment, all his anger, all the insanity of the past three days slipped away, cloaked in simple thankfulness.

He nodded upward at the green canopy above them. "The trees broke your fall." She followed his gaze. They shared a glance of wonder. He felt himself choking up and turned away.

The roar of the river had grown and a trickle of water crept over a rock near his boot. *There is no normal world,* he thought.

He watched the water join another finger of overflow and butt against the scuffed sole of his boot. The water gathered, building up a tiny lake. He stared deep into the pool, feeling light-headed, but he couldn't take his gaze away.

It was as if the world had tilted and a strange light had seeped in from some other sun. In this light, he could understand everything that had happened. All these years he had seen himself as one of the infinitesimal cogs in a harmonious universe. Despite all his practical knowledge of the wilderness and its dangers, despite everything he knew of human nature, he had managed to keep alive the thought, deep down, that the world had made a place for him, in honor of his simple good will.

He nodded, and levered the sole of his boot up, releasing the tiny dam. The little pool of water vanished, spreading into the spongy ground. He knew now what had nagged at him, what they had to do. And he would see to it.

His voice was level as he turned to her. "We've got to move," he said.

He helped her sit, watched apprehensively as she flexed her arms, her legs. She gave him her hand and he helped her up. She grimaced when she put her weight on her bad ankle but was able to take a few exploratory steps. Finally, she turned to face him. She was ready.

"Can we get across?" She nodded at the far side of the canyon. There was no gradual slope there, just a sheer cliff that ended where frothing water now surged. He shook his head.

"We're going back up there," he said, pointing toward the place where the big man had stood, trying to kill them.

"Jack, that's crazy. That's where *he* is."

"And that's why we're going up there."

She stared at him, uncomprehending.

"He'll send someone down here, looking for bodies," he said. "And if they don't find us, they'll never stop looking."

"And what good is climbing up *there* going to do? Assuming we could."

"We'll find a way," he told her.

She stared at him, unconvinced.

"Just trust me," he said. And took her arm.

285

* * *

They descended along the narrow western bank of the stream for a quarter of a mile, struggling over deadfalls, watching the water widen out and grow muddy with runoff, until they came to a place where the rising water met the cliffside. They stared out glumly at the raging water that stretched from one steep slope to the other.

"We could try scrambling along the edge." She pointed to the steep, narrow rockslide that separated the river from the cliff.

He shook his head. The water had turned an ugly brown. Nearby, a huge tree limb surfaced momentarily, then abruptly disappeared as if jerked down by an unseen hand.

She stared at the water in frustration. "Goddammit!" she shouted over the rush of the water. "Goddammit!"

He put a hand on her neck and turned back the way they had come. He shook her gently to get her attention and, when she turned, he pointed at a break in the cliff.

"That's the way we'll go," he said.

It was a cleft in the rock cut by eons of runoff. During snowmelt, a time that now seemed as distant as the Pleistocene, there would be a cascading torrent shooting out of the cliffside to tumble fifty feet or more through the air to the bottom. Now there was barely a trickle of water dribbling down from the break in the rock.

There was also a dead tree leaning near the cleft. It was a huge lodgepole pine. Its trunk was jammed in the talus slope below; its tip was still lodged in the cleft.

Larraine read his eyes then, and nodded. "Piece of cake," she said, and limped ahead without another word.

It took them twenty minutes to get up the rocky slope to the base of the dead tree. Fairchild eyed its base, then glanced up the thirty feet or so to the cleft. He turned to Larraine. "Want me to go first?"

"Yes," she said, grasping a limb and hoisting herself up. "But if it doesn't hold, I don't want to be the one left standing here."

He watched her climb, doing his best to steady the heavy base, which rocked slightly under her movements but held its place. Finally, she reached the top and took a last, breathless step from a slender branch onto the shelf of rock. A scattering of pebbles rained down upon his shoulders, then her voice floated to him.

"It's a mess up here," she called. "But we can make it." She leaned out precariously from the cliff, her face shadowed by the gathering dusk and the tumble of her hair.

He gave her a nod and pulled himself up onto the tree. He hadn't climbed a dozen feet when he felt the thing lurch beneath him. A clatter of rocks shot out from the base. The top of the tree edged away from the side of the cliff momentarily, then fell back. He paused, steadying himself, willing the shuddering of the tree to subside.

When the last tremors stopped, he started to creep upward again, moving slowly, bringing each foot to rest before taking the next step. It seemed to take forever, but the tree held steady.

He was within five feet of the top, close enough to hear Larraine's breathing. She grimaced involuntarily as he reached up to grasp a thin limb near the apex.

He was pulling himself up when the limb in his hand gave way with a loud crack and he found himself wobbling backward. As his weight shifted away from the cliff, the top of the tree swayed back with him. He swiveled his body and the tree wavered, then slid sideways toward the rocks.

He was going into the water, he was thinking, but

287

miraculously the tree caught something and held. He clung to the trunk. His back was nearly parallel to the ground.

He looked up at Larraine, who had reached out to grasp the thin tip of the pine before he went over. Her other hand was fastened on a shrub anchored near the lip of the precipice. Her face was white with strain.

"Jack, hurry." Pebbles skittered out from underneath the soles of her boots. His weight was pulling her inexorably toward the rim.

"Let go," he told her. "Goddammit, let go. It'll take you too."

"Fuck that," she hissed, digging in.

He searched the cliffside for a handhold, found a crevice, and took hold with both hands. The branch he was standing on sheared off with a sound like a gunshot. His boots swung freely in the air and banged off the rock face. He thought his arms would tear loose from his body with the strain. He heard the tree scrape away down the cliff beneath him. Then he felt a hand clamp onto the neck of his shirt.

"Come on," she said, groaning with effort.

He glanced up, jammed one hand further into the fissure, then found a toehold. Larraine scrabbled backward, her hand still locked at his collar. With a last heave he pulled himself over the edge and lay his cheek gratefully against the cool rock.

"Never in doubt," he said, his gaze an inch from the earth.

"Sure," she said, still breathless from the struggle.

Finally, he rose and together they fought their way up the clogged chute of the dry stream, through tangles of brush and deadfall carried down by countless seasons of runoff. The smell of smoke was thick now, and by the time they reached the plateau, they were coughing with it.

"Which way?" Larraine asked. She was bent over in the gloom, gasping for breath, wiping at her reddened eyes.

Fairchild glanced about them. There was no way to tell which direction the flames were actually advancing from. And once they actually saw fire it would be too late. As dry as the forest was, the wall of fire would advance far more rapidly than any human might run.

"Straight up," he said. He pointed back toward the open country they'd traversed at dawn. "The cave," he said aloud.

"What?" Larraine stared at him in surprise.

"The cave where we found the sniper," he repeated. "We're going in there."

"What about that thing that killed him?"

"It's the closest thing to a firebreak we can reach in time." She stared at him, slowly shaking her head as a hot breeze swept over then, bringing visible skeins of smoke along with it. "We're out of choices, Larraine."

He took her by the arm and pulled her away. He thought he could feel the heat of flames at his back.

SKANZ SAT IN the full lotus position, watching without surprise as the two moved out of the cover of the forest and onto the trail leading upward into the rocks. He had arranged himself on a flat boulder just inside the forest where he had found the body of the doctor and was trying to remember what had brought him to these mountains in the first place.

The man and the woman drifted in and out of vision, one moment obscured by drifting plumes of smoke from the advancing flames, at other times as clearly visible as if they were real.

But he had killed them, so how could these apparitions be real? Perhaps these were spirits, returning to the mountain that had spawned them. Perhaps he had the fever to blame for his confusion.

He held up his hands and stared at his blackened nails. In some fashion, it had come upon him too. He thought briefly of the splash of the Indian's blood in his face and supposed that was how it had happened. But what did it matter? He thought of those bloated corpses they'd carried from the ward and shuddered.

Then his mind drifted. It was almost as if he were another person. He knew he'd been upset a moment ago, but he couldn't remember what the cause had been.

He looked back at the man and woman, who were climbing quickly now. He saw the woman stumble and dislodge a flurry of stone over the edge of the narrow trail. It occurred to him that spirits would not need weapons and could not scatter rocks. He considered the possibilities. Had he imagined the episode in the vast canyon? Were these not the same two?

He heard the man call out, urging the woman toward him. The man pointed toward something just above their position on the cliff and then bent to help her climb upward onto a shelf of rock. He watched the man hoist himself up after her.

The two of them seemed to be discussing something. First the man pointed at what was apparently a sheer rock wall, and then he gestured back at the forest. It seemed to Skanz that his finger indicated the very spot where he sat watching, though he knew the man could not see him.

The man bent, apparently gathering something. In a few moments he stood, and a plume of smoke began to rise from where the two stood. *A campfire? Some kind of signal?*

Abruptly, the man stepped forward and seemed to disappear into the rocks. The woman hesitated, then moved after him. She too had disappeared.

Then they *were* spirits? Skanz nodded. A bank of smoke drifted up through the pines behind him, and he turned to look down through the forest. There was a dull orange glow in the sky to the north, although no flames were visible.

Triggered by the odor of the smoke, his thoughts shifted again. Now he was alert, as nearly the creature called Skanz as he would ever be again. He spun back to stare at the place on the mountain where the man and the woman had vanished. The tiny fire they'd built still smoldered on that high place.

They were alive. He did not know how it was possible, and he did not know where they had gone, but they were alive.

He rose and moved out of the forest after them, the handle of the heavy blade solid in his grasp. He stretched. He felt strong once again. He had forgotten the reasons for his pursuit of the two who had vanished into the cave, but it did not matter. Only instinct held, and that was enough. He hurried toward the fire they had set to call him. There was only this final work to be done.

REISMAN SAT IN near darkness in the office of the field hospital, clutching the arms of the chair that Skanz must have sat in, staring out at the same darkening forest. He was waiting for the phone to ring. He'd initiated the call, but you never got right through, no matter what.

He wondered how Skanz had seen the world outside the office. He wondered how the cold steel of the chair arms had felt to him, how the seat had molded to his body. How *did* a madman experience the world? An involuntary tingle raced through his hands, and he jerked them from the arms of the chair as if he'd been burned.

The phone rang and he blinked in confusion before he picked it up. For a moment he'd forgotten he'd put in the call.

"Yes?" He felt groggy, as if he'd just awakened.

"You're in charge now, Alec." It was Schreiber's voice, soothing, reassuring.

Reisman felt a dryness in his throat and swallowed. "He's off the map, you know."

"Yes. The operation is entirely yours."

"Right." He sat up straight in his chair. His hand felt slick on the receiver.

"I have the utmost confidence in you, Alec. Battlefield promotions are made on the basis of ability."

"I appreciate it." He thought his voice had wavered, but it could have been his imagination. He turned from the phone and cleared his throat. When he spoke again, he felt it was with authority. "You read the report from the twins?"

"It does not matter," Schreiber broke in sharply. "If any of them still exist, they are carriers."

For a moment, Reisman thought Schreiber had misread the document. "The report says otherwise. There's the possibility, at least, of full recovery."

"Even if that were so, they would carry *knowledge*," Schreiber said. "Now tell me, either you understand the posture of this company or you don't."

This time Reisman did understand. "Yes," he said. "We'll make sure each of them is accounted for."

"Good," Schreiber said. "I'm counting on you. Many people will be counting on you now."

"I won't let you down," Reisman heard himself saying.

"This will be over soon," Schreiber said. "You'll take some time. There is a little place I favor, an island that one of our Caribbean friends makes available."

"Yes," Reisman answered slowly. "That would be fine."

"We will be in touch," Schreiber said, and the line was dead.

Reisman replaced the receiver and glanced out the window. There was a strange glow surrounding the compound without fully illuminating the area. It was created by the special security lighting that would highlight normal clothing. Anyone trying to cross through the area would stand out like a Day-Glo poster. The perimeter fence was in place now too. There was enough current flowing through it to put any human who made it over the surrounding razor wire into a deep, deep sleep.

A firebreak had been cleared around the area and the wardrooms down the hall had been returned to their former state, ready for some future cadre of smoke jumpers who would risk their lives in defense of the public trust.

They had locked the barn door securely, all right. And he was fully in control, just as he'd wanted to be. All that remained was a little necessary tidying and things could go back to normal.

He leaned back in his chair and massaged his face with his hands. *Back to normal,* he thought, and his laughter echoed wildly about the room.

"Dear God." Larraine's voice echoed in the narrow passageway. She turned away as Fairchild trained the flashlight they'd scavenged from the pack outside.

The corpse of the sniper had been dragged inside the cave and lay jammed across a narrow turn in the path. Its features had been mauled and torn even more savagely than before. Fairchild bent and pried the pistol from the corpse's stiff hand.

"I should be used to it by now," she said, her face still averted.

"No," he said. "Don't ever get used to it." He took her arm and led her on down the passageway, grateful for the surge of cool air that poured over them and blew the stench of the body away.

They moved in silence for several minutes, the air growing cooler and damper as they went deeper into the mountain. At a turn in the narrow defile, he stopped to give her a chance to rest her swollen ankle.

"Do we have to go any farther?" she asked.

"We're looking for a place," he told her.

"What place? For what?"

Suddenly, a sound from far above drifted down the passageway. It was something made of metal glancing off

296

stone. He felt fear, but he also felt satisfaction. "To wait for *him*," Fairchild said. He lifted the pistol in his hand and snapped off the light.

More sounds drifted down the passage behind them. Fairchild heard a strange humming sound, then the clatter of loose stones. "The cat?" Her voice was a whisper. He pulled her quickly along.

They were on a steep slope now that seemed to dive toward the very center of the earth. He snapped on the light. The slope led down into what seemed to be a large chamber.

He flicked off the light again and paused to listen. Nothing.

"Maybe it's gone." Her words were barely audible.

"It's not the cat," he said. He had formed the picture of the big man with the submachine gun in one hand, Isaac's head dangling from the other, and it would not go away. He imagined the man descending inexorably after them.

He turned and pulled Larraine down the steep passage. When the dying surge of air told him they were nearing the entrance to the chamber, he switched the lamp on again.

A few feet ahead, the path fell away into a deep pit. The light glittered off an array of jagged stalagmites that had formed at the bottom, jutting up like fangs. The passageway itself gave out onto a narrow shelf that branched off in either direction, circling the pit like a gallery.

The ringing of metal on stone sounded again behind them. He pointed over Larraine's shoulder, along the narrow shelf. There was a wall of rock that jutted out, nearly cutting off the pathway.

"Get behind that," he told her. "Now."

He waited until she disappeared behind the rock, then snapped off the light and picked his way in the opposite direction along the narrow shelf. When the shelf widened so

Les Standiford

that there was room to kneel, he stopped and drew the pistol from his belt, steadying the weapon with one hand, holding the flashlight with the other. When the man appeared in the chamber, Fairchild would kill him.

Fairchild felt a calmness descend over him as the sound of footsteps echoed nearer and nearer. It was the same calm that had come to him earlier, as he held Larraine in the canyon. He would do this thing. He would see them through.

The footsteps now issued directly from the mouth of the passage. And the strange crooning sound that accompanied them was clearer. The man was mumbling to himself, repeating some kind of unintelligible mantra.

Fairchild was suddenly aware of a strange odor drifting over him, a rank muskiness, like wildness and rottenness mingled together. It was nothing he'd ever smelled before.

Fairchild heard the sounds of rubber soles scuffing over rock, then silence. The man stood now at the entrance to the chamber; Fairchild was certain of it. He tightened his finger about the trigger of the pistol and readied the flashlight. He took a breath to steady himself and pressed the switch.

The beam caught the man squarely: it was the same man who'd fought them at the hospital, the same one who'd killed Isaac, who'd tried to kill them all. The steel of the huge blade he carried glinted in the beam of the flashlight. Fairchild heard soft scuffing sounds from behind him, but ignored them.

He squeezed the trigger, and the big man grunted as the bullet took him high on the chest. He glanced at the wound, then shook it off as if he'd been stung by an insect. Fairchild fired again, but this time his aim was wide. The big man ducked and rushed toward him with incredible speed, raising the blade in a murderous arc. Fairchild frantically swung the gun into position and pulled the trigger, trying to twist away from the blow of the knife. The sickening odor was everywhere. As he ducked down, he heard an unearthly scream from behind him. *Nothing human,* he thought, and then felt something slam against his back.

Claws raked his neck and shoulder and the scream turned to snarls. The sickening wild-rotten odor enveloped Fairchild altogether as he fell forward, losing his grip on the flashlight. He flung out his hands to break his fall and felt his wrist crack as he hit the rocky shelf.

The flashlight clattered over the rocks, sending beams of light bouncing crazily off the walls and ceiling of the chamber. Fairchild twisted onto his side, raised the gun with his good hand, and fired again, blindly. The man's foot lashed out and kicked the gun out of Fairchild's hand.

The light had come to rest, illuminating the man's legs. Fairchild tried to get his feet under him, knowing that the heavy blade would split him open in an instant.

Suddenly, the man lurched backward, away from him, and Fairchild realized that the snarling was mixed with human groans.

Fairchild struggled to his knees. The big man staggered backward along the narrow shelf of rock with a huge cat writhing atop his shoulders, its massive claws shredding the flesh of his chest. The thing tore at the man's throat, trying to sink its jaws into a death grip.

The man flailed at the creature with his machete, hacking at it again and again. Though its back was a bloody mass, the cat seemed unaffected by the blows. It dug its snout in beneath the man's chin, its jaws slashing, spraying blood and spittle.

The big man grunted and dropped the blade, which clattered off the rocks. He grasped the cat's neck with his hands and began to squeeze. The creature screamed in fury and slashed at the big man's arms with its foreclaws, but its grip had weakened.

"Ah, good, ah, good," the man crooned, his breath ragged. He turned at the edge of the narrow pathway and drew himself back, ready to hurl the cat into the pit. The thing swiped at him, but weakly. Its snarls were more like whimpers. "Ah, good, ah, good," the man repeated, as if he were comforting a troubled child.

Fairchild levered himself up the wall of the chamber, disbelieving. The man was like an indestructible machine. He was going to kill this cat, and then he would come for them.

Fairchild forced himself forward, toward the writhing pair at the edge of the pathway. The big man was just leaning into his throw when Fairchild hit him in the small of the back. Both creatures sailed out into the darkness, and neither screamed. The man landed with a gasp. If the cat made a sound, Fairchild did not hear it.

He stood at the edge, his wrist on fire, struggling for breath. Larraine edged along the far path toward him. As she reached him, Fairchild picked up the flashlight and cast the beam down into the pit. The cat lay quietly on its side at the bottom, its eyes two pools of white reflecting the beam of his light.

The big man was not far away. He lay spread-eagled, impaled on one of the jagged spikes of rock, suspended in air as if he were still falling, still waiting to meet the earth. As they watched, his arms contracted slowly inward. His feet sagged toward the ground. There was a last gargling sound and then, nothing.

Fairchild turned the light away and drew Larraine toward him. They held each other. Finally, it was time to go.

THEY LAY RESTING near the entrance to the cave, listening to the storm rage outside. An occasional bolt of lightning illuminated the rain that hammered down in great sheets.

"That'll take care of the fire," Larraine said.

"It's good and it's bad," Fairchild answered.

"Right," she said, but she didn't ask for an explanation. She lay in his arms, shivering as a spray of mist pushed in upon them with the wind.

"It's good because the fire might die down and we can get through. But it's bad because once the rain stops, we'll be easier to track." He grazed his chin through her hair. "But it's also good because it'll slow them down. All the jeep trails turn to muck, nobody drives into the backcountry."

"I thought you were going to tell me something I didn't know," she said.

"Maybe I don't know anything like that," he said.

She sat up and moved away from him. In a flash of lightning he saw her staring out into the storm, her face a mask. "I saw a bruise on your cheek while we were hiking out of the canyon," she said. "I nearly died. I thought, *He's got it again,* and then I realized it really was just a bruise."

She turned to him. "We really are okay, aren't we, Jack?"

He hesitated. "If you mean will we die from that bug,

then I *think* we're all right. But we need to find someone who can tell us for sure."

She put her hand on his arm. "But they'll never stop coming after us, is that what you mean?"

"Only when we're dead," he told her.

"You're so cheery."

"It's my job," he said. "Come here."

She bent toward him and he wound his hand in a twist of her hair. "Jack," she protested. "You're hurting me."

He pulled, hard, then jerked again, until finally a chunk of her scalp lifted free with her hair. She screamed, but he smothered the sounds until she was quiet. She struggled wildly away from him.

"What are you *doing?*" There was pain and outrage in her voice.

"Trying to kill you," he told her. "Take off your shirt."

"Jack—"

"Goddammit, Larraine, it would have hurt more if I told you I was going to do it. Now take off your shirt."

He heard her release her breath, then the soft rustling as she peeled out of the uniform top. He took it from her and began to rip the fabric into tatters.

"Is your head bleeding?"

"It feels like it," she said, still angry.

"Good," he said. "Come here."

He found the spot where he'd pulled her hair out and sponged at the wound with the shreds of her shirt. Suddenly, she understood. He got up and scattered the bloody cloth and bits of her hair well away from the entrance where nothing would disturb them.

"Now for the hard part," he said, already beginning to undress.

He led the way back down the passage until they found

the corpse of the sniper. She held the flashlight while he peeled away what was left of the dead man's clothing and replaced it with his own. He paused, then pulled off his wedding ring. He turned the band so he could see the inscription: JF-LF 6/1/71. Hieroglyphics from a lost world. He bent and forced the ring onto the man's stiff finger. He finished, and stared down at the result.

"Be better if he was scorched up a little," he said.

"He'll have to do," she said.

He glanced up to agree, but she was already on her way out.

Monday, July 25

Joss Humphries had spent the morning tracking a deer, the afternoon lugging it down to his shack and dressing it. It was still overcast and drizzling, but the heat had abated at last and the soft ground had made his hunt easier. He'd taken the animal on park property once again, but he figured he was only thinning a bloated population. Deer died by the hundreds in there every winter, starved out.

He'd have been content to cure the meat from the dead goats, but the vet in Jackson Hole had warned him against it. Joss still didn't know what had killed his little herd, but at least the vet hadn't charged him. Joss had passed up the offer of an autopsy. It would have cost him a hundred dollars, and for that kind of money, dead was simply going to be dead.

He sliced off a hunk of the deer's tenderloin for his supper and laid it on the glistening cutting table. He gazed up at the mountain where you could still see the remains of a fire smoldering. It was a good thing the storm came when it did. The fire had been headed right down the canyon. He might have found himself out of a house, and the Park Service didn't let you rebuild on these leases anymore.

He heard something around back and picked up the lever-action rifle at his side. He jacked a round into the chamber.

He'd been expecting someone ever since the incident with the stranger in Doc Lenzo's office.

"Ease on out here," he said, his voice level. Then he lowered his rifle and watched in astonishment as Fairchild and Larraine labored over the uneven ground toward him. He started forward but stopped when Fairchild held up his hand.

"Don't get too close, Joss."

Larraine nodded, clutching Fairchild's arm. "We'll tell you all about it."

It was dark when they emerged from the shack. Joss had been out to scout the woods nearby and now stood by his pickup motioning them ahead. He'd boiled up bathwater, found clothes for them, stuffed them with venison steaks. They looked almost like a couple of weary tourists.

Joss raised the lid of the truck's false bottom and helped Larraine up. She glanced at Fairchild, grimaced, and then lay down. In a moment he was beside her and the heavy wooden top slammed down.

"It smells like something died in here," she said.

"That's what it's for," he told her.

"Terrific," she said.

The truck started with a roar and soon they were banging down the rough trail toward the highway. Mud and rocks clattered against the underside of their compartment.

"We *are* going to die in here," Larraine called over the whine of the driveshaft. "I can smell exhaust fumes. I'm going to get sick."

"Try not to do that," he told her.

"I mean it," she added.

Abruptly, the truck lurched up an incline, then stopped. There was the wrenching of the emergency brake, then the truck's door creaked open and Joss's footsteps came back toward the bed.

"I ain't seen anything yet," he said, his voice muffled. "We'll just scoot on down the road. Next thing you hear from me, we'll be in Jackson." He paused. "Maybe you ought to knock to let me know you're okay."

"I'm *not* okay," Larraine said, struggling to find a comfortable position.

Fairchild pounded the side of his fist against the wood.

"Good," Humphries said. "Hang in there."

It was better on the pavement. "Thank God," Larraine mumbled. Fairchild nodded. He was beginning to think that their luck had changed, when he felt the truck sway violently. The squeal of brakes rose up beneath them.

He felt Larraine's nails digging fiercely into his shoulder as they ground to a halt. After a moment they began to edge along, the sound of voices from somewhere outside growing clearer as they moved. Another car slowed to a stop behind them.

"A roadblock," Larraine whispered, sounding forlorn. He laid his finger across her lips. He'd left Joss's rifle behind. Maybe it had been a mistake to hide this way.

"Could I see your license please." The voice was hard, unaccented. It sounded as if the man were standing on top of them. A state cop, Fairchild thought. Or at least he hoped it was a state cop.

"Uh, sure," Joss was saying. "It's around here someplace."

There was a clang as the glove box opened and then sounds of rustling cans and papers as if someone were pawing through mounds of garbage.

The driver behind them bleated his horn. "I'm afraid you'll have to pull over to the side," the authoritative voice said.

"I just *had* it," Joss was saying.

"He *never* had one," Larraine hissed. Fairchild clamped his hand over her mouth.

There was a chorus of horns behind them now, but still the truck had not moved. "I'm telling you to pull over," the voice insisted.

"What's goin' on?" It was a third person approaching, footsteps crunching along the shoulder of the road, the voice carrying a familiar Western twang. A *real* cop, Fairchild prayed.

"He doesn't have a license."

"Hell's bells, why don't you just shoot him?"

"I don't need that from you," the tough voice began, but he was cut off when the other cop saw who it was in the pickup.

"Hey, Joss," the man said.

"Howdo, Richard," Joss said. "Man just wanted me to show him this."

There was a long pause. Fairchild realized he was holding his breath.

"This expired three years ago, Joss."

"I been meaning to get in to renew 'er, too."

Air brakes sounded in the background and a long-hauler's horn joined in with the others that were blaring. "Get him out of here," the first voice said, exasperated. "Just get him the fuck out of here."

It might have taken them another hour, but there were no more stops until Fairchild began to see streetlights flicker-

310

ing through the seams of the hidden door. There were sounds of traffic for a bit, and then an abrupt turn and the crunch of gravel under their tires.

The truck stopped and they heard the wrench of the tailgate coming down. Finally, mercifully, the door swung open and they were staring up like freed moles at a sky full of stars.

They had pulled up in a dark lot, alongside a low-slung stone and glass building a block or so away from the main street of Jackson Hole, Wyoming. There was a gamy smell in the air and a chorus of dogs began to bark. A door swung open in the building, spilling yellow light out into the gravel lot. A man appeared there, his face in shadow. He seemed as big as Joss, though it could have been a trick of the light.

"That you, Joss?" The man stepped forward. He wore a white lab coat, and the light glinted off his balding head. Fairchild felt his heart lurch.

Joss's hand clamped reassuringly on his shoulder. "That'd be Doc Gunn," Joss said, and moved them toward the light.

Fairchild and Larraine sat across from one another in the tiny examining room, waiting. Fairchild had already thrown away the little ball of cotton he'd been using to stanch the prick mark inside his elbow. Larraine still held her arm folded tight. Her lips were drawn into a bloodless line and beads of moisture dotted her forehead.

She noticed his stare and forced a smile. "I'm all right." She gave a little shake of her head. "I've never been any good at this."

He moved his chair close enough to take her hand. Warm and slick with sweat, it felt wonderful to him. She tried

311

to laugh. "After all that's happened, somebody puts a needle in me and I want to faint."

"It's okay," he told her. "I'm worried too."

"You are?" He heard the genuine surprise in her voice. And the fear.

"Sure." He nodded at the huge chart that nearly covered one wall at the end of the room. It contained meticulous artists' renderings of dogs of every shape, size, and variety, with little dotted lines connecting them to various spots on a Mercator map of the world. "I'm afraid he's going to tell me I've got distemper."

She laughed then, and it brought some color back in her cheeks. She laid her head against his shoulder, and he wrapped his arm about her.

He studied the picture of the Newfoundland retriever on the chart, a huge, dark beast of a dog, standing on a bluff, dripping from a swim in what he supposed was the North Atlantic spread out below. It looked inviting there. Rugged and wild. And no people around. Not in any of the drawings. At the moment, Fairchild found that appealing.

Finally, there were footsteps in the corridor outside. He felt Larraine stiffen in his arms. The door opened and the big man came inside, his face impassive. He finished peeling off a set of latex gloves and tossed them into a can in a corner, then turned to look at them, his face set.

"I'm just a vet," Gunn began. He glanced at his chart, then turned back to them. "You've both got an elevated white count, which would be normal following a serious infection." He paused. "But I can't find anything else."

Fairchild heard Larraine's breath release. He realized his own stomach had been knotted, as if waiting for a blow to land.

"Nothing we could be spreading to other people?" It was Larraine, her hand still tight on his arm.

Gunn shrugged. "Not that I can see."

"Nothing swimming around, ready to blow up later?" she pressed, her voice urgent.

"I didn't say that." Gunn stared at them for a moment. "From what you've told me, anything is possible. You should have a real workup somewhere. Meantime, if you get sick, then don't go out in company."

Larraine nodded, gratefully. Fairchild stood, his legs unexpectedly weak beneath him. He helped Larraine up, then turned back to the vet, who enveloped his hand in two callused slabs.

"Thanks," Fairchild said.

"For what?" Gunn said. "Anybody asks, I never saw either one of you." Then his face softened. "I'm gonna assume that two folks showed up in the middle of the night in a sweat for a marriage exam. And, as far as I'm concerned, that's privileged information, even for a vet." He was smiling as he showed them out.

Joss leaned against the side of the pickup, waiting. "I thought maybe he put you to sleep after all," he said as they joined him.

"He tried," Fairchild said. "But everything he gave us just kicked us up one more notch."

Joss barked his approval and the dogs took up the chorus. When the sounds had died away, the big man pulled open the truck door and pointed at a grocery sack and a Styrofoam cooler that had appeared on the seat.

"Got you a few provisions," Joss said. In the dome light,

Fairchild saw that he was extending the truck key for him to take. "Didn't figure you'd want to stop if you didn't have to."

Fairchild stared at the key, which glinted in the dim light. "I can't take your truck, Joss."

"Course you can't. I'm giving it to you." Joss cleared his throat. "You leave it somewhere for me when you can."

"Joss," Larraine began, her voice thick.

"Don't you start up with me, missy," the big man growled. He jerked his finger toward the cab. "Just kick 'er on down the road."

He clapped the key and a wad of bills in Fairchild's hand. "Good luck to you both," he said. And then he was gone, a huge, bearlike shadow that moved quickly across the crackling gravel to merge with the night.

Wednesday, July 27

Reisman had ducked into the cockpit of the parked helicopter to get out of the weather. He had a yellow pad in his lap, a list scribbled on it in pencil. He'd drawn a line through every entry but one.

He left off staring at the woman's name and glanced up at the clouds that were piling in from the north. After thirty-six hours they'd finally caught a break in the weather, but it looked as if they were in for more. A soaking mist beaded the chopper's bubble. Two days ago, the heat had been unbearable. Now he wore a down vest that couldn't keep the chill away.

Moving about the clearing were a number of the "contract players"; they were busy stacking the bodies. The pilot was nowhere to be seen. Reisman thought about getting out to look for him. The sky was darkening by the minute. He didn't want to ride all the way back to Idaho through a thunderstorm. Besides, they were finished here.

It had been a grisly scene. A score of bodies littering the forest, most of them burned beyond recognition. Still, nothing could have been worse than what they'd found inside the cave. He stared down at the gold ring in his hand. He shook his head. The poor bastard should have just stayed put in the hospital. At least he could have died with his face on.

317

Suddenly he wanted air and pushed the flimsy door of the helicopter aside. He stood down, grateful for the soft mist on his face. Two of the men struggled through the quagmire and dumped another zippered bag nearby. He turned away. A few more hours and he would be out of this, back at home with a beer, maybe work in that fishing trip. Everything back to normal.

On the scorched and blackened cliffside a hundred feet away, one of the men was making his way down the slope, which had grown more treacherous with the rain. When the man reached bottom and turned, Reisman realized it was Frazoni, the man who'd driven him on the fruitless search for Skanz. Frazoni paused to scrape mud from his boots, then came toward the helicopter.

"We been all through that fucking cave," Frazoni said when he reached him. He was breathing heavily in the thin air. "This is all we got of her." He handed Reisman a sealed plastic bag that contained some fragments of hair and bloody cloth.

Reisman gave him a look. "*All* through it?"

Frazoni shrugged impatiently. "Look, it's a fucking rabbit warren in there. There's little passages, chimneys, crevasses, shit like that all over the place. The goddamn cat could have stashed her anywhere, for when he wanted a snack, right? You want to spend a few days, get some equipment up here, we'll find the cunt." He glared at Reisman. "What's left of her."

Reisman stared back. Earlier, one of the mop-up crew had run some kind of punji stick boobytrap through the side of his boot and sheared his Achilles tendon in two. Frazoni had been walking beside the man, not two feet away. Sometimes, it seemed, there was no justice. Unless you wanted to count what happened to Skanz. A piece of scrap paper nailed to a spindle, that's how Reisman thought of him. He was only sorry he hadn't been there to see the insane bastard fall into the pit.

"We don't have a few days, Frazoni," he said finally. "We're overextended as it is."

"Yeah, well, I just get paid," Frazoni said. "Tell me what you want to do." He gestured at a pile of body bags. "Course, if it was me, and I was worried that I hadn't punched the last ticket . . ." His voice trailed off.

Reisman nodded. "Okay, Frazoni, what would you do?"

Frazoni brightened. Maybe he just liked to feel useful, Reisman thought.

"I'd drop in a few gas canisters on a time fuse and seal off that main entrance with a little plastique." He gave his shoulders a little shrug.

Reisman turned to stare out at the ruined forest. Schreiber would never leave it at this, he knew. Nor would Skanz. They'd want the woman's still-pounding heart, bloody hot in hand, and then *maybe* they'd feel sure.

He heard a rustling sound beside him and turned to see Frazoni wiping his boot soles clean on one of the zippered body bags. He swung his gaze away in disgust. How much of his life would be spent taking advice from creatures like this?

He still held the park ranger's ring in one hand, the bag with what was left of the woman in the other. He tried to imagine what it must have been like for her, in that cave, alone, face to face with that cat.

He turned abruptly to Frazoni. "Do it," he said. And hated Frazoni's answering grin.

The operation was completed within an hour. Frazoni's work was precise. There was a rumble deep within the cave, then a curtain of rock sliding down the face of the cliff to seal it all away, forever. Climb right over those rocks, you'd never know there'd been an entrance to a cave, never know what had gone on in there. A few wisps of smoke curled through the rubble, then all was calm.

Reisman turned back for the helicopter. He saw the pilot lighting a smoke at the edge of the clearing and gestured impatiently for him. He got in the cockpit, donned a set of headphones, and put in his call.

They were hardly airborne when Schreiber came back through. Record turnaround time, Reisman thought. A measure of his new status?

"Yes, Alec?" The line was amazingly clear. Schreiber's voice was beyond calm. They could have been discussing corn futures.

"We've got full confirmation," Reisman said. "The company stands clear."

"You're certain?"

Reisman didn't hesitate. "Absolutely."

There was a pause on Schreiber's end. Then, "That's good, Alec. I'm very glad. You've done a fine job."

Reisman stared down through the side door at the scene in the blackened clearing. They were a thousand feet up now, about to level off toward the Idaho compound. For as far as he could see, the forest was charred and lifeless.

"You've earned a rest," Schreiber said.

"Sure," he said finally. He was more than tired.

"The company is indebted to you," Schreiber added. And then the line went dead.

Reisman replaced the headphones as the helicopter peeled into a turn and picked up speed. There was a grating noise on the floor and the pilot kicked at something in annoyance.

The man turned to Reisman. "You want to stow your briefcase?" he shouted over the engines.

Reisman shook his head. He didn't know what the man was talking about. The pilot juked his thumb toward the back of the compartment. "Strap it into one of the seats or something."

Reisman turned, still puzzled. There was a thin black case jittering about the floor beneath the empty back bench. He stared at it, then turned to the pilot.

"I didn't bring a briefcase," he said.

The pilot turned to say something. Reisman felt a sudden jolt of fear. He had a vision, the cool blue eyes gazing out imperturbably above a polished desk somewhere, waiting. He lunged out for the case but his seat belt jerked him back.

"Schreiber!" Reisman shouted the name like a curse. The pilot stared at him, puzzled. Reisman was still clawing desperately at his seat belt when the explosion came and made them liquid flame across the sky.

"YOU LOOK TIRED, MISTER."

Fairchild had been staring vacantly at the menu. He'd been ready to go to sleep behind the wheel when he spotted the cafe. It was after midnight, and they were somewhere in central Utah. They had to be safe here. If they weren't, he was too exhausted to care.

He folded the plastic jacket closed and glanced up at the waitress. She was nineteen, maybe, her features too sharp to be called pretty, her thin black hair pulled back tight in a ponytail. Still, there was a softness about her eyes. She swiped at her sweaty forehead with the sleeve of a red-checked blouse. She licked at her pencil, her pad poised for his order.

"You look a little frazzled yourself," he told her.

She flashed him a grateful smile. "Yeah," she said. "I been here since six."

Fairchild glanced about the place. A pair of truckers at the counter, one Latino family in a booth across the room. A bus had pulled up outside, and a few passengers were spilling down the steps, dazed from their ride, blinking in the bright light thrown off by the cafe's neon.

The door opened and he saw Larraine enter. You had to go outside to get to the rest rooms, around the back of the place. He caught her eye, then turned back to the waitress.

322

She wore a little tag painted with a stick-figure cowgirl twirling a lasso. *"Panguitch Cafe,"* read the script along the rope. *"Annie"* had been carefully printed inside the loop.

"How about two coffees, Annie." Fairchild nodded toward Larraine, who was maneuvering her way through the tables toward them.

"Sure," the waitress said. She gave him a motherly look. "How about some pie? It's elderberry. Homemade."

Fairchild nodded as Larraine sat down next to him. "Sure. Bring it on."

She gave him another flash of her smile and hurried off toward the kitchen as the bus crowd started through the door. Fairchild turned to Larraine.

"What's your feeling about elderberry pie?" he asked her. He was weary beyond measure, but he was happy. Just watching her come through the door and sit down beside him was enough. Get tired enough and your mind stopped churning up worry. Things reduced themselves naturally to the essentials. Then he registered the expression on her face, and the gnawing fear was back upon him.

"Read this," she said softly, and lay the newspaper down between them.

It was a copy of the *Deseret News,* still warm from one of the steel boxes outside. Much of the front page was devoted to a conference of Mormon elders, but in a lower corner he found it, a two-column box with the headline TRAGIC HOLIDAY IN YELLOWSTONE. "Firefighting Helicopter Crash Kills Two," read a subhead. He saw his name in the short lead graph.

"We're all in there, Jack. Isaac, Dr. Lenzo." Larraine was fighting to keep her voice under control.

The waitress was back then with their pie and coffee. There was a scoop of ice cream on each slice.

323

Fairchild watched her go, then skimmed the rest of the article: He and Isaac had perished while assisting in fire-fighting efforts, it said. Dr. Lenzo had been one of a search party trapped by flames while searching for lost hiker Larraine Keller. She'd been missing for too long now. Officials presumed the worst.

A quote from Perry Christensen closed the piece. "We're lucky we got the rain when we did. Things could have been a lot worse."

"Always the perfect fuckhead," Fairchild said. He folded up the paper and met her gaze. Tears were forming in her eyes.

"They haven't even found that stuff you left for them. This is just what they decided was going to happen."

He turned his palms up on the table. The door to the cafe opened and a man in a dark suit entered the room.

A quaver of outrage had entered Larraine's voice. "You were right," she said. "They can have it any way they want it."

He reached across to take her hand and glanced about the restaurant. Truckers. Bus riders. A salesman searching for a seat. The story in the paper seemed impossible. Something that had happened to other people. In another world. He thought of a stream he'd often fished, saw a trout rising in the mist, felt the press of cool water through his rubber boots.

Outside the cafe windows, the shoulder of a mountain rose up in the moonlight. Its peak was a dim silhouette, miles away. There would be a stream up there. Air cool enough to make you catch your breath.

"No," he told her quietly, firmly. "They don't have *us.*"

He glanced over her shoulder. The gaze of the man he'd taken for a salesman locked on his.

Larraine was squeezing his hand, unaware. "What are we going to do, Jack?"

He held on to her hand and looked out the window. There was a pale sedan he hadn't noticed before angled up close to the building. He turned back to her.

The man in the suit was coming their way, reaching into an inner pocket of his coat.

Fairchild gave her a smile and eased his hand toward the heavy sugar jar in the middle of the table. Larraine saw the look in his eyes and turned.

The man lurched toward them. "Have you heard the news?" he called in a slurred voice.

Fairchild had the heavy jar in his hand. He was halfway out of his seat, ready to strike, before he made out the exploded veins in the man's cheeks, the vacancy in his eyes. There was a heavy growth of beard on his cheeks. His suit was shiny with age. Stains mottled the front of his shirt.

"He is born," the man said. He drew his hand out of his coat, scattering illustrated pamphlets over the table, their coffee, the melting ice cream: Christ knocking on a garden door. A radiant sunset. Sheep and little children on an impossibly green hillside. Fairchild felt his grip relax on the heavy glass.

The man staggered away toward an adjoining table. "Have you heard the news?" he crooned. "The good news?"

The man stumbled on through the maze of tables, still babbling. Fairchild felt his breathing start up again.

"Are we going to run for the rest of our lives?" Larraine's eyes were closed. Her voice sounded as if it were coming from a great distance.

Fairchild sank back into his seat and watched the man lurch out the door into the night.

"We're going to beat the bastards," he said, firmly, still watching.

"How?" she demanded.

He turned back to her then. "We're going to live," he said.

She stared at him, uncertain. He rose, waiting for her to join him. Finally, she stood and took his hand. He loved the touch of her. It was a big, big country. They walked out into the cool dark, together.